Graham is a retired senior lecturer in social work. Having spent his formative years in the Royal Navy, he then developed a career in social work. After working in this field, and after gaining academic qualifications, he then went into teaching. On retiring, Graham has spent his time writing. His first book, *Ships, Trips and Rites of Passage: A Sailor's Tale*, an autobiographical work, was published in September 2022 by Austin Macauley. This second book, *The Pink War*, which is fictional, tackles subjects relating to war, sexuality, friendship, love and loss—subjects rarely tackled by other authors.

Gay and Lesbian Soldiers, Naval personnel, and those who fought in the air, faced extraordinary discrimination during World War II. Yet most found new communities and formed strong long-lasting friendships during this time and thrived, despite the oppression. This book is dedicated to all those who lay down their lives for freedom.

Graham Stuart Tuckley

# THE PINK WAR

AUSTIN MACAULEY PUBLISHERS™

LONDON * CAMBRIDGE * NEW YORK * SHARJAH

A CIP catalogue record for this title is available from the British Library.

ISBN 9781035814916 (Paperback)
ISBN 9781035814923 (ePub e-book)

www.austinmacauley.co.uk

First Published 2024
Austin Macauley Publishers Ltd®
1 Canada Square
Canary Wharf
London
E14 5AA

I would like to acknowledge family and friends who have helped me on this journey and who, through listening 'to' this story as it developed, have encouraged me to complete this work. Without your love and belief, I would not have been able to complete this work.

# Table of Contents

# Foreword

Whilst every attempt has been made to ensure historical facts recorded are accurate, the author does not profess to be a historian and has used these references to provide the reader with descriptive insight only.

The work here within, is fictional; in that any references to characters presented either living or dead are imaginary. The author wishes to state that the main characters featured within the text do not resemble any real-life persons either living or dead. If resemblance can be associated with the main characters, this is purely coincidental.

My reasons for writing this novel is to provide readers with an understanding that people whose sexuality differs from heterosexual were also active members of the fighting Armed Forces during WWII and that homosexuals fought alongside their heterosexual counterparts facing the enemy with courage and heroism.

The novel also sets out to confirm that working class homosexual men living at that time did form, lived, and had full loving relationships in opposition of the laws of that time and furthermore, relationships were maintained.

# Chapter One
# The New Neighbour

Bill Taylor slowly drew on a cigarette as he pulled out the light brown card from the clocking in and out dock at the factory in which he worked. Bill proceeded to push the card into the mouth of the machine recording his daily working hours. The machine made a clunking sound as Bill pressed on the machines side lever, whilst at the same time, ink from the machine recorded Bill's working hours onto his card. Bill returned his card to the docking point then walked towards the factory gate.

Numerous people were replicating Bill's actions scurrying to leave the factory as soon as they could. Some ran, some walked fast, others collected their bicycles and some, like Bill, walked at a steady but determined pace. Everyone was focused on getting home by which ever means they could. Voices were shouting 'Goodnight', with the intention that at least some would receive their communication and they might get a response. Others just shouting 'Goodnight' without waiting for any response as it was the usual thing to do.

Friday nights, always seemed more hectic than other nights when leaving work but Bill suspected that it was just more noticeable on Fridays because of the impending weekend.

At 19 years of age, Bill had worked for Vaughn and Son's since leaving school at 14. Vaughn's produced small drop forgings for the domestic market and Bill was one of Vaughn's best workers. Youth and strength were on Bill's side and his hand eye co-ordination was accurate to a tee, a skill necessary for producing multiple forgings. Standing a full 6' 2" tall, muscular and having a solid frame, Bill was a looker.

His light brown hair was full and well-groomed, and his deep dark brown eyes were symmetrically set into his chiselled facial features. Bill's square chin framed his full lips, and his pure white teeth radiated a warm welcoming smile.

Bill had a quiet nature preferring not to engage in trivial conversation, but which was hard to avoid given his popularity. You could say that Bill was shy, but he did not perceive himself as such. There was a hidden inner strength within him, not immediately noticeable, and rarely seen by others. Bill had a surety about him that was hard to match.

As he walked out of the factory gates. taking his usual path towards the town centre, Bill squirmed as he took in the air, which smelt of rancid sulphur, old oil and burnt coal fumes. His nostrils stung as he breathed. Crossing from the factory gates, Bill aimed for the cemetery which lay opposite. Bill made his way between and around the crumbling sandstone gravestones of the cemetery whistling quietly as he moved. As he walked, he recognised some of the names etched into the stonework of those who had gone long past but whose names Bill had become familiar with over the years and who were akin to living people he knew.

From the cemetery, Bill crossed into Ford Street, which was lined with small, terraced houses. Each house looked identical with their small, sashed windows and highly polished doors, steps, and sills. The Red Admiral polish distinguished residential homes from the small houses that had been turned into workplaces and where cottage industries still produced items for the larger factories within the area. As Bill wandered down the street, he looked at the heavily draped curtains that hung on either side of each residential window and of the many aspidistras' which took pride of place at the centre of those windows.

Bill also looked into the windows of those houses which were now used as cottage industries, and which produced goods for the larger factories. Their windows were thick with grime and dirt and difficult to gaze through, others having their view blocked because of boxes, which had been piled high inside. One or two of these houses were also businesses providing office-based services. Inside these houses one could see desks, typewriters, filing cabinets and the like. All now empty of people at the end of the working week.

At the end of the Ford Street, Bill crossed the road into Chapel Street, where the towns Methodist church stood. The plain sandstone building with its tall arched windows, emulated many of the gravestones that sat in the cemetery. The black caste iron fence which surrounded the building broke only to allow access to the chapels' doors. Dates and times of services were illustrated in gold on a black painted board and the Reverend Wilkinson's name had been underlined to inform people of who was responsible for the chapel's activities.

Passing the Chapel, Bill turned left towards the town's main bus terminal. Bill could see his light blue double decker bus standing waiting for departure alongside other buses waiting to leave. Smoke was billowing from the exhausts of the buses as their engines idled away. People were already boarding busses as Bill approached the bus station and he could hear the voice of the 'clippies' encouraging people to go inside.

"Move along the bus please, move along. Smokers upstairs and no spitting," a young woman's voice shouted from Bill's bus. People scurried onboard to find a seat while others hung on to the grab rails and leather straps that were located all along the inside of the lower deck. Those who preferring to stand tending not to be travelling far.

Bill grabbed the pole located on the platform at the rear of the bus, jumped firmly onto the open platform and made his way up the stairs of the bus looking for an empty seat. Bill could see that most seats were already taken, even through the thick tobacco smoke that wafted from the front of the bus towards its rear. Bill eyed a few empty seats at the very front of the upper deck, making his way forward and passing those already seated.

"Hi ya Bill," came a voice from Bill's left.

"Hi Arthur; You ok mate?"

"Fine ta," Arthur replied. "How's ya dad Bill?"

"He's ok thanks," Bill said. "I'm just on my way to meet him in the Swan. I'm hoping he'll have got a couple of pints in by the time I get there." Bill smirked.

"Good bloke your dad," Arthur responded, "always ready to buy a bloke a drink…good bloke" Arthur mumbled as Bill shuttle towards his seat. Bill sat right at the front of the bus next to a young man who Bill had seen often but who he had never spoken to before.

"You ok mate?" Bill said to the guy he shared the seat with.

"Yes thanks," came the reply. "How are you?" the young man asked, turning to Bill.

"Good" Bill said. "Well, I will be in about twenty minutes, when I get a pint down my neck," Bill smiled.

"I know what ya mean," Bill's counterpart said. "I'm ready for a pint myself. It's been a tough week but I'm afraid it will have to wait," the younger guy stated.

Bill looked at the young man's face smiling. The younger guy had short dark hair, glistening blue eyes, a short, stubbed nose, ruddy cheeks and a beaming smile. Bill thought how attractive this young man was and how, after time, he would still hold his looks in old age.

"You going far?" Bill asked.

"I'm going up to Woodside," the guy replied.

"That's funny," Bill said. "That's where I live. I've not seen you around my area before and I know almost everyone there. Are you visiting someone?" Bill asked curiously.

The young guy smiled and responded by saying, "Actually, I'm moving into the area. Well, my mum and dad are I just live with them, so I'm moving too I suppose."

"Whereabouts you moving too?" Bill asked.

"Short Street, number 6. Apparently, an old woman had rented the house. I believe she died recently. My mum wanted to get away from the area where we currently live because the houses there are so damp; the rents also a bit cheaper in Short Street too," the guy stated with pride.

"Bloody hell" Bill responded with a shock. "I live in Short Street; you must be moving into old Mrs Fosters place. She was a lovely woman, only died three weeks ago; lived alone for years. I live at number 15, just across the road from you. It looks like we are going to be neighbours and it seems likely that we will see a lot more of each other," Bill said happily. "I'm Bill, Bill Taylor." Bill stated, pushing his hand out in greeting.

"I'm Tom, Tom Harris," Tom replied with a friendly smirk grasping Bill's out held hand firmly. "It's good to meet you," Tom sated.

"Likewise," Bill replied. Both Bill and Tom shook each other's hand vigorously, both smiling at each other. Almost instantaneously, both young men recognised that they would become friends. It was as if fate had suddenly thrown them together.

A bell rang out, 'Ding, Ding'. "Hold on tight," the conductress shouted. There was a slight jolt as the bus started its journey. Trundling along, the bus soon picked up speed, then slowed as passengers were dropped off at each bus stop along the way. People on the bus appeared to be in deep conversation with the people sitting next to them, everyone talking about the possibility of another war breaking out in Europe, decrying the actions of Hitler and his Nazi fanatics.

It was August 25$^{th}$, 1939, and tensions in Europe had been building all year. Not only had the British government recognised the potential for another war with Germany, but also the fear that was being generated within the general population. The older generations were particularly scared of a replication of events of the Great War of 1914–18.

The younger generations also feared that should political diplomacy fail, and another war broke out, it would be their turn to fight as their fathers had done previously, defending liberty and to defeat tyranny. Neville Chamberlain had already begun plans for the limited conscription of young men to serve in the armed forces. Chamberlain managing to register almost a quarter of a million men between the ages of 20 and 22 to commence military training. Talk of National Conscription became a continuous focal issue in conversation throughout the country, particularly amongst young men currently under the conscription age and for men in general.

"Things seem to be looking grim," Tom said to initiate conversation with Bill.

"Sorry," Bill replied, not fully being aware of what Tom was referring to. Bill had been looking out of the window, thinking about his father and the pint that was awaiting him.

"This thing with Germany," Tom retorted.

"Yeah it's frightening," Bill replied. "My dad is worried to death about the whole thing. He fought in the Great War, and it has affected him really badly."

"My dad too," Tom said, "still suffers from shell shock. He hardly talks nowadays and never really wants to go out. It's really sad to see him deteriorate into a recluse, when he used to enjoy socialising. He's frightened to death that I'll have to go to war if the government can't sort things out." Bill recognised the pain that Tom was experiencing; he too had to deal with the aftermath of the First World War on his father's health and how his father's mood swings had caused tensions within his family.

"Let's hope that Chamberlain can sort something out," Bill continued. "Have you registered at the Employment Exchange?" Bill enquired.

"Yeah, did it a few weeks ago. Have you?" Tom asked solemnly.

"Yes, just got to wait and see what happens now. I know that there are quite a few guys' already in training. It's just a matter of time and if war does break out, let's hope that it ends before Christmas," Bill stated. "Do you fancy coming for a drink?" Bill asked Tom changing the subject. "I'm meeting my dad in the Swan. It's our local. We always have a couple on a Friday night after work before going home for tea."

"Na thanks, not tonight. Although I would have loved to! I've got to get back to help Mum organise the new place. I heard that Mrs Foster has left the place in a right mess. I guess it must have been because she was old and not able to do stuff around the house. I might pop in for a pint later, if possible, but I don't think that I can make it until around 10ish. Will you be there?" Tom said and asked, hoping that Bill would respond positively.

"Well, I won't be staying until 10, as I usually only have one or two with my dad. I might go back later though, that is if you are coming? It would be great if you could come later," Bill replied. "I can be back in the Swan just after 9 o'clock, if that's ok? That is once I've had my tea and a bath."

"Sounds like a plan," Tom responded smiling. "I'll see what I can do."

Friday night was always the same for Bill; finish work, have a couple of pints with Dad in the Swan, home for tea and a hot bath by the fire, quick change, then back to the Swan. Bill was content with this routine, looking forward immensely to his 'chilling out' time.

"By the way" Bill asked. "How old are you?"

"I'm 18," Tom replied.

"I'm 19," Bill stated. "You don't look 18," Bill continued.

"That's because of my stunning good looks and beautiful complexion," Tom responded, laughing at the same time. Bill also burst into laughter. Both continued to laugh as they neared their destination.

"Here we are," Bill shouted. "Time to get off." Both stood up and ran to the rear of the bus, almost jumping from the top of the stairs to the bottom, landing firmly on the platform below. They both alighting from the bus even before the bus had time to stop, skipping along to slow their pace.

Both young men looked at each other smiling as they began walking at normal speed. "This way," Bill said. "There's a short cut into Short Street from here." Bill led Tom between two houses just a little way down from the bus stop. There was an ally, not much wider than a path by which High Street was linked to Short Street. It was apparent to Tom that the pathway was well used and that small carts as well as pedestrians had used this access for many a year. The ally way led to an open grassed area lined by trees.

"This is useful," Tom exclaimed.

"Yes," Bill replied. "It only takes a few minutes off your journey time, but it's better than having to walk all the way around. It's one of my favourite places," Bill said with a smile. Tom was a little confused by this last comment as he could not visualise why an ally way could possibly be a 'favourite place' but decided not to ask why.

They walked the length of the ally way, across the open green area towards the rear of some other small, terraced houses. To the left was a canal and to the right more fields. On reaching the rear of the terraced houses, another small ally led directly into Short Street.

Almost opposite and to the right, the Swan Pub sat surrounded by waste land. Further down a row of terraced houses stood darkened by the smoke coming from their chimneys. On the other side of the street, more terraced houses stretched the length of Short Street. "I live just down the street to the right," Bill stated. "You're just a bit further down on the left."

"Yes," Tom replied, having gathered his bearings.

"I suppose that you won't change your mind and join me for that drink now?" Bill asked.

"Better not," Tom replied. "I must get home and see what needs to be done at home. I'll probably meet you later though, if you are still thinking about going in the pub after I have finished helping my parents," Tom said with some anticipation.

"Absolutely," Bill responded, in a tone of excitement. "We can celebrate our first meeting and christen your house move at the same time."

Tom smiled saying, "That will be great. See you later. I'll be there about 9:00 o'clock." Tom ran down Short Street to his new residence watched by Bill.

Both Bill and Tom had good feelings about this new friendship. Although not much had been said and although the meeting had been brief; both young men felt a strange connection.

As Tom disappeared, Bill made his way across the road to the pub. On entering the Swan, Bill took a cigarette from his Park Drive Packet, struck a match, and lit his cigarette. Bill felt strangely content. Bill flicked the dead matchstick on the floor and entered the bar.

The bar was full, young men in their work clothes standing three deep to the bar and the older men seated around the small heavy tables which circumnavigated the bar. Some were perched on small stools while others sat on benches with their backs to the walls. Even though smoke filled the bar, Bill could see his father sitting in his usual place with two glasses of ale: one full and the other three parts empty.

"Hi Bill," a middle-aged man shouted from behind the bar.

"Hi Harry," Bill replied. Harry was the Swan's proprietor and had watched Bill entering the pub. Harry, a stocky man was always observant and never missed the comings and goings of his customers. More people acknowledged Bill as he walked towards his dad and Bill nodded in recognition.

The noise level in the pub seemed louder than usual with all men in deep conversation about the situation going on with Germany and the possible threat of war looming.

The mood was sombre and the usual laughter scarce. Bill approached the table where his dad sat and took a small stool. Having seated, he greeted his dad. "Hi Dad, you, okay?"

"Yes, thanks son, you had a good day?" Bill's dad enquired.

"Not too bad, the usual crap. How's your day been?" Bill replied.

"Same as, same as," Bill's dad responded. George Taylor looked tired and downhearted. Although happy to see his son, you would not have guessed by the look on his face. However, Bill had become used to his father's grim expressions and accepted his dad's response without hesitation.

"I've met one of our new neighbours today," Bill stated.

"Oh really," George said, not showing any real interest.

"Yes, I was on the bus home and met a young guy called Tom. He and his family are moving into old Mrs Fosters Place. Tom's coming in for a drink later," Bill stated, trying to start a conversation.

"Oh okay," George replied, again not showing much interest.

Bill and George sat drinking their pints not saying anything more. When they had finished their drinks, George said, "Come on then lad, let's go and get some tea. Your mother will have everything ready."

They stood up, straightened their jackets in unison and walked towards the door. "Will we be seeing you both later?" Harry shouted as Bill and his father passed the bar.

"Yes," Bill said smiling and thinking about meeting up again with Tom. "I'm meeting a mate." Harry nodded in acknowledgment and continued to pull more beer. George didn't respond to Harry's enquiry but Harry knew that it was doubtful that George would return that night.

Bill and George walked home where their evening meal was waiting. Mrs Taylor was busying herself carrying hot water from the outside brew house and filling the tin, galvanised bath that was placed in front of the living room fire. She had scooped the hot water from the copper kettle situated in the corner of the brew house and as she collected the water checked that the fire below was still burned underneath the kettle. As she entered the living room Mrs Taylor shouted, "Don't take too long eating your meal, your bath will be ready soon."

Every Friday night was bath night for George and Bill. After returning from work and the pub, and after eating their meal, it was tradition in the Taylor household that both men would bathe.

First it was George's turn, followed by Bill. Bill could not remember ever having clean bath water, always having to take the second bath after his father. Bill and George's clothes once removed, were collected by Mary, George's wife, who immediately took them to soak in the copper kettle once enough bath water had been extracted.

While George bathed, Bill related his journey home from work to his mother, and his chance meeting with Tom. Mrs Taylor seemed pleased with the tale, stating that she had also had a chance meeting with Tom's Mother, Mrs Harris. Mary informed Bill. They had met at the corner shop, and they had walked together to Mrs Harris's new home. "She seems a really nice woman," Mary claimed. "If her son Tom is anything like her, he will make a good friend."

Bill told his mother that he planned to meet Tom Later in the Swan. Bill also told his mother about Tom's father and the difficulties he was experiencing because of being in the Great War. Bill's mother nodded slightly in recognition, whilst at the same time glancing at her husband who was quietly washing his face with the bath water. "Come on George," Mary cried, "the water will be getting cold, and Bill looks filthy. He needs to get ready too and the kettle is boiling."

George grabbed the towel which Mary had placed on the back of the chair, wrapped it around his waist and as George stepped out of the bath, Bill stepped in the bath as soon as his father was out of the water. Mary thought to herself, *I have two fine men in my life,* as she glanced at the muscular bodies of her son and husband. As Mary collected her 'boys' dirty clothes to take to the brew house, she shouted, "George, your clean clothes are on the armchair, Bill's are underneath." Why she said this, both men did not understand, as every Friday it was routine for Mary to place the men's clean clothes in exactly the same place.

By the time Mary returned into the scullery, both George and Bill had finished bathing, had dressed, and Bill was about to empty the tin bath. "Leave that," Mary said. "You had better think about getting yourself over to the Swan. I suspect that Tom will be waiting for you."

"I'm not going yet; we're not meeting until 9:00 and I'm not sure whether Tom will make it. He will be helping his mum and dad," Bill replied. The Taylor family sat for a while, watching the flames of the living room fire. Mary Taylor picked up her knitting and continued where she had left off the previous evening. The crackle of the fire and the clicking of knitting needles seemed to provide reassuring sounds that allowed the family to relax.

# Chapter Two
# The Possibility of War and the Development of Friendship

Now scrubbed up and looking quite dapper, relaxed, and ready for another pint, Bill looked at the mantelpiece clock. It was 8:50 pm and time for Bill to make his move. Bill stood up acknowledging his parents and said, "I'm off then, see you later." His parents watched as Bill left the house, closing the door quietly as he left. Bill then made his way to the Swan, he smelt heavily of carbolic soap, both from his clothes and body.

The smell of the soap always gave Bill a comforting feeling. He had shaved while his father had bathed and had managed not to cut himself. Bill's face looked firm and clear and there was a glow streaming from his face because of having used near boiling water to remove his whiskers and grime.

As Bill approached the Swan, a voice from behind shouted, "Hang on mate, I'm coming." Bill stopped, turned, and saw Tom running up the street towards him. Bill noticed Tom had cleaned up too, had changed his clothes and had greased his hair. Tom's hair was brushed flat to his head with a cute parting carefully addressed on the left of his head. Bill noticed the speed at which Tom was running and was impressed with Tom's athleticism.

Tom ran with lengthy strides like a rugby player and his 5' 9" tall frame looked firm and solid. Bill could see that Tom's face had become reddened because of running and Bill could see the wide grin on Tom's face as he got closer. "Hello mate," Bill said as Tom slowed.

"Hi Bill," Tom replied smiling even wider. Both looked at each other, their smiles widening to a grin. "You scrub up well" Tom joked.

"You ain't done so bad yourself," Bill replied. Bill eyed Tom up and down admiring Tom's neat clean clothes and his highly polished boots. Bill also became aware of how well-formed Tom's torso was. Tom's upper arms and upper body filling his shirt making it look as if the shirt was just a little too small for his size. Tom's black trousers were also very tight to his frame and the black belt surrounding Tom's waist was pulled tight highlighted Tom's triangular shape.

Tom on the other hand had also eyed Bill's stance. Tom thought how much more handsome Bill looked now that he was all cleaned up. Taller by a few inches than Tom, Bill also had a fine physic, and he too was dressed well.

Looking at Bill, Tom was reminded of Laurence Olivier in Wuthering Heights, but having much lighter hair than Olivier. Even Bill's looks were similar to Olivier. Their quiet observations of each other were disturbed as the door to the pub opened and out fell Jimmy Price. Jimmy looked as if he had had one too many, wobbling past the lads mumbling something inaudible as he made his way towards his own home.

Bill gave out a laugh and said, "Come on then young Tom; let's get a couple of pints down our necks."

Tom gave a slight frown and said, "I ain't that young, I am 18 and old enough to drink."

Bill placed a hand on Tom's shoulder, he laughed again and said, "Come on then 'old man', drinks await." Tom laughed as he was led through the pub doorway into the already crowded bar.

As Bill opened the door, smoked gushed out and heads turned. Harry, the ever-attentive barman shouted, "Come on Bill and bring your mate; two mild, is it?" Bill nodded and pushed his way to the bar closely followed by Tom.

"This is Tom," Bill informed Harry, whilst also informing the lads around the bar at the same time.

"Welcome young Tom," Harry uttered, while pulling the two pints of dark mild ale.

"Tom and his folk have just moved into old Mrs Foster place just down the road," Bill informed everyone standing close.

A few of those standing by the bar acknowledged Tom and a few said, "Nice to meet you" glaring at Tom. Tom nodded and smiled cordially. The introductions were cut short as the lads at the bar returned to the conversation they were having before being interrupted by Bill and Tom entering the bar. It was noticeable to both Bill and Tom that the topic of conversation was deep and disconcerting.

Fred Evans, who was in the group at the bar turned to Bill and said, "We are just discussing the headlines in today's paper. We all think it's very worrying and frightening."

"Why?" Bill asked, "what's happened? I haven't seen a newspaper today."

"Well," Fred said, looking very studious, "the Germans have signed a 'nonaggressive treaty' with the Russians, but none of us here believe it. None of us trust the Russians, or those Nazi's. We all have a feeling that nothing good is going to come out of this. And that Chamberlain doesn't seem to recognise what's really going on. We all know that the Gerry's and the Russians are picking on Poland, and we all think that war is coming whether we like it or not. Even the Irish are getting involved. The IRA have exploded a bomb in Coventry city centre, and it's killed five people. Things are getting bad."

Bill looked at Fred with concern in his eyes and said, "Let's just hope that it don't come to that. If war does come, many of us here are going to be called up and I can't imagine how people are going to feel about that. My dad for sure won't be happy."

"Mine neither," Tom butted in.

Bill grabbed the two pints which had been placed on the counter and replaced them with a florin. Bill gave Tom his pint and they both took a long gulp. Harry gave Bill his change and both lads moved towards the table usually used by Bill's dad. They sat dinking quietly without saying much because of the conversation they had had with Fred at the bar.

Tom then looked at Bill and said, "What will you do if war does break out Bill?"

"I dunno," Bill replied. "I suppose I won't have much say in the matter if I get conscripted, but as far as I'm aware, the government are only calling up those blokes over 22. I've got three years to worry about that and if there is a war, it will all be over and dusted in a flash. There ain't no call for another Great War, the people just won't stand for it."

Tom nodded agreeing with Bill. "You're right Bill. They're all getting worked up over nothing."

Bill and Tom changed the subject and began interrogating each other about work, their likes and dislikes, their friends, family, hobbies, and interest. Both recognised that they had much in common. Both were the only child, both worked in industry; Bill in drop forging and Tom in castings; neither of them had what you would call close friends, and both enjoyed walking and running.

Both enjoyed having a few pints and the occasional cigarette, but neither liked getting drunk and both enjoyed going to the cinema. The evening was going well and as they talked, both recognising that they liked each other a lot. It was Tom who said, "Well, now we have met, I do hope that we become good lifelong friends and not just acquaintances."

Bill smiled and nodded simultaneously, "You took the words right out of my mouth. I was just thinking that."

Tom looked at Bill with a contented smile and said, "It just feels right."

"So, what are your plans tomorrow?" Bill asked Tom.

"Well, I'm helping sort stuff out tomorrow at home. Mum wants me to wallop the bedrooms and staircase over the weekend and we are planning to wallop the living room, kitchen, and scullery next week. You can always come and help if you like," Tom stated with a grin.

"Yeah, I'd like that. I quite like decorating and I haven't got anything planned for this weekend," Bill responded. "What time you planning to start?" Bill asked.

"Well, if we get started early, I should imagine that we could have the lot done in about six hours," Tom said enthusiastically.

"You're hoping," Bill responded. "I guess it's going to take at least six hours just to do the bedrooms, then at least another 4 hours to do the stairs and landing," Bill calculated. "What if I come round about 8:00 in the morning? We should have at least finished the bedrooms before opening time and we can do the stairs and landing Sunday?" Bill stated.

"Sounds fine to me," Tom confirmed.

"What about we also start early on Sunday too? I usually go for a run during the afternoon, usually after dinner. You can come too," Bill said with a smile and in a confident manner. "I usually run along the canal to Jacobs Bridge, cross over into Yew woods and then go around Jacobs's farm to the lake, take a short dip and then return the way I came. Do you swim Tom?" Bill asked.

"Yeah, that sounds great; and yeah, I love swimming. I'll have to make sure I bring a towel with me," Tom replied.

Bill saw the excitement in Tom's face and guessed that Tom had never had someone who he could spend time with. Bill was also excited, thinking to himself that it would be nice to have a mate to chat and share time with. Bill's running and swimming time had always been done alone in the past and Bill of late had been getting tired of being alone so much.

The lads finished their drinks and consumed three more before they set off for home. The lads stopped outside to Bill's house to bid each other 'goodnight'.

"Thanks for tonight," Tom said. "I've really enjoyed myself and have really enjoyed your company." Tom appeared shy in saying this, as if he was saying something out of place.

"Hey," Bill said, recognising Tom's uncomfortable stance. "I've really enjoyed it too and I'm looking forward to the rest of the weekend. It should be fun." Tom smiled, and Bill smiled back. They shook hands and Tom began to run towards his house, turning as he ran to wish Bill goodnight again. Bill stood watching Tom, still smiling and having a feeling of contentment.

"See you at eight," Tom shouted.

"I'll be there," Bill shouted.

Bill walked to his front door and walked into the living room. Bill's mum and dad were still sitting in their armchairs. Bill's mother was knitting and his father was watching the fire, smoking a cigarette.

"Hi," Bill said.

"Hello son," Bill's mother responded.

"Did you have a good night?" Bill's father enquired.

"Yes," Bill said mindfully. "Yes, I've had a really good night. That Tom is a really nice bloke. I'm going to his house tomorrow morning to help him decorate. I'm also going around Sunday too." Bill's dad looked in amazement. Bill was not the type to volunteer to help others although Bill had a good heart. Bill's mother also glanced at Bill as he said this.

"Thought that you would have come in the Swan for a pint," Bill said to his father, changing the subject.

"Wasn't really bothered to be honest." George said. Bill could see that something was troubling his father but decided not to pursue the conversation. "I'm off to bed." George said. "Don't be late Mary," George told his wife as he walked towards the stairs.

"I'm coming with you," Mary said as she folded her knitting and placing it into her knitting basket. "Goodnight son," Mary said to Bill kissing him on his cheek.

"Goodnight Mum; night Dad," Bill said quietly. After his mother and father had gone to Bed, Bill sat in his mother's armchair as it was closest to the fire. The fire was dying but the embers were still spitting slightly. Bill poked the fire and sat back looking at the dying flames and at the ash forming. Bill was content.

Bill realised that he had not felt this content for a long time, even with the worries of an impending war. Bill thought about his day, the journey on the bus, his meeting with Tom.

Their walk down the alley and their time spent in the pub. Bill was pleased with the day and the possibility of him having a 'best mate', something that he had not had before. After about half an hour, Bill got up, switched off the light and went upstairs to bed. He undressed, got into bed, and lay there for what seemed hours, still thinking about his day with Tom and looking forward to what the next day would bring. Bill drifted off into a deep consistent sleep.

# Chapter Three
# Decorators and Dippers

After leaving Bill, Tom ran into his new home. His parents had already gone to bed but had left the light on for Tom's return. Tom sat on a chair by the kitchen table smiling as he removed his boots. Tom could hardly contain himself. What a day he had had, he had found a real friend had felt comfortable in his presence and had found someone who was not only going to help him decorate, but with who he could spend leisure time with too. Tom was hoping that the decorating would not take long so that he and Bill could go running and swimming together.

Tom switched off the lights, climbed the stairs to his bedroom, undressed and got into bed. Tom could hear his father snoring in the next bedroom and heard his mother shift to get comfortable. Tom suddenly needed to use the toilet; he rolled out of bed, reached under the bed for the 'gazunder' relieved himself and then jumped back into bed having replaced the gazunder in its rightful place. Tom pulled the blankets over his shoulders but could not sleep. He lay awake, not moving, his mind taking him through his days journey.

As Tom was recalling the day his smile just got wider; why did he feel like this; why was he so elated? Tom didn't know and couldn't answer his own thoughts but remained feeling happy even without an answer. Tom began to focus on the tasks that needed to be done the next day, running through each task applying times and possible mishaps. Tom began to fall slowly into a restful slumber.

Tom woke at around 7:00 am the next morning feeling fresh and excited. He jumped out of bed, dressed, and put his evening clothes in the tallboy at the bottom of his bed. He ran downstairs into the brew house, washed his hands and face in cold water. He walked back into the house where his mother had started making breakfast. "You were late last night," Tom's mother said, more enquiring than angry.

"I wasn't that late," Tom stated. "I just had a few drinks with Bill and came home before closing time. Bill's coming round this morning to help me decorate," Tom said, feeling incredibly pleased with himself.

"Must be a nice bloke, this Bill," mother said.

"He is Mum. I think that you and Dad will like him a lot. He's 19 and he's an only child like me. His dad was in the war, and he also has problems like Dad. We get on really great, oh! And he also likes walking and running as well." Tom's mother was a little taken aback by the enthusiastic way Tom was describing his newfound friend, but was pleased that at last, Tom was at least trying to mix. After all, Tom had spent too much time being a loner.

By eight, a hot breakfast of fried eggs, bacon and fried bread had been served, eaten and the dirty crockery had been moved. Tom retuned upstairs, moved furniture then began to place old bedsheets around the floor of the main bedroom where Tom's parents slept. Tom collected paint and brushes from downstairs ready for application and began inspecting the walls.

Luckily for Tom, the walls in both bedrooms had Lincrusta wallpaper and although Edwardian in style, the paper had been applied well. The walls had been cared for by the previous tenant but were soiled and dirty, mainly because of the many fires that had been lit and burned over the years.

Tom's mother had chosen a yellow/cream paint for the walls and a white gloss type paint for the skirting, window frames, doors, and dado picture rails. As Tom completed the preparation, he suddenly heard a knock at the front door. Knowing that it was Bill, Tom hurried down the stairs, almost falling due to the speed he was travelling. Tom dived towards the front door to greet his friend. Tom moved so quickly that it seemed that if he did not reach the door within 30 seconds, Bill might disappear from the face of the planet.

"Hello mate, how are you? And thanks for coming. Come in," Tom burbled with enthusiasm. Tom's smile stretched from ear to ear.

"Morning Tom," Bill replied as he stepped through the door.

"This is my mum and dad," Tom said nodding towards his parents. "Mum, Dad, this is Bill."

"Hello Bill, really nice to meet you and thank you so much for offering to help out," Tom's mother said as she moved towards Bill to shake his hand. Bill smiled and nodded. Tom's father looked directly at Bill and nodded, not saying anything.

"Nice to meet you both," Bill said.

"Please call me Joan and my husband is Joe," Joan instructed Bill. "Do you want a cuppa before you start?" Joan asked.

"No thanks," Bill replied. "Just had breakfast and I want to crack on. I'm hoping that me and Tom will finish early enough so that we can go for a run afterwards and possibly go for a swim in Jacob's farm lake."

"Come on then," Tom said, "let's get cracking." Tom led Bill up the stairs to his parent's bedroom and handed Bill a paint brush. "If you do those two walls," pointing to the inside wall and long wall, "which was where the bed would be situated, I'll start on these two, the opposite wall and window wall. We can then meet in the middle." Both lads began painting whilst chatting about Tom's mother and Father. The reason their conversation focused on Tom's parents was because Bill had said that he thought Tom's parents were lovely and had felt immediately at ease when meeting them for the first time.

The conversation then turned to going for their first run after they had finished their work and taking a dip in Jacob's pool. Suddenly, Tom stopped and looking shocked said, "Oh my god, I've just remembered, I haven't got any swim wear or shorts."

Bill said, "Don't worry, I usually 'skinny dip'. No one will see you and it helps in drying off much quicker and I've got a spare pair of shorts you can have for running. They are too small for me, but I think that they will fit you perfectly." The boys cracked on with their decorating completing Tom's parents' bedroom within two hours. They would have completed it within an hour and a half, but had been prevented because Tom's mother insisted, they were topped up with copious amounts of tea and had stopped the boys from working as she admired their work.

The second bedroom, Tom's room, was finish in the same time frame and after cleaning up, they set about arranging the furniture, while Tom's mother made the beds. "It looks lovely," Tom's mother said.

"We'll finish the landing and stair tomorrow," Tom said with satisfaction.

"If you would like," Bill began, "we can do your lounge and kitten next weekend?" Tom's mother was overjoyed at the suggestion and Tom just smiled, looking directly at Bill.

"That would be amazing," Tom's mother added. At that, Tom's father came up stairs to survey the completed work.

"Nice job," Tom's father said nodding as he looked at the walls in both bedrooms.

"It's almost 2:00pm," Bill said. "I'd better go and get changed if we are going to go for that run and swim. I'll grab a sandwich and will be back in half an hour."

"Sounds great to me," Tom replied, looking like the cat that had been given the cream.

Bill left and Tom set about washing the dried paint off his hands and face. Tom grabbed a small amount of cheese from the larder and cut off a chunk of bread. Tom ate his meal quickly and sat waiting for Bill. Bill returned about 40 minutes after he had left Tom's house. Bill had also cleaned up and was dressed in an old shirt and shorts. Bill was also wearing a pair of navy plimsolls and was holding another pair of shorts in his hand.

"Here you go Tom," passing the shorts to Tom. Tom grabbed the shorts, ran upstairs, and put on the shorts given to him by Bill. Within minutes, Tom was downstairs, and he too had dressed similar to Bill.

"Come on then, let's go," Tom cried. Bill looked at Tom in his now new shorts. They fitted perfectly, although a little tight. The waist fitting Tom exactly, but the main body of the shorts gripped Tom's frame. Both lads said goodbye to Tom's parents and walked into the street.

The lads began to jog down Short Street, on into Lodge Street and onto the canal pathway which was accessible halfway down the street. They climbed through a hole in the fence which had been placed by the parish council to deter access to the canal, but which had been broken by kids who wanted to get to the canal. The boys began their run, starting at a pace which moved them quickly, but which did not overexert them. On their left, and on the other side of the canal stood a small wharf where several canal barges were moored.

Two barges had been hauled onto the embankment where repairs were being carried out. As it was Saturday afternoon, the wharf was bereft of workers and a strange quietness hung over the work area. As they jogged along, they saw water voles scampering and swimming amongst the reeds on the opposite bank. Moor Hens and Coots also bobbed in the water, both distinguished by their different coloured head crests; Coots having a block of white on their black plumage, while the Moor Hens topped their dark feathers with scarlet red.

The boys approached the first bridge as the canal narrowed. The old bricks of the bridge were a miss match of Red London and Victorian Staffordshire Blue bricks. The iron work which girdled and framed the brickwork had rusted in parts and there were deep ridges worn into the iron where ropes from horses used to pull the barges had rubbed away the iron over the years. The used ruts shone bright silver and were silky smooth against the rusting untouched parts of the metal frame.

Running down the walls, water had formed ridges of white creamy calcium deposits and on the apex of the roof small stalactites had formed. At the other side of the bridge stood an isolated pub, The Navigation, which was frequented by barge families and which the locals rarely used because of the frequent drunken brawls that happened there at night. On the near side, another pub stood, The Prince of Wales, used by locals and from which barge people were banned. From then on, and on either side of the canal, it was countryside and farmland for the next eight miles.

The boys concentrated on their running, occasionally making some comment about the flora and fauna, and occasionally just glancing at each other smiling as they trundled on. They passed under another three bridges before reaching Jacob's bridge, which they crossed and entered Yew's wood. Yew wood was an ancient wood, spanning several acres. Migratory paths had been formed over the millennia maintained now by people who visited the woods, and which had formed solid trails. Through the wood they trundled taking in the smell of the trees and the damp moss under foot.

They listened to the many birds chirping away hidden from sight in the foliage, only intermittently seeing the birds as they flew from tree to tree. After another twenty minutes of running in the wood, they turned off the main pathway following single file through the shrubbery. Quickly, they entered a large clearing; at its centre, stood Jacob's pool. Surrounded by lush green grass, the pool looked still and the water a greenish brown in colour.

Around the perimeter of the pool, sporadic clumps of reed beds interrupted the smooth shape of the pool. Bull rushes waved their mace like heads of grenadiers in the gentle breeze breaking the even levels of the reeds. There was evidence that wildlife lived and played amongst the rushes, but none could be seen as Tom and Bill continued to circumnavigate the pool. Both boys were sweating profusely and sweat marks were visible under each of the boy's armpits, staining their shirts.

Bill looked wetter than Tom and Bill's shirt also had sweat marks on the back of his shirt making a 'V' shape as the sweat reduced when it reached the lower part of his back. Bill ran on a little from Tom and stopped by a smoothed grassed area located between two large reed clumps. Bill cried out, "This is the place, Tom. The best place to rest and to swim and with no one around to see you."

Tom caught up, stopping next to Bill and looked around. *It was a beautiful spot,* thought Tom, whose breathing was slowly steadying to its normal rate. "Oh wow!" Tom cried. "This is just an amazing place. I've never been here before." Both lads smiled and sat on the cool grass. Nothing was said for a while as both boys took in the quiet and tranquillity of the pool and at the same time calming their bodies.

After a brief time, Bill got up without saying a word and began to strip naked. Tom at first could only look, feeling a little embarrassed but not uncomfortable. "Are you coming for a swim or are you just going to stay there looking?" Bill asked. Tom stood up, healed off his plimsolls, took off his shirt and downed his shorts. Both stood completely naked looking at each other and feeling quite comfortable in each other's presence before running to the edge of the pool and jumped into the cold fresh water.

It was clear that both boys were good swimmers, Bill having a smoother swimming stroke than Tom, who tended to splash as he tried to keep up with Bill. They swam to the centre of the pool where they lay on their backs treading water, floating, and looking at the structures being made by the clouds hovering in the bright blue sky. After a little while, Bill began to make his way back to the shoreline followed closely by Tom. Just as they reached the edge of the pond, Bill stood up, his feet sinking a little way into the jelly like silt at the bottom of the pond. Here the water was only about two feet deep, the water just reaching Bill's knees.

Bill cupped his hands and scooped up water throwing it directly at Tom. Bill laughed as he splashed more and more water at Tom. Tom retaliated by lying on his back in the water and splashing Bill heavily as he kicked. Bill dived forward grabbing Tom and pushed him under the water. As Tom popped up out of the water, he regained his balance and plunged to grab Bill. Bill was surprised at Tom's strength, taking all of his skill and energy to remain standing. Both boys were locked in a wresting hold and the each in turn pushed and cajoled in attempt to duck each other.

Laughing, Tom ran to the side of the pool and clambered out of the water. Bill stood in the water for a while catching his breath before joining Tom. Both lads then fell onto the grass and lay there catching their breath and drying in the warm evening sun. "I'm really enjoying myself," Tom said. "In fact, this has been one of the best days ever."

Bill now relaxed and holding his hands behind his head replied, "Yes. It's been great. We'll have to do it again tomorrow." Tom smiled recognising the feeling of being totally overjoyed which filled the whole of his body.

"I would love to do this every day. It's just a shame that we have to work and that the summer is coming to an end," Tom murmured, as if these words were just thoughts. Bill then rolled onto his side looking at Tom. Bill could not stop himself looking at Tom's firm body, his strong arms, his firm chest, and flat stomach. As Bill glanced, he noticed Tom's manhood slightly raised and pointing towards his navel.

Tom rolled towards Bill, and he too looked a Bill's manly physic, he too noticed Bill's manhood and seemed pleased that they were equally matched. Bill then realised that he too was starting to become erect. To hide his own embarrassment, he began to dress quickly. Tom took a little more time to dress but soon they were both ready for the jog back home.

The run home seemed not to take as much time as the run to Jacob's pool. The evening sun was beginning to cool, and the dappled light reflected on the water in the canal. Little was said between the boys on their return home, but it was clear to both lads that they had really enjoyed each other's company and recognised that their friendship would be strong and long lasting.

As they approached the old wharf, and as they clambered through the hole in the fence, Tom asked, "What time are you planning to come tomorrow?"

"Same time as today," Bill said. "It shouldn't take as long tomorrow to do the stairs and landing, and then we will have time for Sunday dinner before our afternoon run."

"And swim," Tom said firmly.

"Yes, and swim," Bill replied laughing. "We can meet up at the Swan later if you like?" Bill went on.

"That will be great," Tom responded.

"Say nine. Is that okay?" Bill asked in anticipation.

"Absolutely: I'll call for you on my way to the pub."

As they reached Tom's house, Bill said, "I'll see you later mate." Then continued up the street. "Don't be late," Bill instructed.

"I won't," Tom replied as he opened the door to his house. Tom did as he promised, calling for Bill on his way to the Swan. Worried voices greeted the boys as they entered the Swan that night. The discussion about the possibility of impending war echoed around the bar. Saddened faces and arguments abound about Chamberlain's ability to reach diplomatic compromises or to get the Germans to agree to reduce their ambitions were evident. There was a genuine fear in the voices of men within the bar as they depressingly voiced their own views and opinions.

Tom and Bill grabbed their beer from the bar and sat down. "All this talk about war is worrying," Tom said looking directly at Bill.

"Yes," Bill said, "but let's not spoil the day and let's talk about today and plan for tomorrow. Talking about the possibility of war just depresses me." The lads smiled at each other as they retraced their steps of the day. By the end of the evening, they had planned their course of action for the next day, running through times.

How they were going to tackle the decorating of the stairs and landing at Tom's house and their plan to emulate today's run and swim at Jacob's pool. The lads also planned on meeting each day to travel to and from work together and to meet each evening after work. Their conversation was jovial, relaxed, and ambitious; both looked and felt relaxed, yet elated.

Sunday went as planned. Bill arrived at Tom's at 8:30am and they worked happily together until lunchtime, completing the landing and stairs to the Joy of Tom's mother. It felt strange to both lads that during their work time, they felt compelled to keep checking on each other. Each boy catching the other staring and smiling as they worked. Once the decorating was finished, Bill returned home for his Sunday lunch. Tom's mother had also prepared Sunday lunch and had invited Bill to join them. However, Bill stated that his mother was expecting him at home but thanked her all the same.

"Maybe next week," Bill said. After lunch, the boys had a brief time to rest before they met up. Tom was so excited about the thought of going for another run with Bill that he changed into his running gear immediately the lunch table had been cleared. At 2:00pm exactly, Bill was knocking on Tom's door. Tom could hardly contain himself and on opening the door, could see that Bill was equally excited. Their afternoon run along the canal and through the woods seemed even more exhilarating that the previous day and it seemed as if both were running faster to enable them to have more time at their swimming pool.

Arriving at their chosen spot by the pool, the boys spent no time stripping off and diving into the cool, still water. They swam less, spending more time splashing around and play wrestling. Both had overcome any shyness or inhibitions. It felt for both, just so natural to be together naked as they jumped on each other, pulling each other over in turn and having contact with each other's bodies as they locked together. Each boy admired the others form and shape through touch and sight.

Even though the water was chilled, both boys felt a warmth not experienced before. They also recognised that each, was beginning to become aroused. Tom felt a rush of warm tingling sensations gathering around his groin area as his penis began to twitch and swell. Bill on the other hand suddenly realised that he was erect when his member touched Tom's body as they rolled around in the water. Both aware of their own responses and that of their friend, they chose not to say anything.

Once out of the water, they spent more time lying on the grass drying in the warmth of the sun, lying closer together this time with their upper arms, hips and legs touching. It felt natural to both, and each was comforted in each other's presence. Never had either experienced such overwhelming admiration for another human being and neither had ever felt such an intense sense of bonding.

As the rays of the sum warmed them, Tom began to feel his manhood twitching again as his penis began to rise, becoming firmer and ridged. Bill sensed Tom's excitement and he too started to become erect. In realising his excitement was visible, Tom became a little shy. Sitting, Tom grabbed his shorts, pulling them on with speed. Bill's face was flushed, and he too began dressing quickly, starting first with his shirt, allowing more time for his erection to be noticed by Tom.

Both young men had seen each other's excitement and were secretly pleased that their man hoods were of similar shape, size, and girth. Both were well blessed. Both having above average size. Once dressed, they began their trek home. Each running in silence and both having thoughts of what had happened at the pool, especially what had happened when lying on the grass drying together. When they arrived home and before leaving each other, they agreed to meet once again that evening at the Swan.

Tom wanted to say something to Bill about what had happened at the pool that day but chose not to say anything. In his mind, Tom decided that it was best not to broach the subject. The last thing Tom wanted was to cause embarrassment or ill feeling between them. The lad's eyes met, locked together is a short stare, acknowledging each other, they smiled. Bill gave Tom a manly hug before they went their separate ways.

That night, they met at the Swan as promised. Nothing was said of the day's events or of their time at the pool. They drank quietly, chatted little but each was content in each other's company. More content than they had ever been before. As they sat, their knees touched. Neither boy moved, preferring to have this contact. Under normal circumstances, if someone else had had contact in such a way, both boys would have retracted their legs to maintain space, but for Tom and Bill, the closer they were together, the better it felt.

# Chapter Four
# The Outbreak of War and
# a Christmas Surprise

From their first meeting and from their first weekend as friends, Tom and Bill's friendship blossomed, each day their relationship grew stronger. Each weekday morning, they would meet to catch the bus into town for work and at the end of each shift, they met again to travel home together. They completed the decorating in Tom's house and Bill almost became part of the fixture and fittings. Tom equally had become a regular visitor to Bill's house, feeling part of Bill's family. It seemed as if both families had been close for years rather than months and the similarities within each household were virtually a carbon copy.

For the boys, each evening was spent at the Swan and at the weekend they worked together doing jobs around their respective homes, usually working together. Followed by an afternoon run and swim together at Jacob's pool. The excitement they had felt on that first Sunday repeated itself each time they swam together, but both boys took little notice apart from recognising that their sexual reactions was happening more frequently, more quickly and appeared to be lasting longer.

Both boys began to feel comfortable with each other attaining their erections and yet, neither of the boys said anything about this to each other. It was as if, there was an expectancy that each would become aroused and each admired seeing the others manhood responding.

On the 3$^{rd}$ of September 1939, Neville Chamberlain, the British Prime Minister, declared war against Nazi Germany. Britain had given Hitler an ultimatum to withdraw his army after the Germans had invaded Poland. On the day Britain declared war on Germany, Parliament immediately passed more wide-reaching measures, The National Service (Armed Forces) Act, imposing conscription on all males aged between the ages of 18 and 41 who had to register for service. Those medically unfit were exempt, as were others in key industries and jobs such as banking, farming, medicine, and engineering. Conscientious objectors had to appear before a tribunal to argue their reasons for refusing to join-up.

If their cases were not dismissed, they were granted one of several categories of exemption, and were given non-combatant jobs. Conscription helped greatly to increase the number of men in active service during the first year of the war. Because both Tom and Bill were in engineering jobs, both were exempt from conscription at that time, both relieved but still worried that should the war go on longer than Christmas, their positions might change dramatically.

From the declaration of war, nothing much appeared to be happening, apart from one military land operation on the Western front when the French, supported by the British invaded the Saar district of Germany. There remained a general expectancy that the war would be over within the matter of months or even weeks, however, news was still coming in that the Germans remained active in Poland and were also looking further afield.

People became less worried about a repetition of the Great War as military tactics had changed considerably during the intermittent years and modern mechanisation rendered the old type of warfare defunct. People were becoming complacent and more relaxed, referring to this war as a Phoney War.

Bill and Tom continued their routines and their runs and swimming at weekends until the weather began to change later that autumn. The runs continued but the swimming became less as the nights drew in and it became too cold to take the plunge. As the sun moved and nights became shorter, there was also less time to laze about drying in the sun, and so the boys placed a greater emphasis on their running and keeping fit.

More time was now being spent indoors, each visiting each other's houses and becoming more familiar with the others families. By November, the lads were having their Sunday lunches at alternative houses and were being looked at by the neighbours as more like brothers than just friends.

As Christmas approached, plans began to be made to celebrate for the main day and for the coming New Year. Many families at that time began preparations early. Christmas puddings were made well in advance, so too was mincemeat and the pickling of vegetables, such as red cabbage, shallots, small cucumbers, and beetroot. Most families also kept pigs, ducks, geese, and chickens. Pigs were singled out for fattening up along with one goose, the traditional bird of choice for Christmas dinner. Tom and Bill had clubbed together during September to buy two young pigs and several chickens.

They had been industrious in building a stye in Bill's back garden and had also erected a chicken coup in Toms. Their pigs were fattening nicely, fed on oats, apples, and kitchen waste. The chickens were also well fed and were laying regularly. The boys named their pigs Liz and Georgina, after the King and Queen. Their chickens were given names after distant relatives. They had one cockerel, named Hitler. They decided to call the bird Hitler because of the way in which its comb lay to one side of its head, giving it a style like the German leader.

Homemade brews were also on the go. These brews were Tom's father's initiative, and he tended his liquids as if it were gold dust. Alongside beer, Dandelion and Burdock, Ginger beer and Nettle pop was also slowly fermenting. Other products from the garden were stored, including potatoes, carrots, parsnips, and firm fruit such as apples and pears. Soft fruit and tomatoes had been preserved earlier during the summer. Bill's mother had also been collecting the beans from her legume crop and had dried these, storing them in jars. She had quite a collection of dried peas, runner beans and broad beans.

Adding these to small quantities of cheap meat made for a wonderful filling stew. Herbs had also been dried, including sage, thyme, rosemary, and chives. It was if, both households had begun a cottage industry of preservation. On their runs, Bill and Tom had also collected rose hips and brambles, which Tom's mother had turned into jams and syrups. Both families shared whatever they produced and ensured that they never ran short of food. Extra stacks of coal, was also accumulated over the months before Christmas in preparedness for the onset of winter.

As the days drew towards Christmas, Bill's parents had planned to remain at home, preparing as normal. However, they sadly received news that Bill's aunt had become seriously ill. Bill's aunt, who was his father's only sister lived some distance away and because there was a fear that his aunt's life was slipping away, Bill's mother and father decided that they would visit his aunt over the Christmas period.

Bill would not be able to go with his parents because of work commitments and because there was limited space at his aunts for Bill to stay. In truth, Bill really didn't want to go along with his parents, preferring to stay at home and to have Tom close by. Tom's family happily invited Bill into their home to celebrate Christmas and Tom's mother was happy to provide Bill with his Christmas lunch.

In many ways, Bill was more than happy with this arrangement, and he told Tom that while his parents were away, Tom could spend more time at Bill's place. At Bill's invitation, Tom became elated in anticipation, finding it difficult to hold back his pleasure at the thought of being alone with Bill.

During the latter part of the year, the government introduced 'Blackout' and although the blackout meant there were no Christmas lights in the streets. Window boards had to be constructed to ensure that no light escaped from their homes. The boys found timber from a derelict property located about a mile from their home and which had previously been a farmhouse.

In truth, much of the materials they had needed for the pig styes, and chicken coup had also come from this building, including bricks and wire netting. They had also taken an old tin bath from the property to use as a trough and had found a seed holder, which they converted to use for the chickens.

The majority of home decorations for the festive season were still placed around the inside of people's homes, but many decided to make their own. Bill collected holly from Yew wood and had placed this on his mantelpiece, strategically placing candles amongst the small boughs. He had also adorned ivy around picture frames. The green of the holly and ivy added cheer to the dull room and the red of the holly berries accentuated the shiny leaves. Bill also gave lots of holly to Tom's mother, helping her to decorate her home.

Pre-war decorations and glass baubles also decorated make-do Christmas trees which in Bill's case, was a single bough, taken from a conifer, also from Yew wood. A similar bough, but one that was larger, was given to Tom's mother. Bill had dipped some holly leaves into a strong solution of Epsom salts and as it dried, it produced a beautiful, frosted effect.

The boys also collected blown light bulbs and had painted them to use as baubles for the tree. With the fire burning, Bill's house gave off a warm comfortable, festive glow; Tom's place equally looked grand and festive, mirroring Bill's home.

As a present for Tom, Bill had made a wooden potato dibber out of a broken spade handle, carefully shaping the point and varnishing the completed gift to make it appear new. Bill had wrapped Tom's present in tissue paper placing it with care under the conifer bough in his house. Bill had also purchased cufflinks for Tom, thinking that this was more personal. Tom's mother had made jams earlier during the year and Tom had taken two jars also wrapped in tissue paper ready to give Bill as his gift, along with a tie pin purchased from Harry Cooper's, the only men's tailors in town. They too were placed under the decorated bough.

On the eve of Christmas Eve, Bill's parents left to visit his aunt. Bill's parents had left gifts for Tom and his parents and Tom's parents exchanged their gifts before they left. Taking his parents to the railway station was tinged with some sadness as Bill's parents would be away from home for Christmas but was also a high point for Bill as he now looked forward to Tom moving in with him.

Bill had asked Tom if he wanted to stay over at his place while his parents were away, and Tom had accepted this invitation with pleasure. Tom's mother said on hearing about the invitation, "It will be nice for Bill to have you around; saves being on his own and it will give me and your dad some peace and quiet. You can both come round for your all of your meals, so you won't starve."

Saturday 23rd December was when Tom moved in with Bill for his short stay. The boys spent an exciting morning pottering around Bill's house while planned for their afternoon run. They brought in wood and coal indoors from the coal house so that they would not have to go outside into the cold and set up the bath in front of the living room fire, to use on their return from their run. Bill also ensured that there was plenty of coal next to the bedroom fires too and topped up the water jug on each of the dressing tables in each bedroom.

During the latter part of December 1939 an anticyclone brought frosts and fog at night. Day time temperatures had been gradually dropping, becoming much colder as Christmas approached. Temperatures were now well below zero. No longer warm enough to wear shorts for running, both boys found old trousers, which they used as running gear and tied the bottom of the trouser legs with string before setting off.

They also wore old jumpers and hand knitted gloves, as well as hats and scarves. They agreed that on their return from their first run when Tom had moved into Bill's, they would take a bath before going out to Tom's house for tea. Tom built up a roaring fire in the brew house under the copper kettle and filled the kettle to capacity. All the fires in the house were lit, including the bedrooms and the living room fire was well banked up with coal. They set out clean clothes in preparation for their return. Bill also placed towels on the clothes horse near to the fire and stood two large stone hot water bottles next to the fire ready to warm their beds. It was a scene of domestic bliss.

The boy's afternoon run was hard going. The ground solid due the extreme cold and the bighting wind began to cut deep into their faces almost immediately the boys left the house. The run kept both boys' warm, but their hands and feet became frozen, as were their faces. For both boys, the run took an age. Both wanting to get back to Bill's house where they could be warm and to settle down together. As they entered Bill's house after completing their run, they moved quickly to the fire which was now fully ablaze and crackling.

They warmed their hands rubbing them vigorously, and then leaning towards the fire gradually defrosted their chilled faces. After a fleeting time, they both turned around to warm their backs. "We had better fill the bath and get out of these dirty clothes," Bill said.

"I'll fill the bath if you make a cuppa," Tom replied.

"Sounds like a good deal," Bill said, grabbing the kettle off its hanger by the fire and going into the scullery to make the tea. Tom went into the brew house, removed the wooden lid from the copper kettle. A gust of steam rose from the kettle. Tom began scooping ladles of boiling water, carefully filling the galvanised bucket. After several trips to and from the brewhouse, Tom had succeeded in filling the bath and Bill had got everything ready for their brew. They drank their tea allowing for the bath water to cool a little then Bill asked, "Who's going first?" as he dipped his fingers into the bath water testing the temperature.

"You go first," Tom said, "but don't take too long, I don't want a cold bath."

Bill stripped off throwing his clothes by the door to the scullery. Bill stood completely naked standing at the head of the bath. He slowly stepped into the hot water stopping for a short while. Tom looked at Bill directly in admiration eyeing Bill's manly physic. Then Bill began to slowly move to a sitting position, holding the sides of the bath to steady himself. Tom looked at Bill's firm thighs and buttocks as he lowered himself into the water, thinking how wonderfully pronounced Bill's muscles were. Bill looked so handsome, like a Greek adonise, handsome, lean, muscular, and fit.

Tom watched as Bill began to wash his hair, face and neck; his upper arms and forearms were next before standing to wash the lower part of his body. Tom continued to watch Bill in awe. Bill then re-seated himself in the bath where he lay soaking for a short time. "I'll soon be done," Bill stated, enjoying the fact that this was the very first time he could remember ever having clean bath water.

Tom had been sitting in the armchair near the fire while Bill was bathing not realising that he had watched Bill's every move. He had watched as Bill rubbed soap onto his face and hair, then his hands, arms, and upper body. He had watched as Bill stood up to wash the lower part of his body and legs and the special attention Bill had taken when he had washed around his buttocks and groin. Tom admired Bill, the strength of his arms and legs and the firmness of Bill's muscular chest.

He admired Bill's bottom, his firm cheeks and he particularly admired the size of his manhood, which had increased in size through having contact with the warmth of the water. Tom suddenly realised that in watching Bill, he too had become aroused. Tom stood up to begin undressing, leaving his underwear on and throwing the rest of his clothes on top of Bill's. Standing almost naked in front of the fire Tom said, "Want your back washing?"

"That would be great," Bill replied in a dreamy voice. Tom knelt behind Bill and Bill passed Tom the soap. Scooping water from the bath to run down Bill's back, Tom began to run the soap the full length of Bill's back then passing the soap back to Bill began massaging the foam up and down. As Tom progressed, he realised that this was the first time that he had truly touched Bill savouring each and every movement.

The only other time he had touched him was when they wrestled in Jacob's pool but this time, the touching was more intimate. Bill was also enjoying the experience. Tom's firm hands pressing and stroking Bill's shoulders and back. Bill let out a moan of satisfaction as Tom continued to rub. Tom suddenly realised that his arousal had become more pronounced, his erect penis was almost bulging out of his underwear.

Tom began to wonder if Bill had also become aroused but could not see through the soap filled water and because Bill was bent forward in a manner which obscured his manhood. "I think that you had better stop," Bill suddenly said, breaking the moment and sounding a little nervous. "Here, jump, in." Bill stood to his full height resplendent and glowing from the heat of the water. Tom saw Bill was fully erect not making any movement to hide the firmness of his swollen penis.

As Bill stepped out of the bath, Tom removed his underwear showing his swollen manhood before getting into the now used water. His own manhood was at its fullest as he sat in the water. For a brief time, Tom leant forward to hide his erection until it began to subside a little.

Bill dried himself, put on his clean clothes and walked out of the room. Tom washed himself thoroughly but before he had finished, Bill came back into the room with a bucket full of hot water. Bill emptied its contents into the bath where Tom was still sitting and the warmth rejuvenated Tom's semi erect penis into its full hardness. Bill moved to the back of the bath, rolled up his shirt sleeves and began to wash and massage Tom's back. Bill's firm hands caressed Tom's shoulders then Bill ran his hands slowly down Tom's back reaching the top of Tom's buttocks.

Bill manipulated his thumbs in Tom's lumber region before sliding slowly up Tom's back and pressing his thumbs up Tom's spine. Tom let out a grunt. Tom was getting so aroused that he thought that any minute he would totally lose control and ejaculate. Not wanting this to happen, Tom said, "Thanks Bill, I think I'm done." Bill suddenly stopped as if he had been awoken from a deep dreamy sleep. Bill grabbed his towel and began drying his hands and arms while simultaneously, Tom quickly stood up, grabbed his towel, covering himself and began to dry himself at speed.

Tom dressed quickly as Bill began to empty the contents of the bath into the bucket. By the time Tom was dried and dressed, the bath water was almost emptied. Tom then helped Bill carry the bath outside and to hang the bath back in the brew house. Both boys were mindful of each other's reactions when they had been bathing, each having enjoyed the sensations they had given and received, albeit they didn't say anything to each other.

They also enjoyed seeing each other naked and erect but how could they express their feelings? After all, they were two very fit heterosexual guys and to admit that they both enjoyed touching each other and enjoyed getting erect was just the wrong thing to confess. To admit any kind of affection for another man was not only shameful but was also illegal. However, each had come to the realisation that their friendship was much deeper, more profound than just mates.

Bill poured the tea and cut a slice of cake that his mother had made before leaving to go to his aunts. The boys sat for a while before donning their jackets and making their way to Tom's where Tom's parents greeted them. Two bowels of hot stew with crusty bread were waiting for them which they consumed with gusto. "You boys enjoy your run?" Tom's mother enquired. "You both look well-scrubbed up."

"The run was great thanks Mrs Harris," Bill replied. Tom then went on to explain just how hard the run had been. The hardness of the track through their thin plimsolls, the coldness of the wind and how their hands had nearly froze. At minus 14 degrees outside, Tom's mother could well expect Tom's description. The start of the winter in 1939 had been the coldest on record thus far and more freezing weather was expected. Tom then explained how they had built the fire before going on their run and in getting the water ready to take a bath for when they returned.

"It seems that you are well sorted then?" Tom's mother said. "So, what are your plans for tonight" Mrs Harris asked.

Bill immediately responded saying, "Probably a few in the Swan, home to some cheese and pickle then bed." As soon as Bill motioned 'bed', Tom's complexion began to redden. Tom felt the heat in his face change and gave a slight glance at Bill, who was oblivious to what he had implied.

"I'm hoping that we get up early tomorrow morning and maybe take our run first thing," Bill said innocently. "If we leave it until the afternoon, I think that it will be too cold and I would like to spend Christmas Eve mainly relaxing by the fire and listening to the wireless. Of course, we will have to make our usual visit to the Swan, after all, it is Christmas, and we have to celebrate," Bill laughed. Tom joined in with the laughter which detracted the glare of his parents from Tom's very rouged face.

After tea, the boys sat with Tom's dad for a while trying to engage with him. However, Joe was noncommunicative. Joe had withdrawn into himself since the declaration of war, appearing quite anxious especially when the blackout board was put in place and the curtains were drawn. Joe's inner struggle was almost tangible and the boy's empathised with his uneasiness. Later, the boys tried to encourage Joe to join them at the Swan, but they both could see that any persuasion or coaxing would not work, well not tonight at any rate. The boys headed for the Swan around 9:00 pm.

The pub was already full and the noise level so great that everyone had to shout to be heard. The boys indicated to Harry that they wanted two pints and Harry responded by putting his thumb in the air like a Roman Emperor giving leniency to defeated gladiators. Harry also held up a bottle of scotch and waved it smiling. It was Harry's tradition to give all of his customers a small tot of whiskey during the festive season and at any celebration. The whisky chasers went down well with the cold ale, warming the back of the boy's throats as it flowed downward to their stomachs.

After several pints, the singing commenced with Old Jimmy Whitehouse banging out the tunes on the Victorian piano which was located next to the fireplace. It didn't matter that some notes were missing as Jimmy Whitehouse was no concert pianist. Jimmy took delight in playing the pub piano at any opportunity, rocking backward and forward, throwing his head and smiling, showing his hard pink gums where once his teeth had been. By 11:30, most of the customers in the pub were either drunk or well on the way to being drunk with the boys falling into the latter group.

"Let's go home," Bill said, placing his arm over Tom's shoulder. "I've had enough," Bill said with a slight slur.

"Me too," Tom said. "I'll definitely sleep tonight." Bill and Tom said their farewells and walked outside. The sudden sharp drop in temperature combined with the wind chill factor was a massive contrast to the warmth generated in the pub by the fire and body heat of the customers. So cold was the night air that it knocked both Bill and Tom backwards a little. "Bloody hell," Tom cried. "Its bloody cold. Come on let's legit." Both boys ran down the street as quickly and as capably as they could, reaching Bill's house and scrambling inside to reheat themselves.

Inside, the fire was still burning but needed re-banking with fresh coal. The room was warm and the gentle glow from the fire threw shadows as it flickered. Bill switched on the light and made to the windows to ensure that they were totally blacked out. Tom took of his jacked, hung it on the hat stand near the door and slumped in the armchair. Bill placed his jacket over Tom's then sat in the opposite chair to Tom. It was clear to Bill that Tom had drunk his fill without becoming drunk but was now ready to sleep.

Bill chucked more coal on the fire to keep it burning throughout the night. When he had finished, Bill stood in front of Tom and seeing that Tom's eyes were closing said, "Are you ready to go up mate?" Tom responded by saying "Too right I am. I'm bloody done in." Bill grabbed Tom's arms and pulled gently to help Tom to his feet. He held Tom upright for a while looking at his friend's happy face. He then led Tom to the stair well, guiding him forward as he climbed the stairs. Bill steadied Tom firmly by holding Tom's waist.

"I'm not that drunk," Tom stated.

"No, you're not, but I like to know that you are safe," Bill responded laughing. The boys entered Bill's bedroom where a second fire was burning. This fire was smaller than the one downstairs but was sufficient in keeping the room warm. Tom fell on the bed and Bill threw more coal onto the bedroom fire. "We are going to need as much warmth as we can get. It's going to get much colder during the night and into the early hours," Bill said to Tom.

Tom didn't respond but lay on his back smiling. Bill moved around the bed taking off Tom's boots, undoing Tom's trousers and slipping off Tom's bracers from his shoulders. Bill then grabbed the waist of Tom's trousers and began tugging to remove them from Tom.

Tom roused a little and said smiling, "Hang on mate, not too fast, I can manage." Tom wriggled and sat up. He removed his trousers folding them carefully before placing them on the floor.

Bill cried out, "Be careful mate, the gazunder is your side of the bed. Don't get your trousers wet." Tom leaned forward almost doubled up, first looking at his trousers and then checking where the gazunder had been placed. Satisfied that there was sufficient distance between his trousers and the potty, Tom straightens and began taking off his shirt. Bill laughed watching Tom as he also undressed. Both lads wore their vests and under britches and both were still wearing their socks.

They both slid between the crisp cotton sheets and array of blankets. Tom rolled onto his right side placing his head firmly on the pillow and pulled the heavy blankets close to his neck. Bill also rolled onto his right-side shuffling to lock behind Tom while at the same time straightening the blankets so that both were covered and sheltered from the cold. Tom was in a foetal position and Bill emulated this by locking his knees into the cups at the back of Tom's knees.

Bill's groin pressed close to Tom's backside and his chest close to Tom's back. Bill placed his arm over Tom in a brotherly embrace pulling Tom closer. Bill's head was close to Tom's hair and Bill could smell the sweetness of Tom's flesh. Bill's breathing was heavy and the warmth of his breath enveloped the nape of Tom's neck.

Tom, although very sleepy, suddenly felt the strong embrace of his friend and the strength of Bill's body as it pressed against his back. The warmth of Bill's breath on Tom's neck tickled in a gentle way but also sent a tingle through Tom's body. Tom grabbed Bill's arm as it enclosed him pulling it even closer, almost as if he wanted Bill's arm to disappear into his torso.

Tom grabbed the top of the blankets pulling them over his head. Now he was in total darkness. Bill removed his arm from around Tom to emulate what Tom had done, then replaced his arm over Tom's body. Immediately Tom pulled Bill's arm harder towards him.

In the darkness and because of being fully covered, aided by the heavy breathing of both boys and the fire burning bright, Tom and Bill quickly became hot. "Oh fuck," Tom exclaimed. "I need a piss now."

Bill shook with laughter and said, "You're not the only one mate." Bill got out of bed to walk around the bed frame to where the gazunder was located. Tom sat up, leaned forward, locating the trophy before Bill had managed to reach his destination. Both boys were so desperate each held one handle of the chamber pot while relieving themselves. As they were pissing Tom could see that Bill's manhood had swollen slightly above normal size.

Tom already knew that he was also semi erect but didn't give a dam about it. He was happy. Tom finished pissing first and shook himself slowly as not to splash Bill with any urine remnants. Bill finished, placed the now half-filled gazunder in its rightful place and made his way back to his side of the bed. Tom had already positioned himself as before and was eagerly awaiting Bill to get into bed. Both Bill and Tom grabbed the blankets with one hand pulling them completely over their heads and snuggling down.

Bill's arms entwined Tom's body and Tom grasped Bill's hand tightly. Like Ying and Yang, the boys were so close together, locked as conjoined twins that could not be separated. Cuddled together; warm and happy being together each tried to sleep. Around one in the morning, Tom could feel Bill's fully erect monster pressing in the fold of his buttocks. Tom had been fully erect, for what seemed like hours, so erect that it was now beginning to hurt.

Tom pushed his backside harder towards Bill erection trying to get a better feel of the size of Bill. To Tom's surprise, Bill pushed forward as Tom pressed backwards. "You're awake," Bill said quietly.

"Yes," Tom whispered.

"I haven't been fully asleep yet. I just can't seem to drop off," Bill echoed by saying to Tom.

"Neither have I."

"Should I get up and go and sleep in Mum and Dad's bed?" Bill questioned.

There was a long pause until Tom murmured, "No. Please don't go. Please stay where you are."

Both lay still for a while. Bill could feel Tom's chest rise and sink as he breathed. Both boys were breathing in unison, each rising and falling as they took in more oxygen. As they lay together, their breathing became much more pronounced. Tom was still clutching Bill's hand. Bill began to loosen his grip on Tom and slowly drew his now freed hand down Tom's chest towards Tom's stomach. Bill could feel the twitching of Tom's six pack and the ever-increasing speed of the rise and fall of Tom's breathing. Tom didn't move as Bill's hand wondered.

Bill reached the base of Tom's stomach and halted. Tom pushed back towards Bill's ever-increasing erection. Tom's eyes were closed in a dream like state. Never had he felt so aroused. Bill's hand slid up under Tom's vest and the flat of Bill's hand stroked the firmness of Tom's stomach. As he did this, Tom pushed back harder and now began moving his hips in a spiral to experience more of the solid manliness Bill had in Tom's back. Bill's hand slid down Tom's stomach until it reached the welt of Tom's underwear; the short hair of Tom's pubic area just touching Bill's pinkie finger.

Just a fraction lower Tom's thick glance seemed desperate to push out of his pants and for it to reach Tom's finger. Small globules of pre-cum was seeping from Tom's fully hard penis in anticipation. "We shouldn't be doing this," Bill said in a quiet caring way.

"Please, don't stop," Tom murmured desperate to experience more of this overpowering emotion.

"I've never done this before," Bill said.

"Neither have I," Tom replied.

Bill responded by saying, "I know that it's not right, but it just feels so right."

"I know," Tom said emotionally almost in tears. "I know that we shouldn't, but I don't want you to stop. But if you feel that you can't continue, just stop now, please, either carry on or stop completely." Bill hesitated but kept his hand on Tom's stomach and his pinkie finger just inside Tom's underwear.

Bill kissed the nape of Tom's neck and whispered, "I love you, Tom." Tears streamed down Tom's face, who was now finding it hard to breathe.

"I love you too Bill, more than you can imagine," Tom sniffed. Bill pulled Tom even closer squeezing until Tom could no longer take in oxygen and at the same time forced his fingers and hand fully into Tom's pants. Rubbing Tom's pubic hair Bill manoeuvred his fingers around the shaft of Tom's throbbing stiffness and squeezed firmly but gently. Tom let out a moan, whilst at the same time reaching over to grab Bill's monster as it almost exploded.

Tom grappled to get his hand in Bill's underwear and they lay there just holding each other for a short time. Bill still holding Tom's manhood tried to move his wrist to allow his hand to explore deeper into Tom's pants. Tom responded by trying to do the same to Bill. Then Tom let go of Bill, grabbed on to his own pants and wriggled to remove the obstructive item. Recognising Tom's willingness to strip off, Bill also let go and began taking his pants off.

As soon as both were naked from the waist down, Bill reached for Tom's vest pulling it over Tom's head and throwing it out of the bed before removing his own vest. Both now fully naked, Tom turned over to face Bill and both flung their arms around each other. The feeling of skin on skin only added to the sensations each was feeling. Their chests forced together as if in a clamp and their abdomens touching and moving in unison as they breathed.

Both men's man hood pressed hard together and each wallowed as if in a triumph of achievement. Bill's cheek pressed on Tom's cheek; each feeling warmth radiating from one to another. Tom moved his head slightly until his lips touched Bill's. Slowly Tom parted his lips and moved his tongue to taste Bill's hot moist lips. As he did so, Bill parted his lips too and searched for Tom's lips and tongue. Touching together, each tongue explored the others until both tongues entered their opponent's mouths.

Both pressed and flicked their tongues deeper inside tasting the warm saliva that fill both orifices. Harder they pressed their bodies together pushing and easing as if their members were searching to find their rightful place. Bill's hand explored Tom's back and buttocks. The firmness of Tom's body was exquisite. Tom also responded, rubbing Bill's back and pulling him ever closer. Simultaneously, both lads reached down to find their lovers hard penis.

They moved their hands up and down each other's shafts while still locked in a full embrace and while their tongues pressed harder together. Bill's hand moved down to grasp Tom's scrotum and balls, moving his thick long fingers to feel between Tom's legs, searching to find Tom's hot anal opening. Tom squirmed with pleasure pulling Bill's hard length down and placing it between his own legs. Bill pushed slowly moving rhythmically in and out between Tom's legs. Bill's breathing became intense as he moaned with pleasure.

"Oh god," Tom cried, "I love you, Bill."

"I love you Tom," Bill said as his speed increased. Bill now had both hands-on Tom's firm bottom pulling Tom's cheeks apart as he thrust forward. Bill's index finger moved closer to Tom's hot anal opening and began to move his fingers to try to penetrate the tight small hole of Tom's anus. Tom wriggled, trying to help Bill get closer.

"Oh god, this is amazing," Bill said.

"Tell me about it," Tom muttered back. "I've never done this before. Do you want to try to go inside?" Tom asked Bill.

"Ohhh yeahhh," Bill said, "yes, I want that so much; Oh god, I want it to." Then in the same breath said, "I want to but I'm really not sure we should. I don't want to hurt you," Bill continued.

"Have you got any Vaseline?" Tom asked. There was a short pause and Tom was afraid that he had offended Bill, but Bill was thinking.

"I think Mum has some in her bedroom, wait, I'll get it." Bill said jumping out of bed and sprinting into his parent's bedroom. Within a flash, Bill had returned with his prize. "Roll over onto your stomach," Bill instructed Tom. As Tom was obeying this request, Bill opened the jar of petroleum jelly and took out a glob of the paste onto two fingers. Tom lay still as Bill applied the greasy substance around Tom's tight arse opening. As Bill applied the grease, Tom wriggled pushing on to Bill's fingers.

As he did so, Bill pushed gently and entered the awaiting hole. "Ohhh, ohh, ohh," Tom moaned with pleasure.

"Does it hurt?" Bill asked.

"Ohh, no" Tom said, "It feels unbelievable." Bill's fingers went deeper inside Tom's rectum. Bill searched with his fingers like removing cake batter from a small bowl. "Ohhhhh," Tom cried as Bill explored. Bill pushed his fingers to their full depth and pulled back slightly. Pushing in and out he could see that Tom was writhing in ecstasy which prompted Bill to do it even more. The action of having fingers inside Tom and to feel Tom's inner warmth made Bill's cock jerk.

Bill knew Tom was ready to receive something much bigger that his fingers and Bill knew he was ready to give Tom what he wanted. Bill grabbed his throbbing hard on and guided his glans to Tom's waiting hole. Slowly Bill began to push inside. Bill could feel the resistance and so took time to enter Tom. Tom could feel pain as Bill's glans pressed on his sphincter muscle. Tom steadied himself as Bill's erection manoeuvred ready for deep penetration. Suddenly, a popping feeling exploded inside Tom's innards as Bill's glans fully entered Tom's small tight hole.

This felt much different to Bill's fingers. "Wait, wait," Tom cried.

"Wait, don't move," Bill immediately stopped as requested, not moving but not withdrawing. As the pain subsided, Tom asked Bill to go slowly and gentle. Bill did as he was asked taking his lead from Tom. Deeper and deeper Bill drove into Tom, his shaft slowly disappearing into the tight depth of Tom's arse.

"Ohh," Tom cried again once all of Bill's manhood was inside. "Just stay still for a while," Tom asked. Bill lay fully on Tom's back not moving enjoying the warm sensation surrounding his throbbing manhood. Then Bill took the initiative and began to slowly withdraw before pushing back in again at the same pace. The more his did this, the more Tom responded, opening wider at each thrust. Bill started to go a little faster and as he did, so Tom arched his back to take in more of Bill's hot organ. The pressure of Bill's glans rubbing on Tom's prostrate became intense. "Oh god," Tom cried in excitement. I think I'm going to cum.

Hearing this, Bill drove even harder and faster. Tom's arching became more intense accepting Bill with each stroke. Sweat was running from both boys as they raced towards their climax. Bill's thrusting intensified. It was Bill's turn now to say, "I'm coming," and as he did so, Bill's hot sperm shot deep into Tom's lower bowel. Tom climaxed at the same time and his sperm soaked into the crisp sheet below him, both pounding each other until they were empty and exhausted.

Bill flopped on top of Tom as Tom's body fully relaxed. Both were breathing so fast and didn't move. Even when they were breathing normally Bill was reluctant to pull out and Tom was happy for Bill to be still inside him.

After some time, Bill said, "I don't know what to say, but that was the best experience that I've ever had."

"Me too," Tom replied. "I loved it."

"I think that we had better get cleaned up," Bill said eventually, still semi-erect and still inside Tom.

"I guess so," Tom replied. Bill withdrew slowly and rolled off Tom, dismounting from the bed and leaving the bedroom.

Tom remained motionless feeling more relaxed than he had ever felt in his life. Bill returned with a towel and was busy wiping his genitals. Tom rolled over, looked at Bill and said:

"Thank you." Bill just smiled. Tom got out of bed and clambered for the gazunder.

Tom sat on the contraption emptying Bill's liquid from his bowel then grabbing the towel wiped off the excess petroleum jelly from between the cheeks of his arse. Both lads got back into bed and resumed the positions where it had all started. Both boys were happy, relaxed but still wide awake.

"I don't know what to say," Bill said.

"Neither do I," Tom replied.

"We can't tell anyone about this," Bill went on to say, "but I meant what I said to you."

"What's that?" Tom asked, already knowing what Bill was about to say. "I do love you."

"I love you too. I have loved you since we first met," Tom replied. Bill gently kissed Tom and cuddled closer. "Can we do it again sometime?" Tom asked.

"Give me an hour," Bill laughed. Tom began to giggle and laughed along with Bill. "Let's get some sleep. We can talk about it when we wake up. We've got the whole day to discuss it," Bill said contently. Tom turned his head to Bill, kissed him and curled up back in Bill's arms. Within minutes, both were sound asleep.

Early the next morning, Bill awoke to find Tom wide awake. They were still both wrapped in each other's caress. "Morning," Bill said still half awake.

"Morning," Tom replied.

"How are you feeling?" Bill enquired.

"I'm feeling great," Tom answered in a relaxed voice.

"No regrets?" Bill asked.

"Absolutely none," Tom responded. "What about you. You're regretting it, aren't you?" Tom asked, hoping that Bill was feeling the same as him.

"Absolutely not: In fact, I was just thinking how special it was; I just can't fully understand how we got to this stage. I never thought that I would do anything like that, especially with another bloke. I'm still trying to get my head around it and I think it will take me awhile in coming to terms with the way I feel about you," Bill stated.

"I know what you mean," Tom responded, still confused by the night's events. "I never thought that I would allow anyone to do that to me and I never thought that I would enjoy it so much. I'm just wondering what we are going to do now. I would hate to think that things were going to change between us," Tom said in a worried voice.

"Well things have changed, whether we like it or not. We have done things that we are not supposed to do and we have to live with the consequences of that and we have both said openly about how we feel towards each other. It's just so confusing at the moment for me and I expect you feel the same. On the other hand, I don't want to stop feeling the way I do. If anyone ever found out, they would call us 'queers'. I never thought that I was a homosexual and am not sure how to get my head around that," Bill said emotionally.

"Oh my god..." Tom began, "that just didn't entre my head. I've never fancied a guy before, and I never thought that I would allow another guy to do what you did. I just couldn't stop myself. I just want you more than anything else," Tom began to sob quietly beginning to wrestle with the guilt he now felt.

"Hey, you," Bill said, holding Tom closer. "We have both got to work through this. We must both try to accept what happened and never do it again. Stop seeing each other and keep our distance. Or we must work through it. But it's clear to me that I don't want to stop seeing you and I'm not sure if I could still keep seeing you without wanting to do it again, which only leaves the last option, to work through it."

Tom lay quietly still sobbing. "I don't want it to stop but I need time to untangle everything. If we continue, we have to keep our relationship secret from everyone, no matter what." Bill pulled Tom to face him. Bill wiped the tears from Tom's face looking at him intently. Tom's eyes were reddened from crying, looking sad and mournful. Tom looked into Bill's eyes feeling reassured and could see that Bill had meant every word.

Bill kissed Tom's forehead then gently kissed Tom's lips. Tom responded grabbing Bill, holding him as tightly as he could, never wanting to let go. Both were lost in their tight embrace feeling that nothing in the world could mar this moment. "We have to stop now," Bill said firmly. "If we don't stop, we will have to have a re-run. I can feel that we're both getting hard again," Tom laughed knowing that if they didn't stop, that they would most definitely start again.

Tom let go of Bill, rolled out of bed, and grabbed the gazunder from beneath the bed. Tom stood holding the procaine container trying hard not to miss its wide opening. Tom was desperately trying to get his stiffness to go down to pee. Bill got out of the other side of the bed, put on his vest and underwear and after Tom had finished, emptied his now very full bladder. Both boys dressed in front of the now dwindling bedroom fire.

Bill grabbed the poker from the side of the fire raking down the ashes before placing more coal on the embers from the coal bucket. The boys went downstairs and while Bill attended the fire in the living room Tom filled the kettle placing it on the side of the fire to boil. Even with the fires burning there was a strong chill in the air. Opening the curtains, Bill saw that a thick layer of ice had formed on the windowpanes. It was clear that the temperature outside was well below zero and looked set to continue to be cold for the rest of the day.

# Chapter Five
# The Call Up

For Bill and Tom, Christmas Eve was spent at Tom's house. Tom's mother busied herself preparing meals, cleaning in preparation for Christmas day, while Tom's father sat for most of the day staring into the fire. Tom and Bill helped Tom's mother by keeping the fires going, collecting coal and also helped to clear the table and do the washing up. They listened to the radio, especially the B.B.C. news. All day they sneaked quick glances at each other and when they caught each other out, they would hang their heads smiling.

The thought of the previous night still so fresh in their memory. This first wartime Christmas was not much different from how it had been in previous years, apart from Bill staying at home while his parents were away. There were few extra restrictions imposed by government apart from the obligatory blackout regulations which prevented the traditional sight of lit-up Christmas trees in people's front windows, and shop displays were obscured by anti-blast tape on the windows.

In November, the government had announced that butter and bacon were to be rationed, but as yet this had not happened. The Chancellor insisted that money should not be wasted; however, most people who lived in the industrial areas had always had to be frugal to just survive on a regular basis. For many families, Christmas was marked by the absence of many young men who had been 'somewhere in France' with the British Expeditionary Force, and hundreds of thousands of city children had already been evacuated from their homes and sent to live in the country, especially those who lived in London.

Bill thought about his parents who might find that their journey could be curtailed due to travel restrictions, which were beginning to bite; in September petrol rationing had been introduced, and rail travel was now actively being discouraged. Tom's mother had purchased gas masks for her husband and Tom and a Bakelite helmet for Bill as their Christmas presents. She had wrapped these presents and presented Bill with his. "You might as well take this to your house and put it under the tree," she said smiling. Bill didn't know what to say as he wasn't expecting a gift.

"Thank you," Bill said looking sheepish.

"Come on," Tom shouted, "let's take it now." Bill detected the urgency in Tom's voice and stared at him in amazement.

"You might as well," Joan said. "With both of you out of the way, me and your father can have half an hour," looking at Tom and then Bill in turn.

The boys left Tom's place and went directly to Bill's house. It was still bitterly cold outside so going to Bill's house enabled him to restock the fires. As soon as Tom and Bill entered the house, Tom grabbed Bill in a bear hug. "Do you want to do it again?" Tom pleaded. Bill laughed aloud.

"You've been thinking the same as me." The boys ran upstairs, into Bill's bedroom and stripped naked. They dived into bed and explored each other's bodies fully with hands and mouths. After making love for an hour or more and reaching their climax the boys lay still for a while.

"I never want this to stop," Tom stated.

"Me neither," Bill replied. The boys lay in each other's arms. Bill began the conversation about falling in love with Tom. He told Tom that he had never looked at another guy in the way that he looked at Tom and that his sexual interests had previously always been for girls. Tom almost stopped Bill in his tracks, saying that he too had always been interested in girls and that he too had never thought about being with a guy. Both had found it strange that their attraction for each other had come out of nowhere, but each stated that they were happy that things had gone the way that they had.

"I don't think that I will ever want a woman now," Tom exclaimed.

"Me neither," Bill said.

"In fact, I don't think I want anyone apart from you," Tom concluded.

After about another half an hour lying in each other's arms, Bill suddenly said, "We had better get up and tidy up; otherwise, we will end up staying in bed all day."

"I think that I would love that," Tom replied. They kissed each other and Bill jumped out of bed. The boys set about tidying the house, making the bed ready for another night of passion, banked up the fires and emptied the gazunder.

Downstairs, Bill made them a pot of tea and the boys sat chatting. The focus of their conversation rounded on their newfound experiences with each other but this changed to the fear of conscription and the possibility of them being separated and being 'called up'.

"If we do get called up," Tom began, "we will have to try to make sure that we go together."

"That might be difficult," Bill said feeling rather depressed. "I mean, if we are called up, they will probably send for me first, as I'm older than you."

"That shouldn't matter," Tom replied gleefully. "I'll just sign up immediately you get your letter."

"It's not that simple," Bill said looking at Tom directly. "Even if we both sign up together, there's no guarantee that we will be in the same section or division or even in the same regiment. Even if we are, what happens if we're sent to different places on Europe? You could be in France, and I could be sent somewhere else. It just feels hopeless," Bill said mournfully.

Both boys felt as if they had been flung off a cliff. Their elation of becoming friends, sharing time together and now having experienced love with each other was to be shattered because of this dammed war. Tom suddenly looked up, "I'll ask my dad what might happen. I'm sure that if we are in it together, they won't part us. They kept friends together during the Great War, I'm sure."

On returning to Tom's house, Tom posed the question to his father. Joe Harris listened intently; there was visible concern and pain in his face. Tears filled his eyes. Holding back his tears, Joe took time to respond. "Whatever you do, don't go rushing out to sign up. You will hear soon enough if they need you. War is no remarkable thing to happen. I don't want either of you going to war and to experience the things I had to experience and witness."

"It is a dirty, horrible thing and will affect you more than you can ever imagine. Just wait. I'm begging you both to wait. Going to war will not just affect you, it is like a cancer that affects us all and will affect us every minute of the day and for years to come. That's all I have to say on the matter, and I pray that the war will end well before you are called up."

Everyone sat quietly pondering on Joe's every word. Tom broke the silence by saying, "I know that you don't want to talk about what happened to you during the first war, but Bill and me want to know whether they will keep us together." Joe looked at Tom recognising that their friendship might be more than just best mates. Joe had seen for himself during the last war how extremely strong bonds form between two men and the devastating effects that had come from either one or the other being badly maimed or killed.

"If you are called up, I hope to god that you will both be safe and that you will look out for each other, no matter what." The conversation ended there. All day Joe's words seemed to hang over the boy's thoughts. Tom's mother made herself scarce, trying to avoid everyone but it was clear that the conversation had hit home and had shaken her to the core.

All the men had recognised that she had been crying and that she was still feeling raw and heartbroken. After dinner, the boys returned to Bill's house. That night the boy's held each other tightly, not saying anything but sharing their fears in their caress. They made love more vigorously that night, even waking during the middle of the night for more. As morning broke, the boys made love once more before getting up and preparing for the day ahead.

Christmas was quite a Solomon occasion, even though everyone tried to make the most of the day thoughts were of the war and of Bill's parents and his aunt. Presents were swapped, their meal enjoyed, and much time was spent listening to the wireless.

The next few days were a mix of absolute pleasure and delight for Tom and Bill as they spent time together. Tom continued to stay with Bill, even going to work and returning home together. Neither wanted this time to end. Each night both looked forward to the night ahead; to more exploration of each other and just to be able to sleep next to one another.

Just before New Year, Bill received a letter from his mother explaining that his aunt had deteriorated and that because of travel restrictions and the adverse weather, they would be staying longer than expected. Bill was happy because this allowed Tom to stay even longer. Their sexual exploits continued every night, both now having explored each other to the full. They lived, much like a married couple, only secretively.

This was to be the best time of their lives and would remain with them for all time. Bill's parents stayed at his aunts for three more weeks. Sadly, his aunt passed away in early January, so Mr and Mrs Taylor stayed until the funeral and returned as soon as they were allowed and as soon as the weather improved sufficiently. When Bill's parents eventually returned, of course Bill was happy to see them, but was sad because Tom had to return home.

On Tuesday 30th January 1940 on returning from work, Bill walked into his house to find his mother and father sitting around the kitchen table. Both were ashen and Bill could see that his mother had been crying. There, on the table, lying flat, was a letter in a brown paper envelope addressed to Bill. The envelope had a logo printed on the upper left-hand side of a rope forming the shape of a knot and above a crown. The logo was of the South Staffordshire regiment and all three knew what was in its content even before Bill opened it.

Bill sat in an empty chair at the table, picked up the letter staring at the address and logo. No one spoke. They sat for quite a while looking at each other. After what seemed like an age, Bill shot up holding the letter and ran out of the front door. He ran straight to Tom's house, knocked on the door and waited. The snow was falling heavily as Tom's mother opened the door.

"Oh my god Bill, whatever is the matter?" Tom's mum could see by the look on Bill's face that he was troubled. "Come in," she urged Bill.

"No thanks," Bill replied. "Can I have a word with Tom?" Tom came to the door and looked at Bill. Tom thought that something serious had happened and could see the anxiety of Bill's face. Without saying anything Tom grabbed his coat, stepped outside joining Bill, closing the door behind him.

"It's come," Bill said, almost in tears. Tom didn't click on immediately until Bill lifted his hand showing Tom the envelope.

"Oh no," Tom cried. "When and where do you have to go?" Tom continued.

"I don't know," Bill said shaking. Tom realised that Bill had not yet opened the letter staring at Bill's hand which held the now crumpled paper.

"You need to open it," Tom said at last.

"I can't," Bill struggled to say. "I want you to open it for me," Bill said looking at Tom with tears in his eyes. Tom looked in amazement but understood the enormity of the letter and of its contents. Bill handed Tom the letter. Tom carefully tore the letter open. Pulling out the typed note; Tom glanced at the layout and sight read the type and handwritten contents. Tom began to read aloud each work written in the letter. He began:

"National Service (Armed Forces) Act, 1939: Enlistment Notice." Tom stopped and swallowed. He continued, "You should take this notice with you when you report. Ministry of Labour and National Service, Divisional Office: Mr William Taylor, 15 Short Street." Bill looked down taking in each word.

"Dear Sir," Tom continued. "In accordance with the National Service (Armed Forces) Act 1939, you are called upon for service in the British Army, South Staffordshire Regiment and required to present yourself on Monday 11th

March 1940 at 11.00am or as early as possible thereafter on that day, to the Recruit Centre, Aldershot Barracks, Government Rd, Aldershot."

Bill sighed loudly; Tom looked at Bill with tears in his eyes and read on. "A travel warrant for your journey is enclosed." Tom looked at a second piece of paper which was the travel warrant. "Before starting your journey, you must exchange the warrant for a ticket at the booking office named on the warrant. If possible, this should be done a day or two before you are due to travel. A postal order for 4s (4 shillings) in advance of service pay, is enclosed."

Tom looked at the postal order and continued reading. "Uniform and personal kit will be issued to you after joining H.M. Forces. Any kit that you take with you should not exceed an overcoat, change of clothes, stout pair of boots, and personal kit, such as, razor, hairbrush, toothbrush, soap and towel. Immediately of receipt of this notice you should inform your employer of the date upon which you are required to report for service; yours faithfully, Lt/Colonel W. E. (Billy) Gibbons."

Both boys stood silently, Bill looking at the ground, Tom clutching the letter; neither of them felt the cold of the evening air; both were lost in their own thoughts for a while until Tom said, "I think that you had better go and tell your mum and dad." Bill looked at Tom as if lost in a thick swirling mist. Tom recognised the confusion and pain that Bill was experiencing but could not find words to alleviate Bill's troubles. The boys re-entered Bill's house and Tom handed over the letter to Bill's mother. She read the letter, hands trembling before passing it to her husband.

Tears filled Bill's mother's eyes and his father's colour drained from his face, becoming ashen and clammy. Tom could see that this was not the right time for talking and felt a little uneasy about being there. Tom decided it was time for him to leave saying, "I'd better go. I'll pop round tomorrow if that's ok?" No one said anything and Tom took his leave. A feeling of bereavement and loss filled his whole being as he closed the front door behind him.

Tears streamed down his face as he stepped back into the freezing air. He returned home heading straight for his bedroom. After the initial shock of Bill's call up, both families were able to talk more openly about their fears and anxieties. Not least the fact that in time, Tom would also be receiving his letter too.

Bill, on returning to work, did what many others had already done, reporting his imminent departure to his bosses. Several other guys at the factory had also received their letters too and in some ways, this helped Bill to come to terms with the forthcoming events. At least, Bill would not be alone on the day of his departure.

That evening Bill also informed the guys in the Swan, but many had already heard his news. Bill was told that Cyril Squires, Henry Williams, and Albert Tonks were also being called up the same time. It seemed that slowly but surely, the pub was being emptied of its younger generation, some going for active service, some to work as Bevan boys' working down the pits and Harry the barman informed everyone that Doctor Steven's son had been called up to work for the intelligence department. Tom and Bill looked on and listened as conversations around him speculated and informed everyone about their own pieces of news they had received.

Bill and Tom made sure that they spent as much time together as possible catching the odd 'quite' time when either of their parents was out of the house. They didn't have chance to have their 'bed' time together as before but did make love whenever and where ever possible. Their relationship had deepened, each promising to be monogamous and true to each other. Neither of the boys were effeminate in anyway and didn't fall into or fit stereotypical roles of homosexual men. Both had concluded that for them, this relationship was to be life long, however long their lives might last.

As February advanced and March drew nearer the boy's mood became much more sombre. Days were rushing by and soon it would be time for Bill and Tom to part company. Tom's father, since recognising the strong bond between his son and Bill decided to allow Bill to stay over for a couple of nights. He broached the subject by telling Tom that he was becoming anxious and that he would feel better if Bill were around to offer support should he become ill.

So, for two nights prior to leaving home to join the army, Bill stayed with Tom, sharing his bed, making love, albeit very quietly and just being close to each other. The weekend before the 11th March was spent getting Bill's gear ready and travelling to the railway station to swap his warrant for his ticket. On the Saturday, a send-off party was held in the Swan for those guys who would be joining Bill to join up.

The families of the boys and other customers put on a spread and the beer and whisky flowed. Bill had planned to leave early on the morning of the 11th, allowing plenty of time to reach his destination. The first train left the local station at 5:30 a.m. travelling directly to London then a trip across London to board a train at Waterloo. Bill expected to arrive at the barracks by 11:00am at the latest.

On Sunday morning, Bill's case was packed in readiness giving Bill plenty of time for him to spend time with Tom and to say his goodbyes to his parents. Bill and Tom walked along the canal following the trail they had taken on their weekend runs. When no-one was about, they held hands and occasionally kissed. Each promised to write regularly, agreeing to sign their letters with just 'T' or 'B'. That way, they would not draw any suspicion should the letters fall into unwanted hands. They also agreed to enclose a second letter which would be more general, and which could be seen by their parents or anyone else who might take an interest.

Tom would keep Bill informed when his conscription letter arrived, and they both promised to try everything possible to be together as soon as it was convenient. Monday 11th March arrived. Tom had not slept thinking about Bill. Bill equally had not fully rested, primarily thinking about what lay ahead but also about just how much he would miss Tom. Tom was truly the love of Bill's life and vice versa. Tom had agreed to escort Bill to the train station and after would make his way to work. Bill's parents had also wanted to go with Bill and Tom to see their son off, but Bill had begged them to stay home. At 4:00am, Tom left his house to meet with Bill.

At the Taylor's house, the atmosphere was dark and withdrawn. Bill's parents looked heartbroken. Tom knocked on the door of Bill's house and entered. Tom only nodded to Bill's parents knowing that if he were to speak, he would burst into tears. It was bad enough seeing Bill's mother sobbing and Bill's dad with his head low to his chest. Tom picked up Bill's suitcase and said, "Come on mate, time to go."

Bill nodded in recognition then hugged his mother. Bill's mother hung on to him so tightly that Tom thought he might have to prise her off her son, but she let go and continued to sob. Bill's dad stood up to shake Bill's hand then flung his arms around his son.

"God bless you son," Bill's dad said. "Take care and keep safe. Love you son." Bill's dad shook, tears flowing down his face. Seeing his son leave brought back memories of the day he had left his home to fight in the last war.

A sense of déjà vu was overwhelming. Tom opened the door and stepped into the darkness closely followed by Bill. Outside they were greeted by Tom's parents, both hugging Bill in turn. Tom's parents glanced towards Bill's house, seeing Bill's parents standing and watching as their son began his outward journey.

Bill and Tom began the long walk to the station. As they walked along the street, Tom's mum and dad joined Bill's parents. The four stood motionless. Once out of sight from their parents, Tom took hold of Bill's hand. They linked fingers squeezing their palms together. The strength of their grip fusing them as one. There were no other people around to see them linked together but even if there had been it is doubtful whether they would have parted. After a while, Bill and Tom neared the railway station. The station and its outbuildings looked ominous. The silhouettes of the buildings were reminiscent of an old castle and around the periphery dark arches stood.

Bill motioned Tom to walk towards one of these arches and lit cigarettes for them both. Bill past one of the cigarettes to Tom and pulled him into the awaiting archway. Bill grabbed Tom, held him so tight that Tom could hardly breathe. Tom, dropping the suitcase reciprocating the hug Bill was giving. They embraced and kissed each other deeply.

"I love you so much Tom. You are the love of my life. Never forget that."

"I love you too Bill. There is nothing that will ever change that. Please keep safe my love. I need you to come back to me," Tom replied emotionally.

"We will be together again soon and then we will plan our lives together, no matter what," Bill pledged. They hugged and kissed once more before moving towards the station entrance and the platform. Both Bill and Tom thought how sad it was that they had to say their goodbyes hidden in the darkness and in secret.

They knew that others would be saying goodbye to their loved ones in the open for all to see. Wives would be saying goodbye to their husbands, parents to their sons and girlfriends to their boyfriends. The boys had prepared themselves as far as possible, but both knew that they would always have to keep their relationship hidden away from the rest of the prying eyes of others, society, their family, and their friends; theirs had to be a relationship of secrecy.

They lit another cigarette as then walked to the awaiting platform. Within minutes, the train arrived billowing out steam and smoke. Other young men who Bill and Tom knew were also waiting for the train, some alone, some with family members and one or two with their wives and children and some with their girlfriends. The boys walked along the platform envious that they had already said their goodbyes and unable to show their real affection at the point of Bill's departure, however, they did give each other one final hug but more in the style of friends than lovers.

Soon everyone who was leaving boarded the train. Bill made his way along the carriage finding a seat in a compartment to his right. After dropping his suitcase on his seat, he exited the carriage and moved to a window overlooking the platform. Tom had walked along the platform watching Bill find his seat and stood by the window from where Bill would say his final goodbyes. As Bill got close to the window, the train whistle blew, and the engine began to slowly move on its long journey to the Capital.

Tom walked along the platform still fixated on Bill. "I love you," Tom mouthed. Bill reciprocated followed by throwing Tom a kiss. Tom's eyes filled with tears as the steady engine disappeared along the track. Tom stood for a while looking at the empty track not realising that people had already departed from the station quietly, each with their own thoughts, each with their own pain, and each with their own heart ache. Tom walked out of the train station with a heavy heart, drying his tears as he went along.

Bill settled into his carriage along with a couple of mates from his local area but with whom he had not really formed any form of association. They all placed their baggage in the luggage racks, sat down and all began or pretended to begin to sleep. This was not a time for talking nor was it a time to engage in petty chitchat. Now was a time for reflection and a time to reorganise thoughts of what might lie ahead.

Tom walked slowly towards the town and to his place of work. He walked as if he was going to his own execution and impending death. For Tom, it felt that today would be the saddest and loneliest of his entire life. Tom was heartbroken, and yet his heart was also full knowing that he was genuinely loved and that he also absolutely loved Bill. Days would never be the same again.

# Chapter Six
# The Militia

Bill had never travelled far from his home and this journey was the furthest he had ever been from his safety zone. Bill had not slept as others had done but had closed his eyes thinking about Tom. Bill recalling the day he and Tom had met, the times they had worked at home together and of the many runs and swims they had taken together and of their journeys to and from work, but most of all, Bill thought about the times he and Tom had made love together, from the first time in Bill's house that Christmas and the many other times when no one was about.

As the dawn broke, Bill watched as the world shot passed him through the carriage window. As Bill contemplated the times, he had spent with Tom this was the first time that he fully recognised that he was homosexual and that his longings would never be to be with a woman. Neither did he ever want another man; Tom was his true love, his first and one and only love. It was so difficult for Bill to process the enormity of his revelation, but Bill was pragmatic, recognising that nothing would change who he was and how he felt.

Bill realised fundamentally he had not changed as a person. All that he had done, was to fall in love. To him, it was irrelevant that his lover happened to be male. Bill clearly understood that he would never be accepted by society because he loved a man and not a woman but had this strange feeling that there must be hundreds, if not thousands of men just like him, yet how many would never have a male lover.

Soon Bill snapped out of his thought processing as the train began to slow towards its final destination. Arriving in London, Bill, along with the other boys who had shared his carriage all filed off the train and made their way to the underground. There was an air of excitement at being in the capital city even though none of the guys would see much of it travelling underground. They would not be seeing Buckingham Palace; Westminster Palace and Westminster Abby, nor would they see Trafalgar Square or eros in Piccadilly; well not toady at any rate.

They moved from the main line train to the underground train system and then on to Waterloo for their next overland journey. When they eventually arrived at Waterloo to board their train to Aldershot, they were met by a sight that they had not expected. There were literally hundreds, if not thousands of young men averaging ages between 20 and 35 years old standing around waiting for the same train as Bill and his friends. All were bound for the same place. Bill had never seen so many young men together. *Even at football matches numbers had never seemed so large,* he thought to himself, each young man different from the other in stature, confidence and sense of purpose. Bill recognised many who would be destined to lead and many who were so scared that he thought these were the ones who might not make it through any conflicts they might encounter. There were army personnel at hand to give direction and instruction to those who appeared lost or confused. The WI (Women's Institute) was also present, handing out tea and sandwiches from a kiosk located at the entrance of the platform.

The noise level was tremendous. Men talking loudly, station personnel shouting and blowing whistles, Army Personnel shouting orders and the noise emulating from trains pulling in and out of the station. A paper seller shouted, advertised the edition he was selling interspersed with a cry of 'God bless ya boys'. Once everyone had boarded, people scrambled for available seats. Many had to travel standing. Once in a carriage, it was difficult to exit because of the sheer number of men in the corridors. For those who needed the toilet, they had to forcefully push through the plethora of writhing bodies to get relief. Even then, they had to queue for some considerable time. Arriving at Aldershot the throng of young men alighted from the train and moved along the platform like ants taking food and building materials back to their nest. Waiting outside of the station, numerous army lorries were lined up to transport the new recruits to their ultimate port of call.

Career sergeants holding clipboards were shouting to the new militia recruits to come forward and to present their enlistment papers to desks that had been set up at the stations exit. As people moved forward, they were ticked off lists that were set on these tables by army officials, and then allotted their truck.

They were all instructed to move as quickly as possible. Chaotic as it looked, everything was moving like clockwork. Bill, like many others was a little daunted by the whole fiasco but managed to find exactly where he should be. The guys from home who were being enlisted with Bill were all put together, which help enormously.

Bill looked around and marvelled at the mismatch of individuals moving along like sheep. Some looked physically fit while others looked as if they needed feeding up. Some were quite manly, while others looked no older than school kids. Bill thought that he could identify those who had had physical jobs in Civvy Street and those whose only exercise had been pushing pens. Bill laughed as one guy minced along the platform.

Unashamed, this guy was proper effeminate. The young guy wore make-up and had clearly dyed his hair. The red of the henna seemed to make his hair shimmer like copper in the daylight. One of the guys next to Bill said, "Fucking hell, look at the state of him. He's definitely going to frighten the fucking Nazis. He's putting the shits up me just looking at him. I hope to God, I don't have him sleeping next to me."

Bill's group laughed at the comment, but deep-down Bill suddenly sensed a retching in his stomach, thinking about what might happen if the other guys found out that he wasn't as dissimilar to that effeminate guy in that his lover was male. Yes, it was true that Bill did not present as effeminate, but Bill knew instinctively that the henna wearing 'sissy' boy was also drawn to men rather than women.

Once the trucks were fully laden, the convoy moved off to the barracks. The mood in the trucks was jovial and it was clear to Bill that much of the humour was a facade hiding the inner fear of every man on board. Eventually the trucks arrived at the barracks. Bill looked out seeing squad after squad being marched from place to place. Bill could tell those who had been in training the longest by the way that they marched and the way in which they responded to the orders of their sergeant.

Once the trucks stopped and everyone was disembarked, all were made to stand in line and in columns of three. Bill thought, *I bet we look a right shambles.* Men had to respond, 'sir' as their name was called. The sergeant noted missing. Those who spoke quietly were shouted at and told, "Speak up. You're in the bloody army now, not at friggin Sunday school."

After roll call, groups of 24 were then led off by a corporal, who took each group to their allocated barracks. Bill was happy to find that he was with Cyril Squires, Henry Williams, and Albert Tonks. At least, he was not alone. Being with people he knew made the first day less of a trauma. Bill was also relieved that the guy with the henna hair was allocated to another hut.

After being allocated a bunk, the new recruits were instructed to leave their belonging on their beds and taken to the mess hall for lunch. After they had eaten, they were collected again and taken to the quartermaster's store; there they collected bedding. They would be returning later to collect their kit.

Returning to their barracks, they were instructed to make their beds. Some guys had never made a bed in their lives and had to ask for help from those who had at least some idea. The corporal in charge, who had introduced himself as Corporal Lewis, informed everyone that he would be their platoon leader. Corporal Lewis demonstrated how each bed had to be made by making Cyril Squires Bed. Cyril smiled thinking that at least his bed was made properly. To Cyril's amazement, once the bed had been perfectly presented, Corporal Lewis pulled the bedding off the bed telling Cyril to re-make the bed as he had been shown. The corporal then told the men that today would be their easiest day, and that the real work would begin the next day.

Once everyone had settled, Corporal Lewis mustered the guy outside and once again marched them off to the main gym. Inside the gym, the men were lined up by platoon and made to stand in line facing desks that had be strategically place at one end of the gym. There, the men were issued with I.D. cards and given their ID number. Once finished in the gym, they then headed off to the quartermaster's store again; this time to collect their uniforms.

The rest of the day was to be spent tagging each item of uniform so that if lost, each item could be identified, and the owner found. Not all uniforms fitted properly which resulted in some men looking like they had been dropped into hessian potato bags, while others struggled to fasten trousers and tunics. The evening was spent placing all their clothes neatly and in order within their allocated lockers. After dinner, the men returned to the barracks to shower and prepare for the next day.

As the guys had to shower together, all had to strip and place their clothes on their allocated bed. Stripping off together caused some embarrassment but Bill somehow didn't feel that uncomfortable. Bill thought about the first time he and Tom and stripped off in front of each other. The recollection suddenly made Bill long to be with Tom. Only one day away from Tom and Bill was missing him dreadfully.

The corporal mustered his men in the shower area. The corporal was also naked and before allowing them to entre and wash, he himself entered the shower to demonstrate how the men had to wash. Unashamed, the corporal paid special attention to how the men should wash their genitals, backsides, and feet. Many men were embarrassed, but not so the corporal. Being rather well blessed, the corporal seemed to languish the idea of the men watching him wash around his groin area, his penis and bottom.

After the demonstration, all men were ordered to get into the showers and to wash as he had done. After drying, the men were ordered to get into their pyjamas and get into bed. Lights were then switched off. Talking was not allowed. Bill lay quietly awake for some time. He could hear the noises of men crying quietly and of a couple of the guys busing themselves masturbating. Bill was in no mood for either. He was tired and weary from the day's events and soon fell into a deep sleep.

After leaving the railway station, Tom had walked to work. Tears had filled his eyes. The thought of not having Bill around deepened his sadness. How could he feel so lonely already? At work, the day dragged on and Tom put little effort into the tasks he had to complete. The foreman noticed Tom slacking and that Tom's mood was not helping. By the end of the shift, Tom had only completed about two thirds of his work.

The foreman approach Tom enquiring if he was Okay. Tom apologised, stating that he didn't feel well. "Just make sure that you're back to normal tomorrow," the foreman said, patting Tom on the back. "We all have friends who have been called up. Things are going to get worse before they get better," the foreman said empathetically.

This was to be the first day leaving work that Tom had travelled without Bill for months, which added to Tom's sadness. Even when reaching home Tom could not bring himself to engage in chat. After tea, Tom went upstairs to his bedroom. Tom lay on the bed holding his pillow thinking of all the lovely times that he and Bill had spent together. Tom had never felt so sad and so alone.

Suddenly there was a knock-on Tom's bedroom door. "Can I come in?" It was Tom's dad.

"Yes, there's no need to knock," Tom replied. Tom suddenly realised that up until Bill had stayed, Tom's dad had never knocked on his bedroom door. Joe looked at his son and sat on the edge of Tom's bed. Joe recognised the pain Tom was suffering.

Tom's father touched his son on the head and said, "I just want you to know that I understand how you must be feeling," Tom looked his father perplexed. "I too had a best friend before the start of the Great War. Peter Guest was his name. We were inseparable. As kids, we got into all sorts of trouble together, particularly at school. Then we started work together at Harrisons. We were both on the production line. We were thirteen when we started work." Tom could see his father recalling the memories of his childhood. "We both joined up together, thinking that we could rule the world, that nothing bad would ever happen to us."

Joe went on, "Peter was killed 3 days after his nineteenth birthday. We were sent over the top. A bomb landed close to us. The force of the blast sent me flying and I suffered shrapnel wounds. Peter was ahead of me. He was a much faster runner than me and much stronger too. He was closer to the blast and was killed outright."

Joe stopped talking. Tom looked at his father in blank amazement. "You've not told me this before," Tom said, curious as to why his dad should be relating this story now.

Joe went on…"We all can have strong feeling for a friend and I know that with Bill gone you are feeling the loss. I know that Bill is ok but not having him around will be difficult for you. You just must hope and pray that he will be safe, unlike Peter. Then after all this mess has ended, you can start your friendship afresh."

For a time, Tom thought that his dad knew about his relationship with Bill, then realised he hadn't cottoned on to the intimacy of his relationship with Bill. "You'll be fine Tom," Joe continued. "At least, this war isn't going to be as bad as the last one. Things have changed somewhat and men are not going to be used as cannon fodder as they were in the last war. I'm just hoping that if, and when it's your turn, you will have the strength to get through it. Stay connected with Bill. He needs all the support he can get. I have a feeling that Bill will certainly not forget you and will keep in touch as often as he can. If you need to talk, I'm always here to listen." Joe ended his speech, tapped Tom on the head and walked out of the room.

Tom was dumbfounded. Tom's father had never talked to him like that before. Suddenly, Tom's respect for his father grew. Tom loved his father dearly. Tom suddenly understood his father more and why his father was always so withdrawn. *It must have been bad enough fighting for your life during the Great War, but to have your closest friend killed in front of you must be devastating,* Tom thought. By 10:00pm, Tom was in his bed at home and Bill in his bed at Aldershot; both were awake, but both were thinking about each other, both feeling sexually aroused and wishing that they could be together again.

The next morning Tom woke and began preparing for work while Bill, who had been woken at 5:00am, had breakfasted and was mustering with his platoon. All his comrades were now dressed in uniform ready to be marched off for their compulsory medical. Tom at this time, slowly made his way to work without the companionship of Bill. Bill's platoon was joined by another platoon and amongst these was Jimmy Burns.

Bill didn't know Jimmy, but he had seen Jimmy when he had arrived at the railway station. Jimmy Burns was the guy who has minced along the platform and who had been wearing make-up and who had his hair hennaed red. It was obvious to Bill that Jimmy's effeminate ways would not go unnoticed. However, it soon became obvious to Bill that the other guys in Jimmy's platoon were not put off by Jimmy's camp ways.

At the medical centre, both platoons were shepherded into the centre and instructed to strip off. All the guys did as they were instructed and were lined up for examination. Jimmy was the first to strip and appeared to have no inhibitions. Jimmy was about 5' 8" tall, was slim but his body was firm, and he was well endowed. Jimmy was first in line and when called forward, strode proudly towards the Medical Officer (MO).

The look on the medical officers' face was a mixture of shock and disbelief. Presenting himself, Jimmy stood upright and smiled. "Do you have a problem?" the medical officer enquired.

"If you are referring to the way I look," Jimmy replied, "then no I don't have a problem. Do you?" Jimmy asked the MO.

The MO coughed and spluttered then asked, "Are you a homosexual?"

"Yes," Jimmy responded with surety. "Are you?" Jimmy asked confidently.

At this, the MO reddened asking, "Are you being insubordinate?"

"No," was Jimmy's response. "You asked me a question, I answered, and I asked you a question. Is that something with which you can't deal?" Jimmy replied.

Clearly the MO had met his match. It was obvious that Jimmy had dealt with similar enquiries like this in the past and had developed a quick wit to respond to such enquires. The MO then asked, "What was your occupation before joining His Majesty's Army?" Jimmy looked the MO directly in the eye and stated that he was an entrepreneur.

He went on to say, "After leaving University, I went into business. In fact, I now have several businesses mainly in coiffure. Like you, I'm very handy with scissors and I'm quite apt with needles too. I make all my own clothes."

The room suddenly filled with laughter having heard the way Jimmy had responded, which made the MO uncomfortable, the MO was unable to respond. Standing behind the MO a sergeant, who was trying extremely hard not to smile, called for silence. The room fell silent, but all could see that The MO would not win with Jimmy. The MO conducted his examination in silence. During the examination, Jimmy was asked to bend over and to spread his cheeks. As he did so, Jimmy said, "If you find anyone up there, can you tell them we're in the army now and if they don't like it, they had better get out and go home." The MO quickly carried the procedure he was ordered to do and moved to the next guy in line as quickly as possible.

One of the guys from Jimmy's platoon and who was standing close to Bill said, "That guy's got guts. One of the other guys in our platoon called him a queer last night and Jimmy downed him. He's bloody harder than he looks and God, he's so funny. He doesn't give a shit about anything." Bill stood looking at Jimmy. Here was the first person he had ever seen who was openly homosexual and who couldn't give a toss about what people thought of him.

Bill on the other hand decided there and then never to openly admit that he was in love with another man but envied Jimmy in many ways. Jimmy's effeminate ways were not Bill's cup of tea, but Bill did think that he would like to get to know Jimmy just to find out how he had managed to survive in such a hostile society.

Bill did not come across Jimmy again for several weeks and his thoughts of the incident gradually diminished. However, three weeks later when Bill's platoon were again joined together to conduct field exercises. Both platoons were taken to a woodland area, where the exercise would take place. The platoons set up camp and were told that they would be required to remain within the woods for several days.

The platoons would be simulating hand to hand combat and stalking exercises against each other. After two days and following the many exercises, talk in the camp began to focus upon Jimmy and his ability to engage in combat.

It was evident to everyone that Jimmy had courage and determination. He showed little fear and was a fierce fighter. It didn't matter how big the other guy was, Jimmy would tackle them full on. It was clear that Jimmy had learned his craft in self-defence from an early age and could take a punch.

That evening, Bill, along with several others, including Jimmy, was put on spud bashing duties. Few of the guys actually spoke to Jimmy who was concentrating on his duty. At one point, Jimmy joined Bill and commenced pealing copious amounts of spuds.

"Hi," Jimmy said to Bill. "I'm Jimmy, glad to meet you."

Bill felt a little uneasy and somewhat embarrassed but responded by saying, "I'm Bill; Glad to meet you too." Although Bill was not glad to meet Jimmy.

"I've noticed you," Jimmy went on to say. Bill almost choked on his own spittle. "Are you an athlete? You are much fitter than most of the other guys and you don't seem to tire much when running."

"No, I'm not an athlete, but I do like to keep fit and one of my hobbies is running," Bill said feeling extremely uncomfortable.

"Oh!" Jimmy responded. "Well," Jimmy went on… "If we ever end up fighting the Nazis, I hope that you're fighting alongside me, most of the others here have no guts or stamina." Bill was a little taken aback by this comment but could see Jimmy's logic.

Jimmy and Bill continued to peel spuds in relative quiet, then Bill spouted, "Can I ask you something?" and before Jimmy could respond, Bill asked, "Don't you get hassled for being the way you are? I mean being so open about your sexuality?"

"Of course, I get hassled," Jimmy replied, "but I know how to handle myself and usually those people who hassle me the most often have something to hide. One minute they hassle you, coming across all manly and butch, but what they really want are sexual favours. It happens all the time dear. Why? Are you after something?"

Bill became very uneasy, not happy with the way Jimmy had responded. "No, I'm not after anything thank you very much, simply curious. I'm sorry I asked. I was only trying to have a conversation, nothing more," Bill said angrily. Jimmy sensed Bill's inner anger and apologised.

"I'm sorry," Jimmy stated. "I get asked so many times for sexual favours that it just gets a bit monotonous. I really didn't want to offend. Maybe we should start again. I'm not looking for enemies."

"Me neither," Bill said. "I'm not looking for friendship either, I just want to get on with everyone, but I am aware of how others have responded to you, especially the MO." Jimmy smiled accepting Bill's response but also recognised that Bill too probably had something to hide.

"I do hope that we can be friends, plutonic that is?" Jimmy finally said.

"Me too," Bill stated. In Bill's letters to Tom, Bill told Tom of his encounter with Jimmy and although he was happy to have Jimmy as a friend, he did worry that should his relationship with Tom be 'found out', they too would be hassled, possibly ridiculed and made to feel different.

As training progressed, there was little time to think about Tom during the day but at night Bill's thoughts remain firmly on Tom. After three months, Bill's platoon leader informed the guys that they would be allowed leave. Bill was beside himself with joy. Soon he would be able to visit his family but most of all he would be able to spend time with Tom.

Bill began hatching up a plan to meet Tom in London, spending a couple of days together before returning home. Tom was excited about this as he had never been to London and to spend a couple of days uninterrupted with Bill was just the icing on the cake. So it was that on 21st June Bill and Tom would meet in London. Their intention was to book a room in a hotel or boarding house and pose as brothers, taking away any suspicion from their relationship or any questioning about them sharing a room.

Two weeks after the field exercises Bill saw Jimmy again, this time not for conversation but as a member of the audience in the NAAFI bar. He had heard that Jimmy had formed a relationship with a guy called Richard 'Dickey' White, an accomplished pianist who was billeted in the same block as Jimmy. Whether this relationship was sexual, no one knows but they were together an awful lot and had been seen holding hands on occasion.

During some evenings in the NAAFI, Dickey would play the piano, provoking sing-along's as well as providing the troops with music that aided their relaxation. This one evening was to be different. Dickey had arrived in the NAAFI dressed in a white shirt, bow tie and dinner jacket. Dickey moved deliberately to the piano and begun playing Debussy's 'Clair de Lune' followed by 'Prélude à l'Après-Midi d'un Faune' and 'La Mer'. The NAAFI while noisy at first suddenly fell silent, listening to Dickey play as his concert developed. The sound was just beautiful and emotional.

After each piece of music came rapturous applause before everyone settled down again for the next performance. Dickey's final solo piece was La fille aux cheveux de lin (Girl with Flaxen Hair). After the recital, Dickey stood and took a long low bow to his audience to rapturous applause. Even those none-classical music lovers were enthralled. Dickey then sat at the piano waiting for the room to quieten.

As soon as there was absolute silence Dickey began to play the overture to the 'Wizard of OZ' then began to play 'Somewhere Over the Rainbow' made popular by Judy Garland.

As this song started, from outside a voice could be heard singing the vocals. In through the door walked Jimmy. Hair curled adorned with ribbons, wearing make-up and dressed in a white blouse and blue gingham dress. The whoops and howls were deafening overpowering the music and song. As Jimmy reached the piano Dickey stopped playing, looked at Jimmy and nodded. Dickey re-started the song again. Jimmy's voice was pleasant and sounded similar to Judy's.

From then on, Jimmy gave a short concert of Judy Garland songs, including 'Get Happy', 'I've Got Rhythm', 'Easter Bonnet' and 'The Battle of Jericho'. Jimmy sang with so much conviction and heart that Bill thought many of the guys really thought Jimmy to be a woman. One or two even thought it might be Judy Garland in disguise. After finishing 'The Battle of Jericho', Jimmy grabbed a handsome, over enthusiastic guy out of the audience, (with lots of encouragement from the rest of the guys). Although the guy struggled, he was no match for Jimmy's strength and determination.

Jimmy overpowered the guy easily, forcing the guy to sit on chair near the piano previously prepared by Dickey. Jimmy sat on the guy's lap and sang 'Love for Sale' while simulating anal sex. As the song progressed, Jimmy knelt to the side of the guy and replicated oral sex on the poor guy. Although obviously embarrassed, the young guy evidently enjoyed the experience and one of the men standing close to Bill said, "I think that chap is getting a hard on."

Uncomfortably Bill looked to see if the other guy's observations were correct but soon realised this had only be said in jest. After the song, the young guy was released and allowed to join his mates, much to the relief of the guy and to jovial hoots from the crowd. For Jimmy's finale, he announced that he this would be his last song for the night, thanked the audience and Dickey for his help and support and sang 'On the Other side of the Street'.

Bill laughed thinking what an appropriate song to end on. At the end of the concert, the noise in the NAAFI rose to a crescendo and a group of the guys ran to the piano congratulating Dickey while some picked up Jimmy raising him above their heads and began carrying him to the bar. As Jimmy was carried past Bill, Jimmy looked directly at him, winked, and laughed. Bill grinned back and at that moment realised Jimmy knew his secret.

How Jimmy knew, Bill could not comprehend, but the feeling Bill had that he had been found out disturbed him somewhat. The noise from the NAAFI had been such that it alerted the duty NCOs, who once the furores had died down, removed Jimmy and Dickey from the NAAFI, much to the disquiet of the rest of the guys. Apparently, after an investigation of what had gone on in the NAAFI that night, Jimmy, and Dickey were transferred from Aldershot. It was muted that they had both been made to join with the Entertainment National Service Association (ENSA).

Sometime later, Bill heard that Jimmy and Dickey had travelled widely across the globe entertaining the troops for the duration of the war and their relationship flourished. Bill had reservations as to whether Jimmy maintained a monogamous relationship with Dickey, as rumour had it that whilst at Aldershot, Jimmy had engaged with quite a few other guys.

At the end of May, British and French troops became trapped at Dunkirk, Gen John Gort, of the British Expeditionary Force drew up a full-scale evacuation—Operation Dynamo. As well as Royal Navy destroyers and other large ships, the famous 'little ships of Dunkirk' were employed to help evacuate more than 330,000 Allied troops. Talk and action within the barracks began to take on a more urgent focus. The lads realising that the 'Phoney war' was over and that soon, they would be preparing to face the enemy full-on.

During the early part of June that year, Nazi forces entered France moving along the Somme River heading for Paris. The German army reached Paris on June 14. The French government had to abandon the city, the Nazis marched through Paris watched in shock and horror by the Parisians. Then, on June 17, in the southern city of Bordeaux, what remained of the French government decided to seek an armistice. Adolf Hitler, adding insult to injury, insisted that any armistice should be signed in the Compiegne Forest, where, 22 years earlier the Germans had been forced to sign the armistice ending World War I. This escalation of the war sent shock waves through the British Government. The consequences meant that British activities would now also be escalating.

# Chapter Seven
# The Commitment

As June 21st approached, Bill's keenness to meet up with Tom became more intense. Bill had saved quite a bit of money from his army pay so that he could rent the best room for him and Tom. Tom had also been saving and his father had given Tom the money to purchase his railway ticket. Before telling his parents that he would be meeting Bill in London, Tom had indicated his interest to travel to London as soon as he knew that Bill would be taking leave. Tom didn't want to arouse suspicion, so he began by telling his parents of Bill impending leave. In conversations that followed, Tom said, "Wouldn't it be nice if someone could meet Bill on his return?"

Tom's mother said, "That sounds a lovely idea. We could all go to the station and wait for his train to arrive." The sinking feeling in Tom's chest at his mother's response was like being hit with a sledgehammer.

"I was thinking more of someone meeting him halfway, rather than waiting for him to get home," Tom said uneasily.

"I don't think Bill's mum and dad would want to travel too far," Tom's mother said in response, feeling that her suggestion was somehow inadequate.

It was Joe who then piped up, "Why don't you go son? It would be nice for you to meet your mate and for you to travel back together."

Tom recalled what his father had said the night Bill had left for training and realised that his father was more attune to his emotional state than his mother was.

"Well," Tom said, "that does sound like a clever idea, but I don't fancy just travelling to meet Bill then having to catch another train to come straight back home. Maybe we could make a weekend out of it? I could travel down after work on the Friday, meet with Bill on the Saturday or Sunday, or whatever the day Bill is allowed to take his leave, and then return together with Bill."

Tom used this example to test the waters and to allay any notion of what had been already arranged and a way of providing an excuse to be with Bill for longer.

"Sounds fine to me," Joe said flippantly.

"Well, that seems settled," Tom's mother retorted, feeling a little put out. "You men seem to have sorted it," she went on ending the conversation abruptly. Inside Tom was beside himself with excitement. *Well done Dad,* Tom thought, *you're a saviour.* That evening Tom called in to see Bill's parents. They too knew that Bill was coming home on leave. Tom thought it best to inform them of his intentions and to measure their response. Tom explained that he was thinking of travelling to London to meet Bill and to spend a couple of days sightseeing in the capital. After all, he had never been to London, and this gave him the opportunity to explore a little.

Tom also said that he thought it best to go as he too might be called up soon and that this might be the only opportunity he would have to visit the capital should his conscription letter arrive. Bill's parents were sympathetic and thought that it would be nice for Bill to have someone meet him, after all.

"He'll probably want some time away from the everyday training and time to prepare himself to come home," Bill's mother said. Bill's mother had also never seen the capital and thought that it would be nice to explore London with a friend in preference to doing it alone or to be with people with whom he was serving. Tom's relief was evident; both to Bill's parents and his own. Later that night he decided to write a letter to Bill confirming the arrangements. Tom wrote:

*My Dearest Bill,*

*I am hoping that this letter finds you fit and well. I'm doing ok but very bored being here alone without you about. I have been keeping up with the running at weekends and follow our usual path. I sometimes take a swim in Jacob's pool, but it is not the same without you.*

*I am counting the hours until we meet again. I am so excited to think that we will be able to spend time together alone and to enjoy a weekend without interruption from family and friends. The guys in the Swan ask after you and if I have heard from you. I don't tell them that I have letters almost every day, but I do tell them occasionally that I have heard from you and that you are doing ok. I have started making it a habit of going to the Swan after work and having a drink with your dad as you use to do. I think that he enjoys this and has taken some of his worries and concerns about you away.*

*When I receive your letters, I make sure that I get them directly from Sam the postman rather than have him deliver them directly to my home. No one knows that you write to me daily and no one knows that I write to you daily. I think it's best this way. The only person to know that I get regular letters is Sam and he's a good bloke and very discrete. I'm sure that he has some suspicion about us but happily he has never questioned me.*

*I spoke to my mother and father about coming to see you and my father was all for it. He has even offered to pay for my train ticket. Funny, but my dad has some understanding about my feelings for you although he has not said anything specific to recognise the real depth of my love for you. My mother wasn't as keen on the idea of me coming to London to see you as my dad, as I think she would have liked to have met you at the station along with your parents.*

*I have also checked out with your parents that they are happy for me to come meet you in London. I thought it best to tell them and to check their feelings on the matter. They think that it's a great idea and I'm sure that they do not suspect anything untoward.*

*I am thinking of travelling to London after work on the 20<sup>th</sup> of June. Are you able to get way on the Friday? If you are, then we can meet earlier. We also need to find somewhere to stay. I am sure that there will be some sort of board and lodgings close to the station.*

*If you are not able to get away on the Friday, I will still travel down as planned and will meet with you on the Saturday morning. I am just hoping and praying that we can find somewhere that has a comfortable double bed and where the landlady is not nosy.*

*I look forward to your reply and look forward to being with you again my love.*

*I love you Bill more than words can say and hope that as soon as this war is over that we will be able to be together once again.*


*Yours, always and forever.*
*T*


Tom kissed the letter, folded it, placed it in an envelope and wrote the address. Tom had purchased stamps and had kept them hidden in his wardrobe.

Tom retrieved his stamps, took one, licked it and stuck it to Bill's letter. Tom kissed the envelope and put it in the back pocket of his trousers for posting the next morning. As Tom did this, he realised just how empty he was feeling not having Bill around and just how much he loved Bill. Nothing in his life had ever made him feel this way before and his longing for Bill was intensifying as time went by.

A couple of days later Bill received Tom's latest letter mapping out their intended weekend together. Bill could see that Tom had ensured a safe passage and had done so in a way that would not provoke suspicion. Bill checked with his corporal about the leave arrangements and to his pleasure found that leave would be granted immediately following the day's activities on the Friday in question and Bill would be free to go. Bill was elated. He would be able to go to London earlier than he thought and would be with Tom a night longer than expected.

Bill wrote to Tom that same evening confirming that they could meet on the Friday night and asked Tom to meet him at Waterloo Station. Bill had been asking around about places to stay in London and Tansy Lee, one of the London guys had provided Bill with a number of addresses where he could find cheap digs. The excitement Bill felt was overwhelming. If Tom was feeling the same as he was, nothing else in the world mattered. Bill also became aware that Tansy had formed a relationship with another guy from the same barrack as Jimmy, a guy called Andrew Parr.

Both Andrew and Tansy were not what you would call candidates for having a homosexual relationship as both were what many would call 'men's men'; both strong individuals and both good at sports and both married. Bill had admired both men on the sports field as both were keen rugby players. Although their relationship had become general knowledge, no one seems to have taken much notice. It appeared that in times of war, the fact that same-gender attraction was evident within the ranks was very often ignored.

Little was said or done in the way of the army acting against this illegal act as long as the relationship was not affecting morale or training and if any sexual activity was kept private. Bill thought it was the case that the army needed men to fight, whatever their sexual persuasion; for now, the army was not singling out individuals because of being homosexual. What was becoming clear to Bill was that same-gender attraction was rifer than he had ever thought possible. This knowledge still did not persuade Bill to tell anyone about his relationship with

Tom or about the depth of his true feelings. What was happening to Bill was that he was beginning to see his relationship with Tom as being normal rather than being an abomination.

Friday 20th June arrived. Tom was counting the minutes until the end of his working day and was on a high. Tom had managed to persuade everyone at home that Friday was a better day to travel and had also persuaded his boss to allow him to leave work at 1:00pm rather than having to work until 5:00pm. This would allow Tom to get home early and to catch a much earlier train. Bill was also clock watching. To have the opportunity to be with Tom was all that was on his mind. Bill had already packed his bag ready for going on Leave and Tom's mother had promised to pack a weekend bag for Tom so that he would not have to waste time when he returned from work.

1:00pm arrived and Tom rushed to clock out. Tom ran for his bus not realising just how quickly he was going. Tom arrived at the bus station well before the bus was due, standing impatiently. The bus arrived but seemed to be moving at such a slow pace. Tom thought to himself that he could have run home quicker. Once home, Tom took a quick bath which had been prepared by his mother, grabbed some food before snatching his bag. The keenness Tom was showing bemused Tom's mother, but his father just smiled. "I'm off now," Tom said.

"Have you got your ticket and money?" his mother enquired.

"Yes," Tom said, attempting to get to the door. Tom turned, kissed his mother, and went over to shake his father's hand.

As Tom grasped his father's hand, his father pushed a slip of paper into Tom's palm, smiled and winked at Tom. Once outside, Tom looked at the paper to find that his dad had given him £5. Tom knew in his heart that his father was more aware of what was going on than he was letting on. As Tom reached the station and boarded the train to London, Bill was being marched off the parade ground towards the barracks. Once they reached their destination Bill knew that he would be released for leave. A quick shower, change of clothes and Bill would also be making his way to London and on his way to meet Tom.

Tom was halfway to London when Bill boarded his train. In two hours, Tom would be arriving in Paddington and Bill would also have arrived at Waterloo. Bill thought that in the time it took Tom to travel across London he would have time to find digs from the list Tansy had given him and hopefully book a room. With steam billowing from the engine of the train as it pulled into Waterloo, Bill jumped off heading for the exit. After enquiring about directions from the stations master to the street where lodgings could be found, Bill made his way there.

The street he was looking for was around the Elephant and Castle area. Bill found the house given to him by Tansy and knocked on the door. An elderly woman answered, and Bill enquired if she had lodgings for the weekend. The woman, Mrs Price said, "Yes love, is it just for you?"

"No," Bill said, feeling quite uncomfortable. "My, err…my brother is meeting me, and he will be staying with me, if that's alright?"

Mrs Price smiled and said, "That's fine love but you will have to share. I don't have two singles."

Bill almost forgot himself when he said, "That's great." Smiling from ear to ear, then said as his face reddened, "We're use to sharing."

"I guess you are on leave?" Mrs Price asked as she led Bill inside the house and to the bedroom upstairs.

"Yes," Bill said. "I'm still in training at Aldershot but my brother is coming down from the Midlands to meet me. This will be our first opportunity we have had to see London," As Bill said this, he thought to himself, *This is the first time we have been together for a whole weekend away from family and who's bothered about sightseeing.*

Mrs Price showed Bill the room which was small but clean. The iron bed was already made covered with a thick dusky pink candlewick bedspread. The small windows had thick black material hanging as curtains and there was a small fire, albeit not used for some time. Mrs Price pointed out the gazunder under the bed and informed Bill that the toilet was outside in the yard. A small washstand stood in one corner of the room adorned with a wash basin and jug.

The jug already filled with water and in the other corner a small wardrobe. "This is just great," Bill said.

"It will be £5 for the two nights but if you stay longer, £2 per night after that. Make sure that you are back in the evening by 10:00pm as that is when I lock up. Make sure that you close the curtains before you put on the lights. I don't want to have the warden knocking my door. Can you also empty your own gazunder in the morning? If you want tea, I can provide you with a pot in the morning, but you will have to get your own food and drink from outside venues. There is a cafe just down the street."

Bill nodded at Mrs Price's instructions and while she was explaining the rules, Bill took a £5 note from his pocket and promptly gave it to Mrs Price. "I don't want any shenanigans while you're here, so no bringing any women in." Bill was more than happy to agree with that statement but just smiled and nodded courteously. Bill dropped his bag next to the wardrobe and informed Mrs Price that he had to leave to collect his err…brother from the station. "Enjoy your stay and don't forget the rules. Any breakages must be paid for," Mrs Price said finally as Bill headed for the door and in making his way back to Waterloo, where hopefully Tom would be waiting.

When Bill arrived at Waterloo, he could see Tom standing and looking around nervously. Bill's heart raced at the sight of Tom, and he ran towards Tom as if his life depended upon it. Tom suddenly noticed Bill approaching. Tom smiled from ear-to-ear grinning like the Cheshire cat. Tom dropped his bag as Bill neared and both flung their arms around each other in a bear hug. Their instinct was to kiss heavily but both stopped themselves from doing so.

"Oh god, I am so pleased to see you Bill," Tom said.

"Me too," Bill said. "I have thought of nothing else since I left you at the station at home. I've got us a room. It's not far; it's at the Elephant a Castle, about five minutes' walk." Bill grabbed Tom's bag placed his arm over Tom's shoulder and moved him in the direction of their lodgings. "Oh, by the way," Bill began, "you're my brother if the landlady asks. I couldn't tell her that you are my lover." Tom laughed when he saw the serious look on Bill's face. "I don't care what I am as long as I'm with you," said Tom lovingly.

The boys reached their lodgings and went to their room. There was no sign of Mrs Price. Tom dropped his bag next to Bill's and Bill made sure that the door was closed and locked. Bill grabbed Tom and they fell onto the bed in a deep embrace, holding each other as close as it was possible to get, kissing each other with such passion, mouths interlocked, tongues entwined, rubbing, and squeezing each other and both highly sexually aroused.

They both looked lovingly into each other's eyes then parting their lips. Bill said, "Tom, I love you more than words can say. I have never loved anyone so much and I've missed you more than you can ever imagine."

Tom looked at Bill and said, "The feelings mutual. I love you even more than I love my parents. I just wish that this war was not happening. I want to be with you forever." After a time of just staring and smiling at each other, they decided that this was not the time to jump into bed and make enthusiastic, passionate love, and that they would wait and make love when they went to bed like married couples. Although both had the urge to just throw caution to the wind and have sex right there and then.

"Come on," Bill said, "let's explore London." The boys straightened their clothing and left their lodgings.

As it happened, rather than exploring London, they found the nearby cafe which Mrs Price had told Bill about and enjoyed pie and mash for their dinner. They exchanged gossip about home and of Bill's training and looked at each other with longing and yearning. Tom was in awe that Bill had met people who were openly homosexual and fascinated that the army was taking little action to punish those who were quite obviously having relationships with other men. Bill told Tom about the training and the emphasis on keeping fit.

Tom declared that Bill looked bigger, stronger, and fitter than when he left home. Tom told Bill just how lonely he had felt since Bill had left and about his dad speaking to him on the day Bill had gone. Tom also pulled out the £5 note that his father had given him to show Bill. "I think Dad knows about us, but I don't think he will ever say anything about it. It's just a feeling I have and the way he has changed towards me. He just seems more loving."

After eating at the cafe, they found a pub called ironically, 'The Elephant and Castle' and entered for a drink. As they walked through the door, many eyes were watching them suspiciously. They walked to the bar and the bartender walked towards them smiling. "Hello boys. You're new around here, aren't you?" The bartender eyed the boys up and down. This made both Bill and Tom feel uncomfortable, as if the bartender already knew that Bill and Tom were lovers.

Bill said, "Yes, we're only here for the weekend. I'm just going on leave from Aldershot on my way home to the Midlands and my brother has come to meet me. We're intending to see London before we go home."

"Brother, is it?" The bartender said with a smirk. "Don't worry dear, your secrets safe in here. Most of the guys in here are with their brothers too." The bartender said quite loudly and a few of the men standing close overheard; several started laughing. Bill and Tom's uneasiness increased until one of the guys standing down from them said.

"All sorts come in here love. This is my brother Amos. I'm Philip. Amos and I have been brothers for nearly six months." Amos blushed saying.

"Stop it Phil. You can see that they are newlyweds."

"We, we aren't married," Tom blurted out. Then Bill nudged Tom suddenly realising that Phil and Amos were like them and were just joking about being married. In fact, looking around, Bill realised that there were a number of couples like them seated around the pub. Phil then asked Bill if he could buy him and Tom a pint and asked them both to join him and his partner.

Once seated, Phil asked, "How did you find this place?"

Bill responded by saying, "Well we didn't find it because we weren't looking. It's just the first pub we came across. We are staying in digs just down the road and after having something to eat in the cafe we just walked in here for a pint."

"You were lucky. Not many people know of this place; well people know of the place but don't really know what kind of people frequent the joint. You're as safe as houses here," Phil replied.

Although Bill and Tom still felt uneasy, they suddenly began to relax and introduced themselves to their new friends. Phil and Amos took the lead in telling Bill and Tom about themselves and how they had met. Phil worked for the Ministry of War as a civil servant and Amos was a Grenadier Guard. Phil told the boys that he lived local and had he of known, Bill and Tom could have stayed at his place. "I've got plenty of space and have usually got a spare bedroom. Amos is stationed in the Royal Mews and stays with me when he's off duty," Phil said. "I'm one of those lucky buggers who have family connections, and my job is going to be based here in London permanently during the duration of this war."

Bill and Tom found out that Amos, who was from Leeds, had met Phil by chance, in Green Park. Apparently, Phil had been cruising the area for casual sex, had met Amos, who was not cruising for sex, and they had both hit it off almost immediately and had become partners. Phil came from a well to do family; his family had land and property in the Cotswolds and had properties in London too. Phil's father was a Commanding Officer in the Royal Navy and was titled.

Bill and Tom explained how they had met and how they had come to be in London together. The evening went quickly, and Bill had to remind Tom that they had to be back at their digs before 10:00pm. Before taking their leave, Phil said, "If you're around here lunchtime tomorrow, call in for a drink, we'll be here and we will be glad to show you some of the sights. If you like, bring your bags with you too; you can stay at mine tomorrow and Sunday if you want. You will be very welcome." Both couples bid each other goodnight and Bill and Tom left.

On getting to Mrs Prices, both boys were understandably overwhelmed by their experience and thought how nice Phil and Amos had been. What a shock it had been too, finding themselves in a pub frequented by homosexuals and where they didn't have to worry about anyone finding out about them as lovers. The boys crept into bed, made love extremely quietly as not to wake anyone and slept naked in each other's arms. The boys were in heaven. Making love again during the early hours. After waking, washing, emptying the gazunder, they chatted about what they would do regarding Phil's invitation.

After a short while and over breakfast in the café, they decided that they would accept Phil's offer. With some trepidation, Bill informed Mrs Price that they would not be requiring the room for a second night, thanked her for her hospitality, told her that she could keep the rest of the money and the boys took their leave. They met Phil in the Elephant and Castle at 1:00pm and on Phil seeing the boys' bags realised that they would be staying at his place. Amos had not yet arrived, but Phil explained that sometimes, he had to perform extra duties and would most likely meet them later.

After a couple more drinks, Phil took the boys to his house. Phil had a house just off the Old Kent Road. It was a huge Georgian house, four bedrooms, dining room, kitchen, and outside scullery. Phil even had a bathroom and inside toilet. Bill noticed the metal radiator indicating that Phil had central heating for the winter. Inside Phil's house, it was lavishly decorated with comfortable and expensive furnishing, standard lamps were in the four corners of the living room and one wall was full of books in shelves built for the purpose.

There were real oil paintings on the walls and the bedroom given to Bill and Tom was plush. A huge double bed in the centre of the room, a dressing table adorned with male cosmetic items; a large double wardrobe; an ottoman and an armchair covered in green velvet. Long thick curtains were tied back to the window frame, and it was noticeable that once the curtains were drawn, no light would be visible from the main street. This to the amazement of both Bill and Tom was the poshest, most upmarket place they had ever seen.

Not long after arriving at Phil's, Amos turned up. Amos was happy to see that their new friends had decided to accept Phil's offer. Phil made coffee and proposed that they all go sightseeing. "I thought a visit to Buck House might be in order first, then a trip down the mall, taking in Clarence House then through

Marble Arch. We can then go on to Trafalgar square. Tomorrow, if you are up to it, we can take a stroll along the Thames, see the Palace of Westminster and I can show you where I work."

"We can then go on to Piccadilly and the West End. You never know, we could even end up in the Salisbury. Sadly, we haven't got time to take in other places this weekend, but next time you're both in the 'smoke' (apparently, London to those who lived there is known as the smoke) I can take to see other places."

The boys looked mesmerised just listening to Phil, let alone actually visiting all the places Phil had listed. Bill thought just how lucky they were. Most guys back home had never left their home town, let alone visited the nation's capital and most guys would never experience staying in such a 'posh' house. Phil was true to his word taking the boys on their guided tour. First, they crossed the river by bus heading for Buckingham Palace. Imagine, this was the first time either Bill or Tom had seen where the King lived and both imagining what it would be like to live in such a place.

They spent some time looking at the palace before starting their walk up the Mall. Amos pointed in the direction of where his barracks were located and how to get to Green Park where Phil and Amos had first met. As they walked, Phil and Amos enlightened Bill and Tom about cruising areas and how casual sex would take place at night. They also told them about 'cottaging' and how casual sex took place between men in public toilets.

Amos said, "It's amazing how many 'so called straight men' use public toilets to have casual sex with other men. It goes on all the time." Bill and Tom looked at each other in amazement. The sheer thought of having sex with another man in such a public place was abhorrent to both.

They looked at each other both acknowledging without saying, that they would not be doing such a thing. Theirs was to be a monogamous relationship and both wanted to keep it that way. Their relationship was built on love and deep friendship not just sexual relief. Bill said as much to Phil and Amos with Tom nodded if full agreement.

"Funny," Phil said. "That's how Amos and I feel now. We have agreed that from now on, it's just him and me."

As they wondered looking at the sights of London, Phil told them of his life at Public School and how as a boarder, he had his first sexual experience with other boys and how many of those boys still partook in homosexual behaviour.

Bill and Tom were just gobsmacked. Phil named a number of young politicians who had attended his school and who had engaged in sexual activities with their peers. Bill and Tom were really taken aback on hearing this, struggling to process the information being divulged by Phil.

After finishing their tour of Buckingham Palace, the Mall, Clarence House, Marble Arch and Trafalgar Square, Phil took the lads to the West End and to the Salisbury; deciding that it was better to visit there that evening rather than waiting for another day. Here, people of notoriety met, actors, writers, artists, politicians' and the like, some of whom Bill and Tom had heard of but never thought they would meet in person and in a pub. Phil pointed out some individuals of interest and of their sexual antics.

Whilst in the pub, Phil introduced Bill and Tom to a guy call Henry. Henry was a very well-spoken and obviously rich man. His dress was tailored to perfection, (probably) made in Saville Row. Clearly Henry was from aristocracy. Henry was a pleasant man and on introductions, Henry said, "Welcome to Sainsbury's. I call this place Sainsbury's because you get anything in here." Phil and Amos laughed aloud, but the joke was lost on Bill and Tom. Henry was referring to possible sexual partners, particularly the younger men. "Most of the younger who frequent this place are 'rent'. Not expensive but well skilled in their craft."

All this talk about picking people up for casual sex was new to both Bill and Tom. Nothing like this ever happened in the Midlands. It was if they had been visiting a completely different country with completely unfamiliar cultural values. The whole experience was a revelation for both men. After a couple of hours, Phil said, "Right, dinner." They had eaten sandwiches that afternoon bought from a kiosk. Now Phil was taking them to a restaurant for dinner. "Don't worry guys, the meals on me. Bit of a treat for you both."

Phil took them to a sheik French restaurant where he frequently wined and dined his guests. This was a first for both Tom and Bill. As they entered the restaurant, the head waiter walked directly towards Phil. "Bonsoir monsieur Phil. Comment vas-tu?" the waiter said.

"Je suis très bien merci Gaston," Phil replied. "Avez-vous une table pour quatre s'il vous plait ?" Phil asked.

"Certainement monsieur, j'ai votre table habituelle libre ce soir," Gaston replied. Phil responded by saying, "Bon." Gaston then led the party to a table for four. Tom looked and Bill and Bill returned the look. It was clear that Phil was bilingual if not multilingual.

Tom afterwards said to Bill giggling, "He's amazing," referring to Phil. "We have trouble speaking English, let alone another language."

Phil was left to order the food as neither of his other guests spoke a word of French, nor could they read the menu. The two boys had never eaten food like they were presented with, and they struggled knowing what cutlery to use for each course. Amos had been to this restaurant with Phil before, so had some idea what was coming.

"Don't worry about table etiquette, just follow Phil. He's a dab hand at fancy stuff." The meal had five courses, including soup, salad, appetiser, main course and dessert. With each course, they drank wine, a different bottle for each course. Never had they had a meal with so many courses. The boys had only ever been used to having two courses at most and this would only be on special occasions like Sunday's and holidays. After the meal, cheese and biscuits were served along with coffee and Brandy.

Phil paid the bill at the end without hesitation and left a £1 tip for Gaston, the waiter. The price was not known to Bill and Tom, but they knew that it must have cost far more than they could ever afford. They were also taken aback in that the restaurant appeared not to be restricted by rationing. Phil pointed out that dignitary frequented this restaurant and as a result, the restaurant was well stocked by those who were landholder and who owned farms.

Returning to Phil's place, Amos was told to pour the guys a bedtime drink. Before they knew it, between them they had finished off a full bottle of Brandy. "Well," Phil said. "We're off to bed." Grabbing Amos by the hand. "Don't stay up too late, we have a lot more sightseeing to do tomorrow and if you two love birds are going to bang each other all night do keep the noise down. Scream quietly."

Phil and Amos laughed aloud and disappeared upstairs to their room. Amos led the way followed by Phil, who smacked Amos playfully on his backside. Not long after Phil and Amos had gone to bed, Bill and Tom retired to their room. They ensured that the curtains were fully closed before putting on the light. They stared at each other lovingly as they both stripped off, folding their cloths and placing them on the armchair. Both stood completely naked looking at each other as though they were examining fine pieces of art. Both were getting aroused even before getting into bed.

They got into bed in unison and were soon in each other's arms touching where they could with every part for their body. They were truly in love. They made love slowly, exploring each other as it were their very first time together. They took their time to fully engage and to complete their act of physical devotion. Without words, this is what both had been longing for. When both men were fully relaxed, satisfied they remained in each other's embrace. Then Bill said softly, "I never want anyone else in my life other than you Tom. I will be in love with you for all eternity."

Tom stroked Bill's face tenderly saying, "I'm yours forever. Never leave me whatever happens. I promise I am fully committed to you. I will never love anyone else and will never marry. You are my love and my rock." At that, they kissed sensuously, placed their heads facing each other, reached one arm over the other, closed their eyes and slept. At 8:00am prompt, a knock suddenly awoke Bill and Tom from their slumber. They had not moved all night.

"Am I safe to come in?" It was Amos carrying a tray of hot buttered toast and a pot of coffee. Amos was wearing one of Phil's smoking jackets. Amos placed the tray on the dressing table and turned to leave saying, "Phil and I are taking a bath together. When we've finished, do you want me to refill the bath for you two?" Tom without hesitation cried, "Yes please." The thought of bathing together with Bill was yet another new experience yet to savour.

After Phil and Amos had bathed, Amos knocked on Bill and Tom's bedroom door again shouting, "We've finished, and your bath is ready now." Having finished their breakfast in bed, the boys made their way to the bathroom. Viewing the huge bath that had been filled with piping hot water.

Bill looked at Tom and said, "Bloody hell, you could get four in that bath, let alone two." Two large bath sheets had been neatly folded ready for Tom and Bill once they had bathed. Having their first bath together was just the best experience they had had, beginning to wash each other, they giggled. Even the soap was a new experience, none of your carbolic stuff here, this soap was much softer and scented.

"It's a bit different from the old tin baths we have at home," Tom laughed.

"You're telling me," Bill said. "No carrying water from the brewhouse, no stoking up fires or ladling the water into a bucket. Having hot water on tap is definitely a luxury. We don't even have to empty it. It empties itself. Just pull the plug and the water disappears. This is heaven."

After they had bathed, which they both enjoyed tremendously, they dressed and met up downstairs with Phil and Amos. They greeted each other with smiles and Phil and Amos kissed Bill and Tom on the cheek. For both Tom and Bill, this was also a new experience. Having friends kiss you, albeit on the cheek was strange. Phil had prepared a full English breakfast and had set the table. The fine bone China wear and silver cutlery glistened on a pure white tablecloth. In the centre of the table, condiments stood on a small silver tray next to a candelabrum adorned with flowers.

They all ate breakfast swilling down with copious amounts of tea and coffee. After breakfast, Tom elected to clear away and to wash up. Even in the kitchen, hot water came directly from the tap. The kitchen was well stocked, with food and cleaning materials, including liquid to use for washing dishes. Bill arrived in the kitchen just as Tom had completed washing up and began drying the dishes with a towel especially made for the purpose. "Are you happy?" Bill asked Tom.

"Extatically," Tom replied. "I'm even enjoying doing the cleaning up." Both boys burst out laughing.

The day was bright and warm; there were few clouds in the sky, a perfect day for walking. When all four reached Westminster, Phil gave a tour guide showing his in-depth knowledge of the building, its history and of its architecture. They crossed the road visiting Westminster Abbey crossing over Parliament square before proceeding to the embankment.

As they walked, Phil pointed out where he worked and where Horse Guards Parade was located. After a time, the sights became less of an interest as the boys chatted together. "Are you staying overnight?" Phil asked. "You are more than welcome."

"If it's not too much trouble," Bill said looking for approval from Tom.

"That's settled then," Phil replied. "You can travel with me before I go to work and catch your train home. It has been wonderful having you both stay, and I do feel this friendship will last a lifetime." All agreed with Phil's comment. "And…" Phil went on, "anytime you are in London, let me know and I will make sure that you have a place to stay."

Both Bill and Tom were overwhelmed by Phil's generosity and kindness. Who would have thought that a chance meeting in a pub for queers would lead to such a profound friendship! It felt to all four that this friendship had become so close in such a brief time. Amos called the four of them the 'The Four

Musketqueers'. The day passed as pre-planned. It was an exciting day, a day of friendship and of commitment to each other.

During the evening Phil and Amos cooked a hearty meal washed down with copious amounts of wine. Tom and Bill were not accustomed to drinking wine so did not drink as much as their hosts. After dinner and after cleaning up, the boys visited the Elephant and Castle for a quiet drink before returning to Phil's place. Conversation centred on their friendship and how well they had bonded as couples. It was apparent to all four that this friendship would remain firm, and promises were made to keep in touch.

The following morning Amos left the house early returning to barracks before Bill and Tom had awoken. Phil had prepared breakfast before taking Bill and Tom to the railway station to catch their train, leaving them near the ticket office they bid their farewells. Bill and Tom promised Phil that they would return as soon as they were able, parting by giving each other hugs. The boys were content, and the journey home was filled with thoughts about their weekend together.

Tom realised that he would get some stick from work as he should have returned that morning. However, Tom wasn't bothered. Tom had been with Bill and that's all that mattered. When the boys returned home, both sets of parents were keen to know how their weekend had gone and Bill's parents were overjoyed to see Bill looking so well.

Bill's two week leave soon ended. The boys had been able to take runs every evening as the weather held and had occasionally made love near Jacob's pool. Making love outdoors added to their excitement, both recognising the danger element of being found out. The day Bill had to depart was difficult for both Bill and Tom but like any other couple during the war, parting would also be tinged with some fear. Bill had agreed to catch his train early so that he and Tom could leave their homes together. Their goodbyes replicated the time when Bill left the first time for his call up. The arches at the railway station providing cover for them to say their goodbyes without interruption. Bill returned to barracks to continue his training and Tom went back to the grindstone in the casting company.

# Chapter Eight
# Theatre, Conscription and Correspondence

During the latter part of Bill's training, Bill was promoted. He had been singled out as having leadership qualities and was made lance corporal. The men in his troop respected Bill, looking up to him for the calm, solid guidance he provided to them, with added reassurances given when things were getting tough. Bill was a protective lance corporal, always having the welfare of his troops at heart. He recognised the fear that some had about what lay ahead. He told them often, "If you always keep in mind your training and don't panic, all will be fine. It's when people panic and forget what they have learned that puts them in danger." He also added, "If or when we are called into action, just remember that everyone is scared, even the enemy. Being scared is not a weakness but using your fear can help you to focus more on what lies ahead. Use your fear wisely." Of all the things Bill said to his troops, the latter would always remain with them.

Two weeks before Bill was due to be posted, Tom wrote informing Bill that his letter of conscription had arrived and that he would be joining Bill at Aldershot. Sadly, the reality was much different. Tom would be joining at the time Bill was to take leave before joining his regiment. One or two days were all they would have to be able to see each other, but even then, they would not be able to spend time together. What was good, was that Bill would be around to see Tom off.

So it was, Bill took his leave, arriving home the day before Tom had to leave for his training. The boys met at the railway station late evening. Bill of course had to visit his parents so there was little time for the boys to be together. The following morning, Tom left for Aldershot. Another positive was that Bill was able to provide Tom with instructions on what and on what not to do when starting his training.

On 10th June, Mussolini declared war on France and Britain. Mussolini intended to extend Italy's colonies in North Africa attempting to take British and French territories. Rumour had it that it was possible, once their training was complete, Bill's cohort was more than likely to be sent to fight against the Italians in North Africa. On the 1st of August, Hitler instigated the 'Battle of Britain'.

Hitler had ordered that victory should be 'as soon as possible'. Hitler's ambition was to completely obliterate all the RAF flying squadrons and their ground support units, as well as the destruction of the entire British aircraft industry. The Battle of Britain began the following day.

While tensions were high because of Hitler's attack on mainland Britain, there came with it a stronger resolve by the British to quell the aggressor's actions. Bill's focus was to prepare him and his fellow conscripts in readiness for what might lie ahead. Tom was determined to do his part too and to follow Bill's example. So it was that in September Tom attended training at Aldershot and Bill was shipped out to Egypt. When Bill arrived in Egypt, fighting had been on-going since June.

The Italian fort, 'Fort Capuzzo' in Libya had been captured by the British but following this short victory the Italians fought back. The Italian's had just captured Sidi Barrani in Egypt as Bill arrived. Bill was assigned to the 1st Royal Tank Regiment who supported the 11th Hussars. Although in the Tank regiment, Bill was to remain a foot soldier following the tanks as they progressed. The temperature in North Africa affected Bill initially but he acclimatised quickly. He also could not get use to the sand and dust which seemed to blow everywhere and appeared to be ongoing day and night.

Bill also struggled with the smells of Egypt. It was a strange smell which Bill could not describe. He did think though that if any of the Egyptian people ever travelled to the Midlands, they would also find the smells quite strange too. The culture and people of Egypt were so different to that of the British. Their dress, their looks, their attitude, and their belief systems. There was suspicion in the camp of the Egyptians because of what many called their strange ways but Bill soon found that there were lots that were quite likable about many of Egyptians, especially the younger men.

After becoming acclimatised and building up friendships with the locals, Bill set about changing the views of many of his camp mates. Bill soon found that it was only by creating friendships that cooperation could be achieved. Bill also noticed that Egyptian women were kept well away from the British and many were unseen. This subservient way of life for the Egyptian women meant that Egyptian men formed remarkably close relationships with each other. It was to Bill's surprise that he found that on occasion, the Egyptian men also formed sexual relationships with other men.

It became clear that many of the older men had a younger man in tow. Not only as a companion but also to provide instruction and guidance. The Egyptians did not see their sexual activities with other men as being homosexual, but more as a normal part of their cultural heritage. For the Egyptians, same-gender attraction was where two men had formed a 'marriage' type of relationship, were living together and where one man took the role of female, taking on all the duties of a 'wife'. This type of relationship was frowned upon by the Egyptians but on the other hand, they accepted same sex relationships.

Bill wrote to Tom, Phil, and Amos about his observations. Tom was less interested than Phil who found this intriguing and wanted to know more. Tom was more interested in ensuring that Bill remained safe. Phil's letters back to Bill provided information about what was happening on the home front and the progress of the Battle of Britain, and that Amos had been called up to serve in The Far East. Phil told both Bill and Tom that Amos was to be stationed in Singapore. Tom informed Bill, Phil, and Amos of his progress with training and just how well he had settled into army life.

Like Bill, Tom had excelled, and no one was in anyway aware of his sexuality and relationship with Bill. Also, like Bill, he had met others in camp that were open about their sexual orientation, some of whom were having sexual relationships, albeit unseen. At this time, Bill did not know just how long he would remain in Egypt, but he had come to the realisation that he would be remaining in North Africa for some considerable time. Fighting to protect the Suez Canal was the main objective for the British but because of advancements made by the Italians, more efforts had to be put in place to drive the Italians back.

The desert had very few natural water supplies and as a result, water had to be transported in vehicles. Each man's recommended daily ration of 4.5 litres of water was halved because of logistical problems in getting water to the numerous troops who were continuing to arrive. Each man was only allowed 2.25 litres per day for drinking, washing, and shaving. The other half went for cooking and topping up vehicle radiators. Visibility everywhere was poor, hampered by heat haze and the continual dust and sandstorms.

Although the troops were fit, adequate drinking water and medical supplies were not always readily available, and many began to suffer from dehydration and diarrhoea. There was also a distinct lack of co-operation between the armour divisions and infantry, meaning that both the infantry and the armoury divisions ended up fighting almost separate battles.

As a result, the infantry did not receive the support it might have done, and the armour division frequently fell victim to well-co-ordinated enemy attacks. The British counter-offensive which began in earnest in December 1940 resulted in the Italians suffering heavy casualties. Bill, along with other British troops were ordered to move along the coast to capture Tobruk. Being by the coast had its advantages. There were less dust storms and the frequent gentle ocean breeze helped to cool the intensity of the sun.

Bill's first actual experience of battle was frightening. It seemed to come out of nowhere. Bill's platoon were taking 'point', when they encountered a large contingent of Italians, who had not been expected. The Italians had become aware of the British movements and had lay in waiting to ambush the British. When the shooting started, Bill quickly took charge of his platoon, who followed his orders to the letter.

Responding to Bill's orders allowed his men to take cover and to out manoeuvre their opponents. So many Italians were either killed or wounded and more ran for their lives. Luckily, none of Bill's men were killed or injured. However, having to deal with the stress of fighting suddenly became Bill's main objective once this initial action had ended. Firing at and killing or maiming other humans was difficult for everyone. Killing another human being, especially your first, is always the hardest.

Bill remembers firing at the enemy not knowing if he would be shooting at a hardened soldier or a recruit like himself. The thought of killing a young man in his prime and who would have been as scared as him, troubled Bill for a brief time. However, as the battle raged, Bill became accustomed to the fact that someone had to die, and he was fixated on the idea that it would not be him.

From then on, going forward was hard and eventful. All the men had suddenly become more acute to sights and sounds, their preparedness pronounced. The heat of the day and chilly night by contrast also affected many. Camps had to be set up along the way even during the fighting. When there was reprise, the troops had to 'dig in', creating makeshift homes. Holes covered by camouflage net became their sanctuary. On several occasions, Bill was dug in with sappers Cyril Hamilton, a broad set, overweight guy from Lancashire and David Worrall a short young youth from Liverpool.

David was what you might call a 'pretty boy;' Jet black hair, blue eyed and who had an olive skin tone. While Cyril found it easy to sleep at any time or opportunity, David, at night, found it more difficult. David would chill easily, was often scared, and would frequently shout out in his sleep. This did not bother Cyril so much as he was a deep sleeper; nothing seemed to wake him until he was ready. Bill however was more sensitive.

Bill took pity on David and one night, as David moaned in his sleep, Bill placed his arm over David to comfort him. David immediately snuggled up closer to Bill which resulted in David falling into a more relaxed sleep. Bill immediately thought of Tom and how they had snuggled together. It took all of Bill's resolve to control his physical and emotional responses. Lying so close to David was so comforting for both him and David. David wriggled consistently while he slept, which made it difficult for Bill to sleep but Bill had no regrets. Bill made a conscious decision to look after David, protecting him as much as he could.

After this first time, whenever David was with Bill, he would make sure that he lay close to him to offer reassurance. When sleeping, they always ended up in a foetal position with David's backside pushed into Bill's groin. Bill became aware that David enjoyed spooning Bill and David wanted more from Bill than just a cuddle. But Bill had committed himself to Tom and that is the way it was going to stay.

During one fierce fight against the Italian's David was wounded slightly in the arm, by a flying bullet. David was quickly patched up by the medics and was ordered back to duty. This injury added to David's night-time anxieties but did not seem to affect him during battle. In fact, David developed greater resolve to punish the enemy. Following more movements forward and more skirmishes, Bill, Cyril, and David commenced digging their hole for the night and fixing up their camouflage netting.

Bill was aware that David was keen to get the hole dug as deep and as wide as possible. David even prepared shelf like structures within the dugout so that the men could have a bed like space. Bill saw how David had laid out the dig and realised that Cyril's bed space had more distance from those prepared for David and himself. When the lads settled for the night Cyril soon fell into his normal deep sleep. Bill and David ended in their usual position. As the night achieved its darkest, David slid his hand around his back, to grab hold of Bill's now erect manhood. David knew that Bill was always erect as they cuddled. David was also erect having Bill at the back of him.

"What are you doing?" Bill asked quietly.

"I know that you are excited, and I know that you enjoy having me cuddled up close to you. I thought you would like some relief?" David stated bravely. "You really turn me on Bill and I'm not new to this kind of stuff. I also think that you have also tried it too."

"Maybe I have or maybe I haven't," Bill replied. "I have a lover at home." Bill went on, "I promised that I would keep faithful and that's exactly what I am going to do." Bill thought that this would be an end to the matter, but David became more inquisitive and even more intent to achieve some sort of sexual gratification.

"Is your lover male or female?" David enquired.

"None of your business," Bill said, not wanting to deny or admit the relationship he had with Tom. "Let's just leave it there and get some sleep. I have no problem cuddling up to you but that is as far as it goes. I really like you David and I guess in another time and place I would have gone further, but not now." David accepted what Bill had said without responding. What they both now knew, was that both preferred men to women.

The following day, Bill's division was ordered to push forward attacking the Italians. Thankfully, there were few British troops killed or injured, but many Italians were. The sight of the dead Italian's brought home to Bill the horrors of war, as many of the Italian bodies were of young, handsome men. Now gone forever, their lives snuffed out in an instant. Bill thought of what lives these brave men would have had if there had not been a war, their loves, family, ambitions, and lifestyles.

Bill shed a tear on seeing one such victim, a young man about 18 years old, shot in the chest, through his heart, but his face was angelic and his torso lean and muscular. Bill thought to himself that this boy would be mourned by his parents, siblings and friends in the same way that if anything ever happened to him or Tom, they too would be mourned.

Back in Aldershot, Tom had also been propositioned by one or two men, especially when he was showering, and after the majority had left the shower block. One guy, Ernie Corby was always on the prowl. Ernie originated from Leicester. Ernie, who was 25 years old had offered Tom oral sex. Ernie was a nice guy but did not make friends easily. Ernie suffered with a pronounced lisp, finding it difficult to be accepted, especially during group conversations. It had become well known that Ernie, had performed oral sex on several of guys, trying to gain their friendship.

Tom was not sure whether Ernie really enjoyed performing oral sex but was doing so on the promise that whoever he 'gave head' to would become his friend. Sadly, most of the guys just wanted to 'off load' and once Ernie had completed his task, would be ignored by the recipient, until the next time they wanted relief. A Birmingham youth also propositioned Tom, Shadrack Joins, Shed, to his friends. Shed came from a Romani family and was rough and ready. Shed was a keen fighter and was as strong as an Ox.

Shed had tried it on with Tom one night on the way back from the NAAFI, pulling Tom into a darkened area near the stores. It had taken Tom every ounce of strength to get Shed off him, but Tom managed to get away. Before reaching their barrack, Shed broke down pleading with Tom not to tell anyone what had happened. Shed confessed to Tom that he had always been attracted to men but within his own community this was a definite no-no.

Should any of his family ever find out that he was homosexual he would end up dead. Shed told Tom that if he was ever found out, he would have had to run and hide for the rest of his life. Shed said that in his community, anyone with the slightest inclination towards same-gender relationships would be ostracised, beaten badly (to the point of death), and banned from his community and family for life. For Shed, death in battle was better than admitting his true feelings.

Tom empathised with Shed's predicament and promised to keep quiet; but could not make sense of how someone like Shed, who was such a fierce, hardened individual, could ever think about having sex with another man. Tom then thought about his own situation. He and Bill were not your average homosexuals, in fact both Bill and Tom thought that they were fully heterosexual, until they became friends. Even now, Tom and Bill never acted like any of the other homosexuals they had come across.

After the incident with Shed, he and Tom became good friends and Shed stood up for Tom at every opportunity. Shed would follow Tom around, standing next to him like a personal bodyguard. Shed also invited Tom to visit his family. Shed told Tom that he would be most welcome, and that Tom would be given a caravan of his own to stay in. Although Tom was grateful for the offer, Tom never accepted the invitation.

In their letters to each other and to Phil and Amos, both boys related their experiences in full detail, writing in a way that would not arouse suspicion, should any of their letters be opened by officials or if any of their letters went astray, it would mean that their secret would put in the open for all to see. Phil and Amos also informed Tom and Bill of their escapades too.

All four would smile and giggle when they received letters from each other, knowing secretly how things must have been. Amos's letters tended to arrive in bulk, due to the way postal services ran for people when at sea. Amos had started his journey to Singapore on a troop carrier sailing from Southampton. He had stopped off at the Ascension Islands on route and in Cape Town, South Africa. Then was transported to India, before commencing the final leg of his journey to Singapore.

In December, and outnumbered, the British in North Africa made a counter-offensive, pushing the Italians back five hundred miles. The Italians suffered very heavy casualties and Tobruk was captured. Bill and his troops fought hard, sustaining few losses but heavy casualties. Ron Asquith, one of Bill's troops, was shot in the leg. When Ron suddenly went down in the Sand, Bill ran to Ron's aid. A bullet had penetrated Ron's leg but there was no exit hole. Bill had to cut away Ron's shorts to get at the wound, which he dressed using field bandages.

What shocked Bill was that when he cut through Ron's shorts, he found Ron not to be wearing any underwear and Ron's man tackle popped out. This would not have been so bad, but Ron had a raging erection. As Bill applied the bandages, Ron moaned out. Bill was not sure whether this was because of Ron being in pain or whether he was enjoying being erect and touched at the same time. Ron was taken off theatre by medics, then transported to the nearest field hospital. The doctors decided not to remove the bullet stating that it would be more dangerous to remove it than to leave it where it had lodged.

Ron was stitched up and a few days later returned to fight alongside his mates. After this incident, every time Ron saw Bill, he would smile and wink his eye. Bill could do nothing but laugh. Sadly, not all of Bill's platoon survived. Herbert Riley was one such man. Only 23 years of age when he died. Bill saw as a mortar exploded near to where Herbert was taking cover. The blast propelled Herbert almost ten feet into the air. Sand and blood spayed out like a firework expanding in a display. Herbert landed with such force, his body bouncing along the ground.

Bill heard Herbert expelling air from his lungs in a dull 'Uhm' as he finally came to rest. Bill responded in his usual way, rushing to Herbert's aid. What he saw was a gaping hole in Herbert's abdomen, his innards spewing out of his young body. Herbert's left leg was missing, and Bill could see the mix of flesh, muscle, bone and torn remnants of Herbert's shorts. Blood spurted from this gaping wound, clearly coming from the ripped artery. The look of Herbert's face would haunt Bill for the rest of his life.

Herbert stared as if in disbelief, shocked and horrified, knowing that he was near to the end of his life. Herbert looked at Bill desperately hoping that Bill would make things right. Bill gazed back at Herbert with tears streaming down his face. Bill knew that he could not do anything to stem the bleeding, nor could be put back Herbert's intestines, which pulsated as they lay on the hot sand. Bill grabbed Herbert's hand in an act of reassurance but knowing that this act could not change the fact that Herbert would die.

Herbert's breathing became intense, short, and grasping. Then nothing. Herbert stopped breathing, lying motionless, eyes staring as he gave up his life. Bill stayed with Herbert until medics arrived and was urged to go back to his troops as the medics did their job, closing Herbert's eyes before covering him with a blanket, Bill moved away. The medics moved Herbert's body onto a stretcher, running to move evidence from the battlefield.

Unfortunately, not all those who were fatally wounded, received such care and attention, as many would have to be left where they fell until it was safe to return, too late to save them, but necessary to remove their bodies. In some ways, having to leave those who were killed was better than having to try to deal with those who were in the process of dying. At least by leaving these brave men, the individual impact was not so great.

Christmas and New Year came and went. Seasonal celebrations were held in Egypt within camps, but these celebrations were not as the troops would have liked. Many however, were simply happy to be still alive. Bill celebrated Christmas and New Year in his dug out, while Tom on the other hand had been granted leave and would be spending time with his and Bill's family. On his way back to the Midlands, Tom decided to stop over to stay with Phil for a few days. The Battle of Brittan had raged and had been won, yet the jubilation was short lived as the Blitz on London had commenced.

When Tom arrived at Phil's, he saw for himself the misery that people were going through. Lucky enough, Phil's place was still standing and had not yet been affected by the bombing of London. Phil was not at all in the Christmas spirit. One because of the bombing and secondly, his parents had insisted that he should stay with them over the Christmas period in the Cotswolds, which Phil had politely declined. Phil's parents were aware of his sexuality and of his relationship with Amos, both of which they found abhorrent and made their views known to Phil. Phil told Tom, "If they can't accept me the way I am and cannot accept Amos as my lover, then they can both go to hell."

Phil was also becoming ever more concerned about Amos. News had it that the Japanese were building up forces in Manchuria (Northeast China), and there was a possibility that at some point Japan would enter the War, making it more likely that Amos would be forced to engage in combat. Furthermore, letters from Amos were arriving less frequently, due to difficulties with the postal services but also because Amos had more responsibility due to him being promoted to Sergeant.

The time that Tom spent at Phil's was done quietly; both enjoying each other's company and having time to share their worries and concerns, but Tom felt sad for Phil. It was nice to be friends together during the Christmas period but there was an emptiness within Phil's house without Amos and Bill being around. Phil told Tom that he was having more pressure put on him by his superiors and that because much of his work was secret, he was not able to share his burden with anyone.

Tom could see that Phil found difficulty in coping with these extra duties but tried to make Phil aware that everyone was experiencing their own mental torments because of the war and that Phil would be wise to remember this. Sadly, Tom's words were not enough to alleviate Phil's feelings of inadequacy and sense of doom. Phil remained feeling lost, troubled, and scared. Tom's time at home, although pleasant, seemed empty without Bill. Tom was happy to see his parents and he did spend a considerable time with Bill's parents too.

Tom tried hard to keep Bill's parents feeling positive, but they knew that unwelcome news could come along at any time. Conversation in the Swan was always about what was happening to the troops overseas, especially in North Africa and the bombing of London. A number of bombs had been dropped in the local area killing six people. Dave Race, one of the youngest guys in the Swan, told how on the night of the bombing, he, his mother and two younger brothers had been sleeping. They had been awoken by the sound of the sirens, and Dave had found his bed suddenly occupied by his mother, and two younger brothers.

Dave laughed as he recalled hearing the whistling of the bombs as they fell from the aircraft, the noise of the explosion and of his mother, who suddenly turned to God for help; praying out loud, "Oh God, please let it miss us, please let it miss us, please…" Dave then went on to say that the next morning, he and his two brothers attempted to visit the bomb crater, but were not allowed to get close. He said that the Police had cordoned off the area and would not let anyone see. Not everyone in the pub found Dave's story compelling; morale in the Swan appeared to be under strain.

New Year celebrations happened but not in the usual sense of the word. At midnight on New Year's Eve in the swan, whisky was passed around in the usual manner and a toast was made. Everyone stood in silence for one minute in remembrance of those who had been lost, killed, or injured in action. There were more tears than smiles as the realisation became clear, that this war was going to be more prolonged than had first been expected. Now moving into its third year, some even spoke of it lasting longer than the Great War, or World War I as it was now becoming to be known. Times were hard for everyone.

# Chapter Nine
# Escape from Rommel

In December 1940, Rommel formed a counter offensive in Egypt, after obtaining reinforcements from Tripoli. Now the British began to retreat. After the elation of making ground and capturing so many Italian troops, Bill's heart sank. It was apparent that the British had overstretched their resources making it easier for the Germans to make ground.

Bill's efforts during the earlier part of 1941 had not gone unnoticed. His commanding officer had requested that Bill kept his company busy by providing keep fit classes when the opportunity arose. Bill took up the gauntlet and threw himself in providing sports activities for many of his men. Bill even set about organising competitive games, coordinating a day where company was set against company. Prior to the games, some of the finest, fittest men who excelled in different disciplines were provided with extra training sessions, all overseen by Bill.

Bill looked at these young men wondering if any were like him, but never broached the subject. Bill had noticed that one or two seemed to be eying up their competitors not for their athletic prowess in their chosen sport, but because of their attraction to one another.

These were strong, good looking, healthy, heterosexual athletes. However, rumour had gone around that some had been involved in mutual masturbation and some had even found Egyptian boys who were willing to give sexual favours in return for gifts of cigarettes, chocolate or even tins of corned beef. This was confusing to Bill. He had become attracted to Tom and vis versa and as a result, neither of them had considered a heterosexual life after their union was formed.

These athletic boys seemed to want the best of both worlds yet still retaining their heterosexual status. Trying to understand all of this was confusing, mainly because there was no one to explain these issues to Bill, or for him to go to anyone for him to discuss this to find answers. What Bill was certain of, was, that whatever the sexual preferences of these men, each would fight as hard as they could for their country, and each were prepared to support and die for each other.

The games were held during early spring of 1941 and were a resounding success. Sprinting, medium distance, long-distance running, relay, tug of war, shot-put (Using stones), boxing, wrestling, long-jump, high-jump and even shooting were all on the itinerary. Hundreds of spectators cheered their champions on to success and failure. Improvised medals had been made by local craftsmen and strung on ribbon in assorted colours to denote first, second and third place in all events.

The commanding officer presented the prizes making the whole experience look professional and truly symbolic. One particularly fine athlete was Tony Smith. Tony was a good all-rounder. Blond-Haired Person, muscular and well-tanned, Tony could outrun the field, was good at track and field events and had turned up at every training session Bill had put on. Tony often watched Bill after completing his training event, sitting on the side-lines. Bill had noticed that Tony had not only watched Bill instruct others but seemed to undress him with his eyes.

Bill felt a little uneasy at first, having someone look at him so intently. At times, Bill almost felt naked as a result. Bill also noticed that Tony's bulge appeared to swell in his shorts, when watching Bill, which led Bill to consider that Tony might fantasise about him at night and might masturbate with visions of Bill in his head. Bill had certainly thought of Tom while masturbating and occasionally had thought about other guys too, including Tony Smith. *How strange the mind works,* thought Bill, suspecting that most virile men would also sexualise others while satisfying their own personal needs.

After the games, Bill had no more contact with Tony and wondered to himself if Tony would survive and just how many others of these young men he had trained would survive and how many would be captured, lost or injured so badly that their lives would change forever. Bill's emotions were a mix of pride and sadness. Bill's own thoughts made him think about his and Tom's fathers. They too had witnessed similar and more horrific things which had affected them in a much more devastating ways than this war. Their war had been much different to Bill's experience of war, yet they too must have seen, if not experienced the same emotional traumas.

Earlier during the year, Benghazi was lost, resulting in the British troops having to retreat. Retreating from anywhere was difficult for the men to take in. Ground was won, then lost again, making the whole experience even more difficult to bear. The Eighth Army now had to establish a line of fortifications and minefields to halt Rommel's forces. Bill was given responsibility of getting his men to lay anti-tank mines.

Setting out these mines was not as easy as Bill had first thought. The mines, which had to be off loaded from lorries were man handled and set into position following a detailed plan. The area in which these mines were laid extended for miles, each having to have a pit dug, then laid, covered with sand, before being activating.

Rommel began his offensive at the end of May, not long after the games Bill had orchestrated, and which had been completed. This began with the Italian infantry attacking at the front while Rommel led his panzers round the edge of the fortifications to cut off the supply route. Rommel went on to capture Sidi Muftah and Gazala, which was held by the British but which then had to be abandoned.

Fighting the Italian infantry was severe. Bill and his men ended up falling back to the port at Tobruk. Rommel was able to take Tobruk and its port; 35,000 British troops were captured in a last-ditch attempt to hold the enemy back. Bill and his men, including David and Cyril were amongst those captured. Bill was furious with himself for allowing the Germans to capture him and began to immediately plan his escape.

Moving 35,000 prisoners of war is not easy logistically. German and Italian guards had to be posted at strategic distances to ensure that all captives complied. However, the Italians were a little over lax with their duties than were the Germans. Bill was lucky, in that his division were being controlled and guarded by the Italians, and not the Germans. Bill realised that with careful observations, his plan of escape might come to fruition.

David and Cyril who had gotten to know Bill's ways well, soon realised that Bill was plotting something. David and Cyril challenged Bill, who after some persuasion let his plans of escape known to his buddies. On hearing what Bill's plans were, both David and Cyril wanted in. The bond that they had built over time between the three men had become too strong for them to be separated now.

Bill told his friends that he had noticed that the Italian guards often dropped their guard at night and were lacking sound self-discipline. Many of the Italian guards were fatigued, lacking focus and frequently fell asleep when on night watch. Bill thought that it would be easy to escape and avoid capture if their timing was right, and if they stuck together. It was agreed by the other two, that Bill would take the lead and the others promised that they would follow his every command when the time was right and whatever the outcome.

So it was, several days later, and at night, as the columns were halted to rest, Bill, David, and Cyril saw their opportunity to make a run for it. Bill had waited until the columns were halted along a road in open country. For as far as the eye could see, all along the edge of this road were small hills to either side. Lucky enough, this road was known to the locals as al-wadi sghir 'the small valley', which described it perfectly. Bill recognised that having halted here, the three of them would have the best opportunity for their escape.

Bill informed David and Cyril that their chance of escape had come, but they had to wait for the guards to be distracted. Then, and only then, could the three men make a dash for it, disappearing over one of the sand hills situated to their right. Their timing had to be perfect; ascending the hill which was located behind them would not be too difficult, as it was not too high and there were boulders scattered on its slopes. The men would easily scamper up the incline and hide, if necessary, behind the boulders strewn on its incline. Then, would be able to roll down the opposite side of the hill lying prone to the ground when they reached the bottom. From this position, they had planned to move from one scrub bush to another, keeping low and quiet, using the darkness as cover.

As luck would have it, that night was particularly dark and visibility restricted. The boys having made their escape over the hill, were able to snake along the open sand on the opposite side of the hill on their bellies in the increasing darkness that lay before them, stopping only occasionally to see if there was any movement from behind, or if any alert had been called.

Luckily, all was quiet, and there was sufficient rocks and shrubs around to take cover. They moved forward at speed, like snakes after prey, quickly covering the ground to become virtually unseen from their escape point. Once at a safe distance, and as dawn was breaking, the men quickly covered themselves with sand and remained as still as possible. That night, the weather had also been in their favour. Clouds hid light from the moon and stars. The night being darker than usual and a sandstorm aided their invisibility.

The next morning, after the column had moved forward, the coast became clear. However, it had been almost ten hours before the men felt safe to move.

Bill, David, and Cyril then dug themselves out of their temporary graves and headed East back towards Egypt, running, stopping, lying prone, observing, and using their wits. As the afternoon passed and as night drew on, the boys moved south of Tobruk skirting El Adam to the West. The lads moved some distance from the road to ensure that they had the best opportunity for no detection.

They eventually crossed the border of Libya on the Libya Plateaux heading for Salum, south of Sidi Barrani. Their hope was that they would be able to find a fishing village where they might steal a small boat and sail to Alexandria. Although scared, exhausted, and lacking food and water, the boy's spirits were at a high. David recalled that on the night of their escape and after digging their shallow graves, he had wanted to piss. He told Bill and Cyril just how difficult it had been to retrieve his penis from his shorts and how he had wriggled to ensure that when relieving himself, he did not get his shorts wet. "You have to keep a sense of decorum," David said smiling.

"Stuff that!" Cyril exclaimed. "I just pissed my pants when I needed to. At least, the piss was soaked up by the sand, and the heat from this sun soon dries you out."

"That's all well and good," David replied, "but at least **I** don't smell of piss. The Germans will be able to smell you a mile off," he laughed, putting Cyril down.

As the days passed and their journey progressed, the boys came across a number of small villages, where they were able to get fresh water and scavenge food. These raids taking place in the dead of night to avoid any detection. The men becoming quite adapt at foraging and stealing. *Funny,* Bill thought, smiling to himself, as he stole fruit from outside one of the houses in a village they passed, 'If my mother could see me stealing, she would want to cut off my fingers. She hated the thought that anyone should steal'.

At this first village, they also found clothes drying on rocks and took these to cover their uniforms. The Kamis or Gamis they took were wide garments with large sleeves that is frequently only seen on Fellahin, also known as Egyptian farmers. With materials wrapped around their heads, from a distance, they could easily have been mistaken for natives. Their journey, which was always taken by night, took days. The men always keeping low during the day and moving silently through the dark nights. On the sixth day, they neared Mersa Matruh.

They were travelling north of Zawyet Umm El-Rakham now and headed for the coast. Before they reached Mersa Matruh, they came across five Felucca fishing boats moored at the water's edge, close to a small settlement of houses. Next to one of the feluccas. was tied a small wooden rowing boat. The boys decided that this was to be their target and with effort, they would be able to travel virtually unseen and unrecognised.

Keeping hidden, they waited until well into the early hours before making their break. Bill had to swim out to the tied vessel, un-tether the rowing boat from the felucca, before bringing the boat closer to shore. There, Cyril and David waded into the sea to meet Bill. They mounted the boat as Bill steadied it, then once Bill was aboard, they silently rowed their stolen boat towards the lights of Mersa Matruh city.

Before daybreak, they managed to find a small cove. The cove was small enough just to hold the boat close to the rocks where they would wait for nightfall before attempting to pass Mersa Matruh. Here they ate food that they had taken and water they had gather, using a sheepskin drinking sack, left in the open at the first village they had come across. Then slept. It felt that this day of all days had given them the opportunity to fully recuperate. Bill said, "With luck, we will now be able to proceed towards El Alamein and then move on towards Alexandria."

Ever optimistic, Bill's enthusiasm encouraged Cyril and David to build up their spirits. The next night they began their long sea voyage, keeping as close to the shore as was possible and only venturing out to sea when there were villages in sight. As they were passing Mersa Matruh, they could see the lights of the city and they could hear voices in the distance. Rowing carefully and quietly and keeping at a safe distance from the shore they manoeuvred along the headway. Before dawn, they looked out and searched for another safe place to stop and rest.

Once they were comfortable in knowing that they were out of sight from watchful eyes, they again foraged for food and water. Bill found a well near to mud-built houses that were near to the headland. Bill managed to fill the sheepskin water carrier, which he made off with. David had moved closer to the houses where he found chickens roosting in a small outbuilding. With care, David was able to grab one of the resting chickens and quickly dispatching it by pulling its neck then running through a reed bed to make his escape.

Cyril was not so lucky in finding food, but did find a small fishing net, which he took in hopes that they would be able to catch fish along their escape route. It took the boys another four more days of travel and hiding to reach El Alamein.

Once past this port, the boys would be insight of Alexandria where hopefully, they would be able to report back to the main British command. The men knew that the British still held Alexandria and that they had built a large force there.

The march with the detained prisoners and their escape was now beginning to take its toll on the boys, especially Cyril. All three were weary; exhausted from rowing, having minimal sleep and having to manage without substantial food, some of which had been rancid, which made them all feel weak. Cyril, not being the fittest of the trio had come off worst and his mental stability had dwindled considerably. Cyril had slowed the other two and had to be watched, when sleeping, as he trended to cry out in his sleep.

Frequently, Bill had to gag Cyril from crying out, disturbing everyone's sleep even further. David was always close to Bill, curling up together for comfort after Cyril had eventually settled. On occasion, David and Bill became more intimate, touching each other but never having any sexual activity together. They had kissed on occasion and had held each other's swelling members. But Bill always ensured that when David became too aroused, he would stop, allowing David to relieve himself. Bill also relieved himself too but always had Tom on his mind when doing so.

When they eventually reached Alexandria, the boys discarded their stolen attire and made their way by foot to the nearest British post. They decided to shed their stolen items on the outskirts of the city before walking, as to not draw to attention to themselves. Once reaching the city, they reported to the nearest commanding officer, after having to go through various checks. There, they relayed their story to their superiors. They were congratulated by one of the majors on their bravery, courage and British grit, then ordered to rest up for a few days.

A sergeant Boswell led the men to the barracks and after eating a hearty meal, they were allocated beds. David made sure that he would be sleeping next to Bill and pulled his bed so that it was touching Bill's bed. Cyril just fell onto his bed, not taking any notice of David's antics and fell into the deepest of sleeps. In fact, Cyril did not wake until late afternoon the following day. David and Bill chatted before they both slept with David edging so close to Bill that they soon ended up both in the same bed. Further orders would not be given to the courageous three for several days, and so they took this time to build up their reserves.

Rommel and the Deutsches Afrik Korps were only seventy miles from Alexandria. The situation was getting so serious that Churchill himself made the long journey to Egypt to discover for himself what needed to be done. Churchill then updated the command structure, placing General Harold Alexander in charge of British land forces in the Middle East and Monty (Montgomery,) took command of the Eighth Army.

At the end of August, Rommel attacked at Alam el Halfa; Montgomery responding immediately by ordering his troops to withdraw to El Alamein. Bill, David, and Cyril, once deemed fit, were dispatched back to El Alamein. Ironic thought Bill, we have recently escaped passing this bloody place, and here we are again, back in the same bloody place, that's what they mean by déjà vu? He smiled to himself. Montgomery made sure that Rommel and the German Army was unable to make any further advances into Egypt.

During the fighting, Cyril was fatally wounded, suffering a direct shrapnel hit to his head. His loss to both Bill and David was profound. Cyril had been a great mate, and the three had planned to be lifelong friends after the war. Bill and David made sure that Cyril's body was well cared for. They wrapped him in a blanket and even helped stretcher him to the transport, which took him away to his final resting place.

That night, in their dug out, Bill carefully packed up Cyril's belongings and wrote a touching letter to Cyril's family. Bill then placed all of the packed belongings in Cyril's empty bed, speaking softly to Cyril as if he were still there with him and David. David slept closer than ever to Bill that night.

Bill also wrote to Tom, telling him about their escape and of his transfer back to El Alamein and the loss of Cyril. Bill spoke of how hard it was to cope with Cyril's death. Bill also confessed that he had not deterred David from sleeping in the same bed as him.

Bill knew that Tom would understand about him allowing David in his bed, and he also knew that Tom trusted him enough to know that nothing untoward would ever happen. In Bill's letter to Tom, he finally wrote, **"After all that we have been through, Cyril, David, and I, this had to happen. Life is so unfair. I miss you more now than I have ever done and love you unconditionally."**

For the next six weeks, Bill and his men helped with the unloading of vast quantities of weapons and ammunition. Large numbers of Sherman MS and Grant ME tanks 1,351 in total and 1,900 pieces of artillery were stockpiled; 195,000 men also arrived on troop ships. On 23rd October, Montgomery launched Operation Lightfoot with the largest artillery bombardment seen since the Great War. The attack came at the worst time for the Germans as

Rommel was on sick leave in Austria and his replacement, General George Stumme had died of a heart-attack during the 1000-gun bombardment of the German lines.

Rommel was ordered back to Egypt by Hitler. The Germans defended their positions well and the Eighth Army made little progress. When Rommel returned, he launched a counterattack at Kidney Ridge (27th October); Montgomery now returned to the offensive and the 9th Australian Division created a salient in the enemy positions, which they managed to hold despite a series of German attacks.

Montgomery, ignoring criticism from Churchill made plans for a new offensive, Operation Supercharge; and on 1st November, Montgomery launched an attack at Kidney Ridge. After initially resisting the attack, Rommel decided he no longer had the resources to hold his line and on the 3rd November, he ordered his troops to withdraw. However, Hitler overruled Rommel and the Germans were forced to stand and fight. Montgomery ordered his men forward.

The Eighth Army broke through the German lines and Rommel, in danger of being surrounded, was eventually given permission by Hitler to retreat. Those soldiers on foot, including large numbers of Italian soldiers, were taken prisoner. Rommel had managed to take Sollum on the Egypt-Libya border but was left with only twenty tanks. The British recaptured Tobruk on 13th November, bringing the battle at El Alamein to an end.

During the campaign half of Rommel's army was killed, wounded or taken prisoner, numbering over 100,000-men. He also lost over 450 tanks and 1,000 guns. The British and Commonwealth forces suffered 13,500 casualties and five hundred of their tanks were damaged. However, of these, 350 were repaired, and were able to take part in future battles. Following the battle of El Alamein and to Bill's relief, he was informed that he would be returning home for some well-deserved leave and was promoted to Staff Sergeant.

Bill immediately wrote to Tom informing him of his impending leave. Bill was to sail back through the Mediterranean and would dock in Portsmouth. Tom, who had now been posted to London, was beside himself with joy. Tom was going to make sure that he would spend as much time as possible with Bill; even meeting him in Portsmouth. Tom took no time in telling Phil, who had also received a letter from Bill the following morning telling him of his impending leave. It would be great that at least three of the four 'musketqueers' were back together again, but sad that it could not be all four.

# Chapter Ten
# The Far East

After receiving his papers, Amos had readied himself for his transfer to Singapore. He had little time to get ready, only 4 days before departure. His call-up papers came as a surprise to both him and Phil, with Phil taking the move harder than Amos. They had only two days together in all, most of which was spent in bed. Every waking moment, the boys seemed to be in an embrace or were locked together making love. Amos had notified his family by post about his posting and on his decision not to visit before leaving. Afterall, it would have taken almost two days in travel. Phil and Amos decided to say their goodbyes at Phil's house, preferring to keep their relationship under cover. They realised that should they meet at the railway station; their cover would have been broken. They parted in tears, promising that they would keep in contact by mail and that on Amos's return, they would commit to a long-standing relationship.

Amos's journey to the Far East was long but adventurous. Amos had never been abroad, nor had he ever travelled by sea. When the ship stopped at the Ascension Islands, their first port of call, no one was allowed ashore. The ship refuelled and took on board provisions before setting sail for Cape Town. In Cape Town, the men were given the opportunity to spend time ashore, many exploring the sights and sounds of the city and surrounding areas.

The cultural differences between South Africa and England were mesmerising and Amos soaked up as much as he could in the brief time the ship was there. Amos made a point of writing to Phil describing what he had seen and experienced in this new land. He also made a point of telling Phil about some of the guys he was travelling with and of those he suspected were having same sex relationships. After only five days in Cape Town, the ship set sail for Singapore.

6,736 miles from London and 5,129 miles from Cairo, Amos landed, and he began settling into Selarang Barracks in Singapore. These new barracks built in

1938, was part of the Changi Garrison. Changi Garrison was a heavily fortified coastal defence where most of the British forces were based. Amos had docked in Sembawang some eighteen and a half miles from Changi along with a number of other troops. This deployment had not been Amos's preferred choice of places to be but on his arrival, he found Singapore to be a beautiful place.

Exotic plants everywhere and the tropical weather suited Amos to the ground. The cultural mix of Chinese, Malay and Indian people fascinated Amos. People who lived in Singapore were polite and always appeared happy. Selarang barracks not only offered space, and which was extremely comfortable, but was serviced by many Singaporeans who seemed to work tirelessly to maintain the barracks in tip top condition. Near to where Amos was to be stationed was Changi beach.

Changi beach offered soft golden sands and warm waters, which appealed to Amos. Singapore city was not too far away either and its vibrant and cosmopolitan sprawl provided everything a young man could ever wish for. The food stalls offered new and exciting things to eat and, Amos loved many of the new flavours on offer. Shops and bars were plentiful and a vast array of entertainment available. One of the most appealing of places to all the British soldiers, sailors and air force men was Bugis Street, offering market stalls during the day which then converted to outdoor restaurants and bars at night.

This 24-hour metropolis provided for every possible need a man could wish for, including prostitutes and rent boys. Amos loved the atmosphere of Bugis Street, which became his favourite place and where he found time to relax. Amos would have preferred to have remained in London, but Singapore was a close second best. Amos wished that Phil could have been here with him. *Phil would love it here,* he thought to himself and, *Phil would have loved the rent boys especially.*

Amos hoped that one day, he might have the opportunity to bring Phil here for a holiday. Amos's letter expressed his longing to be with Phil and how he would have wanted Phil to be with him to experience the wonders of the sub-tropical Island. Temperatures in Singapore averaged thirty-two degrees and at night rarely dropped below twenty-five degrees. The hustle and bustle of Singapore provided a great morale booster.

One night Amos was lying in his bed feeling hot and sticky. He found it difficult to sleep so whiled away the hours thinking about Phil. Amos smiled to himself as he recalled his first night with Phil, he remembered saying to Phil that first night just how hot and sticky he had become following their night of passion. Smiling, Amos visualised in his mind how Phil and he had met. Amos had never thought of making love with a man before meeting Phil, nor would he have done so if it had not been for that chance meeting in Green Park.

The night Amos met Phil had been for him, quite a boring night until their meeting. Earlier, that evening, Amos had chosen to go out alone and had wandered the streets of Central London, finding himself at last around the Shepherds Market area. He had called into the Market Tavern for a couple of beers and had sat alone. Amos recollected that on that night, he had wanted to be alone and had refused invitations from his mates to visit Soho.

Normally, Amos would have only ventured out with others from his troop, but that night had been different. After calling into the Market Tavern, Amos drank more than the couple of beers as he had planned to have. He had drunk his beers too quickly and felt quite inebriated. He then decided to take a stroll through Hyde Park and onto Green Park to see if he could sober up a little. About halfway through Green Park, Amos was caught short, desperately wanting to empty his now over full, stretched, bursting bladder. He recalled looking for a public toilet, but none were in sight.

Then he saw some bushes and decided that they were his best option to relieve himself without being noticed should anyone pass by. Amos had walked to the bushes and made his way a little deeper into the thick shrubs hiding from the walkway. Amos remembered that he had difficulty opening his button flies and so had opened his belt to gain easier access. Amos ended up with his trousers halfway down his legs and attempting to hold them in position with his knees. As Amos began to urinate, a hand came through the bush from behind, reaching out to grab his manhood.

Shocked and in full flow, the hand touched him and held him, manoeuvring his penis to direct the now forceful flow. "Wow" he remembered crying out. Why Amos did not move, he could not say, but allowed the hand to direct the now forceful flow. *Amos put his inactive response to being a little drunk,* he thought, *he had drunk quickly and more than he had anticipated.* The hand around his active urinating penis was the last thing he had expected; yet Amos did little to stop the mysterious hand from manipulating him.

The sensation was not at all unpleasant. In fact, it was highly stimulating and fun. The stranger's hand then began to move; pulling and pushing up and down on Amos's shaft until Amos reacted becoming erect. "What should he do?"

Amos recalls thinking. The sensation was just too nice to stop the hidden person for doing what they were doing and whose hand was providing Amos with so much pleasure. The bushes moved and the figure moved to stand closer. The figure made his way to the Amos's side. Amos stood frozen and speechless.

It was at this point that Amos realised that the figure was male. The figure exposed his own erect penis and with his other hand was masturbating. Only after a short while, both men climaxed and stood looking at each other. The stranger spoke first. "Thank you. I needed that. I've not seen you here before." Amos was amazed at how well-spoken this guy was and curious about what the man had said.

"What do you mean; you haven't seen me here before? It ain't a place I would usually visit at night," Amos stated.

"I only needed a slash, and this seemed the best place to do it. I've never been here before and have never had a bloke wank we off before." The guy looked at Amos figuring out that this was the first time Amos had been approached for sexual favours.

"Didn't you know that this was a cruising area"? The man asked.

"I don't know what you mean," Amos replied.

"Green Park," the guy said. "Green Park is well known as a place where guys meet at night for casual sex."

A little embarrassed Amos stated, "Well I've never been here before and I didn't know that men met up for this kind of thing. I've never let any bloke do that to me before, and I do find it a bit strange. In fact, I'm shocked that I even allowed you to do that to me. I'm angry with myself for allowing you to do it." Amos said quite firmly.

The stranger said, "Well there is a first time for everyone I suppose. Did you enjoy it?" he asked.

"I'm not sure now," Amos retorted, getting a little angrier.

"Well, I'm sorry," the man went on to say. "Perhaps I should apologise but I have to say, you were amazing. I'm Phil," the guy said pushing out his hand offering Amos a handshake. Amos struggled to shake Phil's hand due to him trying to pull up his trousers and secure himself. Both men stood as if time had stopped; Amos looking at Phil's hand, not knowing whether to accept the apology being offered or even to respond to Phil's handshake at all.

Amos had no idea why he hadn't just hit the guy or why he had grabbed his hand and shook it.

"Apology accepted," Amos found himself saying.

"Look," the guy said, "let's start as if this had never happened and think of it as if we had just met. Can I ask you if its ok to invite you to my place for a drink; nothing more, just a drink?" Amos still confused accepted Phil's invitation. Why he had accepted this stranger's invitation, Amos had no idea, but almost felt obliged to accept Phil's offer. "I don't live too far from here. Only five-minute walk," Phil said encouragingly.

Actually, Phil lived about two miles away but the walk was covered quickly. "What's your name?" Phil asked.

"Oh…I'm Amos," Amos replied. Amos looked at Phil now taking in his build and good looks. Amos somehow felt attracted to Phil and it was clear from the look on Phil's face that he was attracted to Amos.

Phil and Amos walked the short distance to Phil's place. Phil had talked consistently as they went along their way while Amos listened intently. Phil was eager to give a good impression and provided Amos with a tour guide as they walked. It seemed to Amos that Phil was full of knowledge and that he was 'posh'. Phil spoke with a noticeably clear upper crust accent, like many of the army officers he had had contact with. Amos was aware that his accent bore the locality from where he had been born and bought up.

Amos was intrigued by Phil, never had Amos wanted to listen to someone as much as he did Phil. Phil was worldly wise, relaxed, did not appear to have a care in the world and was happy and content with everything. Amos envied Phil: his ability to make friends so quickly, his relaxed manner, his dress sense and his surety all contributed to his attraction to Phil. So it was, that Amos and Phil began their friendship.

Phil told Amos that he frequented Green Park only occasionally and that he found the experience exciting. "I think it's the danger element that I like the most," Phil told Amos. "Why did you go to Green Park?" Phil enquired. Amos told Phil that he had been walking around Shepherds Market and had called in to the Market Tavern for a drink. He told Phil about him staying longer in the pub than anticipated and had decided to walk through Green Park on his way back to the barracks.

"Oh my god!" Phil cried, "you're in the army. How fabulous. You must tell me about it." Phil then went on to tell Amos that he lived alone and that he had had numerous sexual encounters with men. He told Amos that his first sexual experiences had been when he was in Boarding School and how, since then, had always been attracted to men. Phil went on to say that somehow, sex with men was for him, more enjoyable than sex with women, albeit that he had not had many sexual experiences with the opposite gender.

Amos was shocked but excited by Phil's openness and honesty but fascinated to hear more. Why he was so interested in Phil's sexual exploitations Amos could not fathom out. His mind was in a mess but funnily enough he felt very secure and relaxed in Phil's company, far more relaxed than he had ever been with anyone else. Before he knew it, Phil was leading Amos to his front door, taking his key from his pocket Phil opened the door and invited Amos inside.

Amos was in awe of Phil and of his home. It was huge, compared to Amos's family home back in Leeds. Amos's parents lived in a two up two down terraced house which was damp, cramped and not pleasant, although it was homely. Phil's place was spacious, very grand and everything inside look expensive. It was clear to Amos that Phil came from a well to do family. Inside Phil invited Amos to take off his coat and to take a seat.

"What would you like to drink?" Phil asked. "I don't have beer, but I do have a broad selection of wines and spirits. Maybe you like champagne?" Phil laughed. Amos was startled.

"Champaign? I've never tried it, it's not what us Army blokes are used to, well not what us squaddies would normally drink, and we wouldn't ever think of drinking it at home. I've only ever drunk beer and the occasional whisky," Amos confirmed.

"Champaign it is then," Phil stated with another laugh. "This can be our celebratory drink. Our first meeting drink." Amos could not understand why he felt so relaxed around Phil, it was a strange feeling, Amos really didn't want the evening to end. By 2.00am, Phil said, "Well, I must get to bed. I've got work in the morning."

"Yes, I'd better get going too," Amos replied. "I'm on duty at 8:00am and I can't be late."

Phil then went on to say, "You are welcome to stay here if you like, I've got two spare rooms, or you can double up with me. Don't worry I'm not going to take advantage of you again, and if you don't want to stay that's fine. I really would like to see you again though, if only for a drink."

Amos thought for a little while then said, "Well if you don't mind, I'll stay." Shocked by his reply, Amos had to internally process what he was saying. Then he suddenly said, "I'm quite happy to double up too; it will save making two beds in the morning." Both boys laughed, even though Amos was still unsure of why he was responding the way he was. Phil grabbed Amos's hand pulling Amos to his feet. "Come on then," Phil said as he led Amos upstairs. After using the bathroom, the boys stripped off and got into bed. As Phil had promised, nothing happened between them that night and both fell asleep curled up together; both feeling comforted, safe and happy.

The following morning Amos was woken by Phil who had already made breakfast and presented Amos with a tray. The tray held two boiled eggs, buttered toast, jam, and a cup of steaming hot coffee. "It's 7.00am," Phil said. "If you are to be back in time, you had better get your breakfast and move sharpish." At that, Phil left the room going directly into the bathroom. Amos finished his breakfast and followed Phil into the bathroom washing himself once Phil had finished. Amos dressed and took the empty tray downstairs. "Leave it in the kitchen," Phil shouted. "I'll clean up when I get back from work." The boys left the house together, making their way to their respective places of work. As they walked along the street, Phil asked Amos, "Will you come around tonight? I'm back home by 6:30pm and it would be great to spend another evening with you."

Amos smiled and without hesitation replied, "If that's ok with you? I can be at yours by 7:00pm."

Phil clapped his hands as if in triumph. "Seven it is then, don't be late." Phil walked off, turning, and waving back at Amos. Amos returned the wave smiling. He too felt a sense of triumph but was also still very bemused.

That evening, as promised, Amos turned up at Phil's. Phil had prepared dinner, eating heartily, and after washing up together, both sat drinking whiskey in Phil's lounge. By 10:30pm, the boys were in bed ready to make love. This was a first for Amos and Phil took the lead. By the next morning, Phil and Amos had made love four times, taking it in turn to wake each other through foreplay.

Neither of the boys had planned for this to happen but both had hoped that something would happen. Nor had they formally said that they were in a relationship, it just happened. The longer they were together, the deeper and stronger their love grew for each other. Amos virtually moved into Phil's from that day on, staying overnight when it was possible and staying for longer periods over weekends and during Amos's leave. Both young men were tall, Amos standing at 6' 2" tall and Phil 6' exactly. Both men were handsome and together they looked a striking pair.

Phil and Amos had been a couple for several months before meeting up with Bill and Tom, but after their first meeting, it was as if it was meant to be. Both couples just hit if off from the beginning. For Amos, Bill and Tom became almost like family. After Bill had been sent to Egypt, Amos and Phil remained in contact with both Bill and Tom by letter.

Tom was able to visit Phil and Amos several times while Bill was away, particularly during the time Tom was in training. Amos recalled informing Bill and Tom of his deployment to the Far East and begged both boys to keep in contact and to keep an eye out for Phil. Amos had continued to write regularly, ensuring that their relationships would endure.

Being in Singapore during those early stages of Amos's deployment was relaxing and fun. Amos was soon able to fall into the general lethargy of the colonial forces stationed there, enjoying the relative tranquillity the barracks offered and the contrasting life of Singapore. Amos felt at home in Singapore, the weather particularly suited Amos and he soon made friends with some of the locals, especially those who frequented the same bars as him. Amos loved Changi beach and the nightlife provided in and around the city.

The food was particularly good too and Amos did not hesitate to try out the mix of Malay, Chinese, Indian and European cuisine. When walking, Amos also took time to soak in ambience of this wonderful country. There was an abundance of exotic trees, shrubs, and flowers, which Amos loved. Amos had, from being a young boy, been a lover of gardening. Here, in Singapore, his passion for flora and fauna grew.

Amos often wishing that he could be able to grow such things in his garden in blighty. Amos also relished the rains that fell. Often, when it rained, the water would come down so strong that it was difficult to see a yard in front of where he was going, but the rains were refreshing and warm, unlike the cold rain of England, which tended to chill the body to the core, even in summer.

After being in Singapore for a year, Amos's bliss was interrupted. Information came to everyone's ears that there might be an attack by the Japanese. The Japanese had begun an expansion of their territory, aiming to take Malaysia. However, in the eventuality of the Japanese attacking, the British forces were considered to become victorious as the British had superior numbers and were also seen as a greater fighting force.

Singapore had also been designed as a formidable fortress and thought to be impregnable. This arrogance by the British was to contribute to the eventual downfall of the British forces in the Far East. When the Japanese did eventually attack, it was symptomatic of their military prowess. The Japanese soldiers were ruthless, brutal, fearless, savage and fast moving.

The attack on Singapore happened at speed and with such ferocity that it took the British forces completely by surprise. As the Japanese moved forward, they executed many rather than taking prisoners. Like a hurricane, the Japanese swept through Singapore leaving shock and destruction in their wake.

At the beginning of December, on the same day that Japan attacked Pearl Harbour, the Japanese simultaneously bombed the Royal Air Force bases to the north of Singapore along the Malayan coast. The Japanese eliminated the Royal Air Force's ability to retaliate or to protect occupying troops. The Japanese tactics had been well thought out. Even before any Japanese soldier set foot on Singaporean soil, Britain's naval and aerial capabilities had been destroyed.

The Royal Navy's response in sending her battleship the 'Prince of Wales' and the battle cruiser 'Repulse', ended with both ships being torpedoed, sinking into the tropical waters off the South China Sea. Singapore was left defenceless. Singapore's only hope was left to the British Army and Commonwealth forces in a bid to hold their ground. Lieutenant General Arthur Percival was in command of the British forces at the time having 90,000 men at his disposal.

Percival commanded British, Canadian, Indian, and Australian forces which made up the army's fighting force. Fighting started in the north of Malaya with the Battle of Jitra, which began on the 11th of December and ending on the 12th. Percival's forces were humiliated. The Japanese quickly moved south, moving through the jungle from Kota Bahru travelling six hundred miles towards Singapore. Following this battle, British forces were forced to retreat to Singapore, falling back over the causeway at Johor Bahru; the causeway at Johor Barhu, separating Singapore from mainland Malaya.

The Japanese were unstoppable. Percival ordered his men to spread over 70 miles in order to face the enemy. The spreading of the British forces so thinly resulted in them being unable to repulse the Japanese forces. Quickly Percival's troops were completely overwhelmed. It took just seven days for Singapore to fall to the Japanese. Percival surrendered to prevent further loss of life. Before the surrender, Amos was ordered to defend the causeway at Johor Barhu.

Amos, along with the other men in his division fought bravely, but the number of Japanese quickly overwhelmed them. The division lost a considerable number of men and many more were wounded. They fell back towards the naval dockyard, still fighting then were pushed through Singapore to Changi. Carnage was the only way to describe what the Japanese left in their wake. It was estimated that over 100,000 people in Singapore were taken prisoner. 9,000 of which were to go on to die building the Burma-Thailand railway.

During the fighting and immediately afterward the Japanese murdered many civilians, decapitated allied soldiers, some prisoners were burnt alive and hospital patients slaughtered where they lay. Those prisoners that survived the initial carnage were subjected to three years of pain and torment: many would never make it back to their homes.

Amos had remained in Singapore to the very end, becoming part of the last fighting group. Percival had surrendered and Amos along with others was taken prisoner. The Japanese killed many of Amos's comrades as he watched. He expected that he would also fall to a similar fate, preparing for the worst. Fear gripped Amos every time the Japanese gathered those that were left. He had never been one to fear much, but the unknowing of whether he would live or die played on his mind. Luckily, the worst that Amos received was sever beatings.

He bore these beatings without shouting out or showing signs of retaliation. Frequently, as others had been beaten, they had attempted to fight back, not in retaliation, but as an automatic response. They were the ones who were immediately shot. Those who screamed at the beatings given by the Japanese, were seen as being weak, their punishment tended to be further beatings or were made to work harder. The breaking of the British soldier's spirit seemed to be the Japanese's favourite pastime. Although his body was battered and bruised, all Amos could think about was Phil and just how much he loved and missed that man.

Amos had swellings around his head and eyes and thought he might have several broken ribs. Amos continued to have and withstood many more beatings but remained defiant. He managing to stand and march even after each thrashing, joining the other men of his battalion but the pain from the relentless onslaught of thuggery began to take its toll.

After some time in Changi, which had now been turned into a prison of war camp by the Japanese, Amos was ordered to muster along with fellow inmates. All had thought that this muster was part of the now daily routine, however, on this particular day, all of the men mustered were led away, being marched out of the camp.

The men were surrounded by guards heading in the direction of the naval dockyard. Unbeknown to him and the rest of the men, they were destined to work on the Burma-Thailand railway. The men left camp in the clothing they stood up in, some without shoes, others just wearing shorts. None carried food or water or medical supplies. After spending weeks in Changi Prisoner of War Camp, Amos, along with several hundred soldiers, airmen and sailors were heading to be put on what the Allies called, "Hell ships" and transported to Burma. Amos left Singapore on 14th May 1942 to be eventually disembarked at Victoria Point, in Burma.

One in five of the prisoners onboard his 'Hell ship' did not survive the cramped, disease-ridden journey. The bodies of those who died were left to rot amongst the living, then disposed of by throwing them overboard whist at sea. Amos began to suffer dreadfully during this journey. His wounds became infected, and he contracted other bacterial infections that zapped him of his strength.

Amos's mental health also began to suffer because of what he had witnessed, yet the thought of Phil gave him strength. What with the severe beatings, lack of food and water and his constant sea sickness, Amos began to lose weight rapidly. On their arrival in Burma, Amos along with other prisoners of war was disembarked and force marched into Burma's interior. The march was gruelling. The pace was set by the Japanese who had no time for straddles. Prisoners were beaten regularly to make them keep up or shot on the roadside if they were unable to continue.

Each time one of the men was shot, Amos would initially jump in fear, fighting back tears and any reaction. However, after a while, his reactions stopped when hearing gun shots but his internal fear remained. This played on his mind constantly, affecting him in such a way that he began to withdraw into himself, becoming quieter and refusing to talk to his fellow prisoners.

The prisoners were given little water or food on their journey and in the humid heat many more men fell ill. After five days of marching and exhausted, they eventually reached the P.O.W. camp. Only a third of those prisoners who were transported with Amos survived to reach their destination.

Facilities at the camp were inhumane. Sleeping areas were literally just open coverings with palm fronds as roofs over solid dirt flooring. Beds were made of bamboo and any bedding available was sparse, dirty and not fit for purpose. Toilets were simply holes dug in the ground which had to be dug by the prisoners themselves and the washing facilities were communal outdoor showers. Prisoners were only allowed to shower once a week at most, sometime not at all.

Food was rationed to a small bowl of rice; on occasion, as a treat, a bowl of soup might be given and very rarely, some meat, often rancid, was found within the soup. Many more men died as a result of malnutrition, starvation and disease; if it hadn't been for some of the locals sneaking food into the camps, and the men making traps to catch rats, snakes and insects to eat, many would have died earlier. Living in these appalling conditions was bad, but to Amos, it was much better than having to be force marched.

Phil had heard the news about the fall of Singapore but had no idea if Amos was still alive, was well or had been captured. The last letter Phil received from Amos was just after the fall of Singapore. Amos's letter had been sent just days before his capture. In this last letter, Amos had told Phil how he had met several guys who were, like him and Phil, attracted to men. Amos said that of those he knew, few spoke openly about their sexual orientation but that all were great blokes.

Amos spoke proudly of these men and of their heroic actions and of the way they were trying to keep the Japanese at bay. Amos expressed his love for Phil and how much he was missing him. Phil read Amos's letters over and over, praying for his safe return. Little did Phil know that no more letters would be sent, and all letters written to Amos would never reach their destination.

Amos was made to work on the Burma-Thai railway where he formed strong bonds with his fellow prisoners. However, Amos soon learned that to form any strong friendship was futile, as many of his loyal friends would die through over work or were killed by the Japanese either through starvation or because they just were not productive enough.

Amos had built a strong relationship with a guy from Shropshire named Sam Baker. Sam confessed to Amos of his sexuality and Amos had happily told Sam about Phil and his relationship with him. Often, they would laugh at some of the exploits both had done in the past and Amos loved to hear Sam's stories. Sam was a brilliant storyteller. Sadly, Sam was killed by the Japanese after a high-ranking officer had noticed that one of the guards had taken a liking to Sam and Sam was seen to be giving the guard 'The eye'.

Such friendships or relationship was abhorrent to the Japanese and the officer had the guard shoot Sam through the head in front of the whole camp. The Japanese guard was also never seen again and what happened to him remains a mystery. Amos was beside himself with grief. He shook as the execution took place and Amos withdrew into himself again.

Six months later, Amos contracted malaria and dysentery. As medicine was not provided, Amos suffered dreadfully. Initially, his illness began with headaches, stomach cramps and diarrhoea. No matter what Amos did, he could not shake the symptoms. Eventually Amos became delirious and in his confused state, would often cry out at night, shouting for Phil.

As none of his fellow prisoners knew who Phil was, they presumed that Phil must be Amos's brother or some other relative. Amos's fever intensified; his body raked with disease. He lost so much weight that he would have been unrecognisable to family and friends in England. Now less than six stone in weight, face drawn and ribs protruding from his chest, Amos fell into a coma and died, as so many others had done before him.

Amos's body was laid to rest in the camp cemetery with a simple wooden cross marking his grave. Even before the war ended, Amos's cross along with all other P.O.W.'s epitaphs who had been buried there, were removed. All marks of respect were hidden by the Japanese to eliminate evidence of the whereabouts of their captured troops, in an attempt to hide the atrocities, they had carried out.

At his burial, the men who dug the grave laid Amos gently into his resting place. Neither of the men knew Amos personally, but both shed tears for his loss. On completion of the burial, both men stood to attention, saluted, before moving on to the next corpse awaiting disposal.

# Chapter Eleven
# London

After completing his training, Tom was re deployed and stationed in the Capital. Tom's commanding officer during training had moved to London and had decided to take Tom along with him as his batman. Tom's commanding officer had taken a real liking to Tom and had chosen him specifically because Tom had been outstanding in all that he did during training, but Tom thought maybe he had been chosen because his commanding officer had a secret crush on him. Tom was not particularly happy in becoming a batman as he desperately wanted to be sent to Egypt, hoping to be closer to Bill. The only advantage of being in London was that he was able to meet up with Phil, who provided a spare bed for Tom whenever he was off duty and to be able to at least socialise and talk about the things they had in common.

The Blitz, which had destroyed many parts of London's infrastructure, had left its mark on the population. The Blitz, which was a shorten form of the German word 'Blitzkrieg' (lightning war), had begun on the 7th of September 1940 and ended in May the following year. This had come about in part, because of the German air force changing its strategy of bombing the British air force (Battle of Britain) and realising that this strategy was just not working.

It had been reported that around 2,000 people had been either killed or wounded in London's first night of the Blitz and by the end, 32,000 civilians had been killed and 87,000 seriously injured, along with military personnel. Birmingham and Coventry had also been hit heavily, causing Tom to worry about his and Bill's parents.

Lucky enough, no shells had hit where Tom and Bill lived but several areas close by had received direct hits, including factories in Tom and Bill's hometown. Tom knew that a number of people had died as a result and several more injured. It was to Tom's relief that things were not worse. Still, Tom's parents' spirits were up, knowing that the Blitz had ended, and that Tom was safe in London.

Phil had also been one of the lucky ones, in that his house had been left intact and he had come through the carnage unscathed. When Phil heard that Tom was being posted to London, he took no time to invite Tom to stay and wrote of his excitement at seeing Tom. Phil also wrote to Bill and Amos. In each of his letters he wrote, Phil gives details of the carnage in London and about how many times Tom had stayed at his place. Phil was meticulous in telling the boys of every conversation he had had with Tom and what they had been doing together.

The people of London played an enormous role in protecting the city. Many civilians, like Phil, who were unwilling or unable to join the military, joined the Auxiliary Fire Service. Phil, although not required to join any of the ancillary services, decided that he must also play his part and became a Fire Warden. Phil would often have to go out at night leaving Tom to his own devises until he returned. Tom, when off duty and when he stayed at Phil's place, took on the household chores and became a proper little homemaker.

Phil would laugh at just how efficient Tom was. Even Bill had to laugh when he received letters from Tom and Phil which described Tom's pernickety ways and his diligence. Phil had even purchased a pinafore for Tom to wear about the house. Tom saw the funny side and took to wearing his latest item of clothing with pride.

People who were unemployed were drafted into the Royal Army Pay Corps and alongside the Pioneer Corp, were given the task of salvaging and cleaning-up London. Alongside his other duties, Phil also had a remit to link with the local authorities to monitor progress of the clean-up and to report back should the military need to be used to remove bombs or to help demolish dangerous buildings and to remove dead civilians. Pre-war, there had been dire predictions of mass air-raid neurosis and that many civilians would require psychiatric support.

As it happened, these predictions were not borne out. The government had grossly underestimated civilian adaptability and resourcefulness. Because of the many new civil defence roles, the people of London seemed to have gained a sense of fighting back rather than of despair.

Up until the fall of Singapore, Phil had become more motivated and determined to do his part in protecting the city, but on hearing that Amos was in danger, had been wounded or even killed, Phil's mood began to change. Letters from Amos had stopped, and Phil could not find out any real details about where Amos might be. Even the Red Cross could not provide answers. Of course, with Phil not being a relative to Amos, no letter had come from the Ministry of War informing Phil of Amos's predicament.

Having no letter as to whether Amos had killed in action, wounded or had been taken prisoner added to Phil's stress. The only good news at that time was that Bill would be coming home from Egypt and would be able to spend time with Tom and Phil; as well as being able to be available to visit his family back home. When Bill eventually arrived in London, he was greeted at the station by Tom and Phil.

Tom had tried to get leave to meet Bill in Portsmouth, but due to pressures at work, Tom was not able to do so. Both lads took it in turn to hug Bill on the station platform; Tom clinging on to Bill as if his life depended upon it. Although happy to see Bill, Phil's heart sank, thinking that he was alone, without Amos and not being able to express his feelings to the one person he loved most.

For the next few days, Bill stayed with Tom and Phil at Phil's place. Bill looked leaner than when Tom and Phil had seen him last and it was apparent that Bill had been witness to many atrocities, which Bill found difficulty to talk about. Bill also saw the change in Phil. Empathy was all that Bill could offer, recognising that neither he, nor anyone else could take away Phil's worry and concern.

Bill and Tom could only imagine what Phil was thinking or feeling. Bill, Tom and Phil spent as much time together as they could. It had been a blessing that the pubs had not closed and a further blessing that beer was not on ration. Even through all the carnage that had occurred so far, the boys were still able to have fun together. Even the pubs tried their hardest to ensure that for just a brief time, normality could be achieved.

"It's funny," Bill said to Tom one night in bed, "this separation has made me love you more. If it hadn't been for you, I don't know how things would have panned out. Having you on my mind all the time really helped me to keep focused. I never realised just how much our relationship would affect me and never thought that I could love anyone as much as I love you."

"If anything should happen to you, I don't know what I would do. I can see how Phil is being affected by not knowing what has happened to Amos and I think that I might be the same if you were missing."

Tom hugged Bill for a long time, then broke the silence by saying, "We have to make sure that we are both safe and must do everything in our power to be together once this fucking war is over." The boys kissed and made love. Their love making although vigorous, was more tender than they had ever been together. They touched each other more, savouring each second, each sensation and revelled in the joy of just being together.

Following Bill's brief stay with Phil and Tom, Bill had to travel to the Midlands to see his and Toms family. The boys had agreed that it was only fair that Bill should share his time with all those he loved most dearly. After his leave, and having one more night in London, Bill was posted back to Aldershot. Tom was also expected to do more work, which meant less time was spent with Phil or Bill. Phil had been trying hard to get information about Amos from Amos's parents, but to no avail.

Amos's parents had no real understanding of Phil and Amos's relationship, but they had suspicion that something was not as it should be. Why would a high-class guy like Phil take an interest in their son, when his background was so different to Phil's? As a result, Amos' family decided to ignore Phil's letters and enquiries apart from writing once to Phil asking not to contact them again. Phil attempted to get information through contacts at work and through the British Red Cross, but nothing could be found.

Phil's depression began to get worse, resulting in him becoming more of a recluse when Tom was not about, never venturing out when not working and having less and less contact with his parents too. On the occasions that Tom was able to visit Phil, Tom noticed that Phil was taking less time to keep his house neat and tidy, something that Tom thought strange, as Phil had always been fastidious in maintaining cleanliness.

Even Phil's personal hygiene was becoming less important to Phil. Tom found that when he visited Phil, he would have to suggest to Phil that he needed to shave, take a bath, take a haircut and even to change his clothes. Tom spent more time cleaning and looking after Phil more than enjoying each other's company. Afterall, with Phil the way he was, Tom became chief cook and bottle washer.

One evening, when Tom visited, Tom knew that he had to broach the subject of how Phil was feeling and about him not getting news about Amos. Tom was not the type of person to be empathic in his communication although he did feel deeply for Phil and his situation.

"Phil" Tom started, "I know that you have been struggling lately and it's obvious that you are not coping very well. I think that you need to talk about how you are feeling. I'm really concerned that you are not looking after yourself and that is just not you. Each time I visit, you seem to have gone down further each time. You look depressed and you have changed so much. I don't like what's happening to you, I am really worried, and I seem to be spending all my time just cleaning up."

"I'm fine," Phil said in an angry tone, "stop fussing, you sound like my fucking mother." Tom was shocked by Phil's response, as Phil had never spoken so abruptly in the past.

"I'm not fussing," Tom said quickly, "I'm worried about you, and I have noticed how unkempt you have become, and it has become a real effort to get you to do anything," Tom went on.

"What the fuck do you mean?" Phil shouted. "You don't have to come here if you don't like what you see; no one has asked you to give an opinion," Tom was gobsmacked by Phil's outburst. Tom looked at Phil angered because of the response he was given.

"I'm only expressing concern," Tom muttered. "I do care about you, and I hate to see you going downhill." Phil looked at Tom as if Tom had suddenly grown in stature. To Phil, Tom looked as if he had grown to double his size. Phil's eyes suddenly became terrified. Phil physically shrank into himself, lowered his head as if cowering away from Tom, then suddenly began shaking uncontrollably, bursting into tears, sobbing so deeply that his breathing was affected.

Tom suddenly felt Phil's pain and anguish. Tom reached out to Phil who stepped back in fear. "It's ok mate," Tom said gently. "It's ok; I'm only trying to help." Phil looked back at Tom, but he appeared to be in a trance like state, not knowing if Tom was truly there to help or to cause him pain. Tom could not fathom out what was going through Phil's mind. They were friends. The last thing Tom would do was to hurt Phil.

Phil turned and went upstairs to his bedroom. Tom messed around the house for a while hoping that Phil would eventually come downstairs. A couple of hours passed, but still no response from Phil. Tom then decided that it would be better for him to return to barracks and try again the next time he visited. Before leaving, Tom went upstairs and knocked of Phil's bedroom door. There was no answer. Tom stood for a while listening, hoping that he would hear Phil mumble something but there was no sound.

"I'm going now," Tom called quietly through Phil's bedroom door, still no reply. "Phil are you ok?" silence: not even the sound of sobbing. "Phil…Can you hear me, Phil? I'm going now. I'll call in tomorrow. Just to check if you're ok." Still not a peep from Phil. Tom grabbed his bag from his bedroom, stopped again by Phil's room to listen as he went past, then crept down the stairs making his way outside to begin his walk back to the barracks.

The following day, Tom called at Phil's, but it was much later than he had expected. Tom had been called to report to the administration office, where he had been given new orders. Tom was to be posted; he would be going to Italy. As soon as he was given his orders, he immediately wrote to Bill and his parents. Tom had two more weeks in London before being shipped out.

In his letter to his parents, Tom only informed them that he was well and that he had been given a posting to Italy. In his letter to Bill, he raised his concerns about Phil and of his posting. Tom begged Bill to try to come to London before his posting; Tom was desperate to see Bill and need to be with him.

When Tom eventually arrived at Phil's, Phil was still in his smoking jacket. It was obvious to Tom than Phil had not engaged in anything that day. Phil had not gone to work, had not washed, or dressed and had not even made himself a drink. Phil looked dreadful. Tom tried to chivvy Phil up, but Phil was not responding. Tom made him tea, which he left to go cold before attempting to drink it. Tom made sandwiches, which Phil did not touch and when Tom tried to engage with Phil, there was nothing but blankness.

Tom told Phil about his posting, but Phil did not respond. Tom stayed the night retiring to his bedroom. Phil slept on the settee. When Tom got up the next day to go back to barracks, Phil was still sitting there, had not moved and seemed to be staring at the same spot he had been staring at the night before. Tom sat in the armchair opposite. Tom did not say anything; he did not want a repeat performance of the previous time he had visited and thought it best not to make matters worse.

Tom tried to show how much he cared through his eye and body language, but Phil was not taking any notice of Tom. At last, and just before Tom was about to get up to leave, Phil said, "He's dead."

"What do you mean he's dead?" Tom blurted out in shock and annoyance.

"Amos; Amos is dead. I know it. I can feel it in my heart," Phil said in a cold slow voice.

"Don't be silly," Tom replied. "You don't know what has happened. There's been no news. Or have you had a letter from someone?" Tom asked seeking confirmation.

"My heart is telling me that he's gone. I have had no news from anyone about Amos and can't get any information. That's the problem. No one will tell me anything. Who gives a fucking toss about the queers? Their love isn't important. Their love isn't real. They are an abomination, misfits and queers," Phil went on. "Who gives a toss about us and how we feel? Amos's family haven't even got the decency to respond to my letters. I bet they know what has happened to Amos, but their own fucking pride will stop them from letting me know anything about him. It's wrong, just so fucking wrong."

Tom was dumbfounded, shocked, and stunned by what Phil had said. Tom had listened wide mouthed realising what Phil had said was, in the most part true, especially about people's general attitude to homosexuals, and their relationships. Tom realised that in reality, no one would be bothered to insist on telling a man that his male lover had died or seriously injured first. Maybe they would mention it in passing, but not in the same way if the news were to be given to a girlfriend or wife.

Family, friends, and authority would just ignore the fact that two men could feel as heterosexuals felt. They would much rather ignore everything and keep it quiet than have to face the reality that two men or women for that matter, could ever be in a loving relationship. Tom realised that what Phil was saying would be the same for him should anything happen to Bill or vis-versa. Of course, Tom and Bill's parents would acknowledge that either one had gone, but they would never acknowledge their relationship or the love they had for each other.

After all, how could they understand the love Tom and Bill had for each other, or the love that Phil and Amos have, to all, they were all just abominations. The reality of what they all were came as if one of Hitler's bombs had just landed on Phil's house. It came from nowhere and shattered all the beauty around. Tom stood up; tears fell from his eyes.

Tom lent over, kissed Phil's forehead while at the same time Tom touched Phil's head lovingly. Tom needed to see Bill; the urgency now even greater than ever before. Tom left Phil, both still crying. Tom could no longer face what Phil was going through and Tom needed space to process this new reality.

When Tom returned to barracks, a letter had been delivered from Bill. Bill had managed to get leave the following weekend. Tom was also able to take leave and Tom made no hesitation in asking Phil if they could stay with him. When Bill arrived, he saw for himself the state that Phil was in and recognised what it must be like for him. Bill had seen similar loss when in Africa.

He had witnessed when someone had been killed or seriously maimed and what it had done to friends, especially if that guy had a secret lover who was also serving in the same place. Although Bill was more pragmatic than Phil, recognising that plans should always be put in place, he urged Phil to wait until he had confirmation on Amos's situation and to be a little more positive.

Phil tended to be more emotional than pragmatic and could not see the world through Bill's eyes. Sadly, Bill also had an uneasy feeling about Amos, suspecting that the worst had truly happened. Bill had heard first hand of some of the atrocities being carried out by the Japanese even if what was being said was hearsay. Bill knew that there must be some truth in those rumours. *Those poor buggers*, Bill thought to himself, *Poor Amos. Please God: please let him still be alive,* he thought.

Conversations that weekend were subdued, muted and sparse. However, the intensity of Bill and Tom's love making was greater than at any other time. In bed, Tom and Bill continually told each other just how much they loved each other and they both promised to make sure that should anything untoward happened to them, they would insist that each would be told.

They both hatched a plan to carry a letter with them at all times, sealed within an envelope and with each other's names and addresses written boldly in capital letters, with instruction that the letter should be posted immediately. Bill also tried to reassure Tom about what he might find in Italy and what he must do to try to keep safe.

"You must always stay alert, keep your head down and whatever is happening around you. Keep focused and don't take risks. You will have time after the event to become weak and emotional" Bill instructed Tom. "I want you back safe and sound and I want you with me for the rest of my life," Bill said tenderly.

"I want you too," Tom said. "We must stick together. No one else will ever understand what it is like."

The weekend ended far too quickly. Tom and Bill asked the guys in the pub to keep an eye on Phil and asked them to write to keep them informed on Phil's progress. Both had a feeling that Phil would not be writing as often has he had in the past. Bill reassured Phil that he would be back as soon as it was possible, concerned that Phil was not responding to anything he or Tom had suggested. Bill left Phil having a real uncanny feeling in his stomach but was more concerned about Tom and what lay ahead for him.

Tom was equally concerned about Phil but had started to keep in mind Bill's words, to focused on his own deployment ahead and to remain safe. Tom saw Bill off at the train station and for the first time, both had kissed each other in public. Tom returned to his barracks in preparedness for his deployment and for the horrors which were to come. Their parting at the railway station was the hardest parting they had ever experienced. The future for all four men was now in the hands of the gods.

# Chapter Twelve
# Tragedy at Home

With both boys now currently stationed in England, both Mary and Joe and George and Joan were content in the knowledge that at least for the time being, both of their children were safe. Since Bill's call up and following Tom's call up, both sets of parents had become closer. They shared what many other parents were sharing, in that their children were facing atrocities which no one should ever have to face. Bill and Tom's parents were lucky in some respects in that their proximity to each other aided their support and the fact that both families were similar, were able to form a bond like no other families. The fact that George and Joe had similar backgrounds having both served during WWI and now both still suffering from the consequences of being in battle helped.

Almost immediately after Bill had been called up, Mary began to call in to see Joe and Joan more frequently. Mary had encouraged Tom to visit more too, and once per week until his call up. George and Mary were invited over to Joan and Joe's for dinner on a regular basis. This was then reciprocated and became a regular occurrence for both couples. From them on, firm friendships became even stronger, and after Tom was called up, the bond between the families became solidly fixed.

Mary and Joan were the first to make this companionship work. They shared food items, helped each other carryout everyday tasks such as washing, cleaning and doing their shopping together. Both women encouraged their husbands to work together in their vegetable patches, look after the pigs and chickens and help each other when repairs were needed to be carried out.

Joe also started to go to the pub with George for their early doors drink and often travelled together when going to work. George worked in the same factory as Bill had done but worked in the finishing shop, hence George never travelled to or from work with Bill due to them working different hours. Joe worked for the local water company overseeing purification and distribution which was located at the opposite side of town to where George worked, but they caught the same bus.

After the boys had left home, the women decided to contribute to the war effort as best they could, initially joining the Women's Institute (WI) and then after gaining employment. Joan getting a job as a machinist, working the lathes at a munitions factory making cases for bombs and small casings for bullets. Mary on the other hand worked in the powder shop of the same company. Gun powder was shipped from a local storage area to the factory where women on Mary's line would fill the casings made in Joan's section.

This suited both women, as they were with each other more and were able to even take breaks together whilst at work. As one can imagine, when the women were together, the core of their conversations were about their sons. Whereas when George and Joe were together, they tended to circumnavigate talking about Bill and Tom focusing more on the general aspects of the war, their responsibilities as husbands and of their own experiences of war.

In many ways, Gorge and Joe were a therapy for each other, opening up to talk about the atrocities they had both witnessed during WWI. Like most men who were not required to become involved in active service, George and Joe enlisted as Fire Wardens and became part of the Home Guard. Fire wardens were usually stationed inside buildings to watch for fires caused by incendiary bombs and to extinguish the fires before they could create too much damage.

Wednesday and Friday evenings were especially good times for both the men and women. The men worked their gardens together and looked after their livestock before going on duty as wardens while the women went into town to meet at the Women's Institute. One evening there was an air raid warning. The siren sent out a distinctive wailing noise. Bombs had been dropped in the town and on the very munitions factory where Joan and Mary worked.

The noise of the explosion reverberated for miles as the munition factory erupted. The factory still housed workers as shifts covered the twilight and night hours as well as the day shift. Lucky enough, Mary and Joan were at home when the mayhem started. People still working within the factory had little chance of escape and those living within the vicinity of the factory had little time to take cover, as there was neither apparent activity in the sky nor any distant thumping of exploding bombs.

There was commotion in the streets as the bombs were dropped. People ran for cover, many heading towards the bomb shelters. Others ran towards Anderton shelters erected in gardens. There were Shouts of 'Fire' and the piercing sound of whistles being blown. George and Joe both ran into their respective homes, quickly grabbing their coats and opening their front doors. "What's happening out there?" Mary shouted.

"It looks as if one of the factories in town has been hit," George cried. "I would imagine that there will be a right panic going on. I'd better go and see if I can give them a hand." At that, Joe turned up at George's house.

"I'm going downtown to see if I can help," George exclaimed.

"Me too," Joe replied. The women stood together in the doorway of Mary house as they watched their husbands run to where the explosions appeared to have happened. After, twenty minutes or so, George and Joe arrived in town. They saw immediately that it was the ammunitions factory that was ablaze. Both men felt a sickening feeling build within their stomachs as they realised that had the bombs been dropped just a few hours earlier, their wives would have still been working and would have stood no chance of surviving.

When they finally arrived at the munitions factory, the whole site was ablaze, and the fire was quickly spreading to other building close by. The fire department were working flat out to quell the main blaze at the factory while others were attempting to put out smaller fires. Joe and George were called on to try to tackle a fire that had started about fifty yards from the main scene, and to try to prevent further spread. Other incendiaries were lying in the road and gutter, burning brightly like white flares. More were burning in front gardens spaced along the street.

George and Joe wore their heavy overcoats over thick scarfs. Their coats reaching well below the top of their wellington boots and their faces hidden behind balaclava helmets pulled down over their ears. Their metal hats protecting them from falling debris. George and Joe's training as fire wardens had instilled in them that when fighting incendiary fires, that they were to use sand to extinguish these fires as water reacted to the chemicals causing them to burn much more fiercely.

"Where's your bucket of sand?" a voice shouted to Joe and George.

"Sand? Ain't got no sand, the only thing we have are a bucket and access to water," George responded.

"You're not supposed to use water," the voice said, "It'll blow up! Leave the incendiary fires, they will burn out themselves. Just concentrate on the buildings," the voice shouted. George managed to get his hands on a stirrup pump located next to one of the fire engines while Joe managed to access one of the main water pipes running along the road.

While fighting the fire, George began jumping around as though his boots were on fire, poking his stirrup pump at the burning building. Within 20 minutes, Joe noticed that the incendiary bombs along the road had begun to burn out, some of them now just empty shells, their red heat fading in the darkness.

"Hurry up!" George shouted to Joe, "It's almost out!" referring to the fire in the building they were working on. "Well done, Joe! We've almost managed to handle this fire ourselves." Joe lifted his balaclava and gave a big grin.

"Weren't nothing, we were just doing our job." he said modestly.

The fire in the munitions factory was still blazing and the heat intensifying. George nudged Joe encouraging him to look towards the factory. In the darkness and within the glow of the fire, he had noticed a number of bodies which had been pulled from the burning building and laid out on the pavement across the street. Ambulance workers were busily assessing each body and reverently covering them each with a blanket.

"Those poor sods," George said to Joe with tears in his eyes. "Any of those poor sods could have been either Joan or Mary." The reality hit both men hard, but this only spurred them on to do more. Suddenly, a huge explosion erupted from the munitions factory as the gunpowder store caught fire inside the building. Bricks, metal, wood, glass, and mortar flew in all directions but mainly upwards. The noise was deafening as the power of blast blew people off their feet.

Some working closet to the building were blown back several feet. Luckily enough, no one was killed from the explosion, but several of the fire fighters and ambulance crew sustained injuries, mainly from flying glass and shrapnel. As luck would have it, this second major blast functioned as a fire extinguisher, as the building collapsed the main fire ball was reduced. After some commotion, the fire brigade along with those people supporting them, including Joe and George, managed to start to take control of the fire.

Everyone appeared to regroup quickly and became organised once again. The men on scene worked tirelessly to control the mayhem and to prevent a further spread of the fire. George and Joe were exhausted but their will to succeed never wavered.

It was not until dawn the next morning that Joe and George were told that they could return home. More people had arrived to take over from those men who had worked during the night. The Chief fire officer thanked George and Joe for their assistance telling them, "You have done enough guys. You are exhausted. Go home now and take a rest. You could not have done more; your contribution has been noted and very welcomed. You have done an excellent job. Thank you."

Both men nodded in recognition and began walking home in silence, hoping to catch their wives before they set out for work and to inform them that it would not be of any use even attempting to return to their place of work because of the events of the previous night. As it happened, both Joan and Mary had already been informed that it was the munitions factory that had been hit and all night they had sat wondering what the outcome had been regarding their husbands.

On returning home, George, Joe, Mary, and Joan sat in the Taylor's house taking stock, had breakfast together, talking over the events that had taken place overnight. Mary and Joan were physically upset knowing that some of their work mates had been killed and that it could easily have been them. What happens now, no one could say but all four knew that they would do everything in their power to help rebuild and push forward.

It took several days for the munitions site to be made safe and for the final body toll to be accounted for. Some of the workers were never found, as when the bombs hit, their bodies were totally obliterated. The town recognised the efforts made by the emergency services and those civilians who had placed themselves in danger to help during this major emergency. The mayor called for all those involved to attend the memorial service which happened a few weeks later and thanked them personally for their efforts.

Tom and Bill became aware of the incident initially through the reporting of the event by the B.B.C. Both hearing the news on their radios. Thankfully, George and Joe had recognised that their sons would be extremely worried about their parents and as soon as it was possible, both George and Joe sent telegrams to Bill and Joe telling them that they were all safe and well. The relief for both boys was all consuming, as they would have both found it difficult to return home at that time.

# Chapter Thirteen
# The Italian Campaign

In January 1943, the allied leaders, whilst in Casablanca, Morocco, decided to use their massive military resources based in the Mediterranean to launch an invasion of Italy. The objective was to totally remove Italy from the war and to secure the Mediterranean Sea. Then with luck, Germany would divert some of their fighting divisions from the Russian front and others from northern France. The plan then was for the allies to be able to cross the English Channel and to land in Normandy to liberate France.

So it was that Tom had his first real deployment and was shipped out to initially to Malta, arriving in May 1943. Tinged with excitement and trepidation Tom looked forward to being able to contribute to the war effort but was mindful of the dangers that lay ahead. Going to sea for the first time was not a joyful experience for Tom, especially as their ship crossed the Bay of Biscay. Although late spring, the crossing was rough. Tom found that he did not have sea legs, vomiting continually as the ship progressed.

Tom had never felt so bad. Tom's seasickness worsened when others from his battalion were also throwing up. Relief for Tom did not come until the ship entered Mediterranean waters and even then, Tom continually felt queasy. Tom had not eaten properly for days, feeling weak due to the lack of food and because of his continual wrenching. "Thank God I didn't join the Navy," Tom mused.

Unbeknown to Tom, that on his arrival at Malta, he, along with his compatriots would, on 10th June 1943, be involved in operation Husky and the commencement of the invasion of Sicily. However, the days before the planned invasion, Tom would at least be able to enjoy what Malta had to offer. Having evaded enemy ships through the Mediterranean, he, along with the other men, disembarked in Malta. When docked, Tom almost immediately began to recuperate, gathering strength and being able to eat normally once more.

Tom was able to take time to explore Malta's grand central harbour and St Angelo. Tom loved the Maltese people and the fun offered in some of the still standing and open bars. Tom's favourite place was a street known as 'The Gut'. Here, small bars were crammed together, the place heaving with British, Commonwealth and American troops. Frankie's bar was a particular favourite for Tom as Frankie was a very outwardly acting homosexual.

Frankie, who owned the bar and, who was the main attraction, flaunted himself around, constantly joking and giggling and frequently sitting on the knees of those who took his fancy. Frankie took his pick of sexual partners for the night, all of whom confessed to being full-blooded heterosexuals but would still end up in bed with Frankie at some point during the night.

Frankie's preferred choice were American G.I.'s who looked stunning in their tight-fitting uniforms. G.I.'s tended to get drunk faster than their British counterparts and who were more adventurous in bed. Unlike the British, the Americans were happy to try anything, apparently not being satisfied with just the missionary position, nor did they have that **'wham, bam, thank you mam'** attitude to sex, unlike the British who tended to have fixed sexual orientations.

The Americans would try anything Frankie suggested; albeit that Frankie did not actually suggest anything, he just got on with what took his fancy at that time. Frankie preferred to take the female role if the other guy was big and muscular and aged over twenty-five. Younger men, it is said, lost their virginity to Frankie and ended up being quite subservient in bed to Frankie's whims.

On several occasions, Tom also got chatted up by Americans, Australians, Canadians, and the occasional Brit. Tom of course was flattered but did not show it and never took up on any of the offers made, although he did engage in mutual masturbation several times with guys in the barracks. Most of the men were more interested in the brothel that was situated opposite Frankie's Bar, where the girls would be working almost none stop, giving more than sexual favours to their customers.

Many of the men who visited the brothel ended up with a variety of venereal diseases, including Gonorrhoea; Chlamydia; Herpes; Syphilis and Pubic lice (Crabs) as well as many other quite nasty things. Thankfully, Tom, through caution and piousness, evaded trips to the clinic and the embarrassing examinations and treatments on offer. Whilst in Malta, Tom also came across a number of other men who were having longer term sexual relationship with other men; the commonality of which surprised Tom.

Tom often wondering how it was that homosexuality was more common than anyone would admit too and why, if it were so common, should it be kept secret and punishable by law? Tom was simply happy to know that he had Bill as his partner and that he had friends like Phil and Amos. Tom just hoped that Amos was still alive and at worst had ended up in a prisoner of war camp.

Two days before the invasion of Sicily, Tom, along with his company had been briefed on the plan of action and were to board a troop carrier the next day. They were be transported to their drop off point and would be landing via landing craft on the numerous beaches of the island.

Here they would have to make their way as quickly as possible up the beach to the headland. They were told to expect heavy firing, so were urged to keep running, keep their heads down and not stop until they reached the top of the headland. Once at the top of the beech it was secured. They were then made to muster and were given further instructions of where to go next.

The combined air and sea landings involved 150,000 troops, 3,000 ships and 4,000 aircraft, all directed at the southern shores of the island. The day before the assault a summer storm blew up causing serious difficulties for paratroopers and the operation was nearly cancelled. However, the storm also worked to the Allies' advantage.

The Axis defenders along the Sicilian coast had judged that no commander would attempt an amphibious landing in such inclement weather and were caught with their guard down. By the afternoon of invasion day 150,000 Allied troops reached the Sicilian shores, taking with them 600 tanks. The landing had been supported by a shattering naval and aerial bombardment. As a result, Allied troops encountered light resistance. Tom was lucky in that his group did not encounter any enemy fire and as a result, reached their goal in quick time.

When Tom first landed on the shores of Sicily, all he could remember, was the words Bill had said. "Keep going, keep your head down and concentrate of what you are doing, not on the things that are going on around you." Tom did exactly what Bill had said. He alighted from the landing craft head down but eyes focused forward and ran faster than he had ever run before. The run up the beach reminded Tom of the first days he had run to the pool with Bill.

The excitement to reach the pool enabled Tom to give that extra push. In Tom's mind's eye, he could visualise him and Bill running together. Tom's heart was pounding against his chest, his breathing heavy and strong, the air being inhaled seemed to cool his inner chest enabling him to take in more oxygen.

Others in his platoon struggled to catch Tom. Many cried as they ran. The fear of being attacked almost made them freeze to the spot, but they were driven on by their sergeants and officers.

Momentum was paramount, even when at times it was slow. Tom soon found himself at the beach head without firing a single shot and ahead of the main group. Tom sat for a while, wondering what to do next. He wanted to move forward but had been ordered to remain once the primary objective was accomplished. When everyone arrived at the designated point, an officer began separating groups and individuals.

Tom was ordered to join with Montgomery's veteran forces. This force was ordered to move up the east coast of the island. Other groups followed different routes. The Italians, once recognising that the allies had landed, retreated as fast as they could. Many Italians lay down their arms surrendering to this new aggressive force.

Within two weeks, news came that Mussolini's Italian fascist regime had fallen, and that Mussolini had been arrested. Furthermore, the troops had been informed that those in charge of the Italian forces were in talks with the Allies to secure an armistice. By August 17, 1943, the Allies were stunned to find that the enemy forces had all but disappeared. The battle for Sicily was complete, but the Allies had failed to capture the fleeing Axis armies which undermined their victory. The battle for the rest of Italy would now be much harder to fight and take much longer than had been expected.

Tom had already written his letter to Bill in anticipation of possible injury or death and kept this letter close to his heart. Tom had ensured that should the worst happen; his letter would be sent. Most nights, Tom wrote to Bill mapping out what had happened each day and of his involvement. He also expressed his concerns about oncoming actions. Tom was relieved that to this point in his war, things had not been as bad as he had previously thought.

Tom also told Bill about Montgomery's veterans who had been brought over from Africa and he wondered if there were any guys who Bill might know. Tom wrote stating how much he thought that he had change since landing in Sicily. He felt more mature and certainly more battle hardy, albeit he had not yet been in a significant battle. There had been the occasional skirmishes, but nothing too disastrous. Tom also wrote weekly to his parents and occasionally to Bill's parents. When writing home, Tom always made out that everything was fine and that he was in good spirits.

He made light of some of the action that had taken place, always stating that he had been at a far enough distance that he had not been in danger. The truth was somewhat different, as on several occasions, Tom had been involved in several minor skirmishes and had been in the line of fire. In Bill's response to Toms letters, Bill tended to concentrate on issues relating to Phil and how Phil was not improving.

Bill also prepared Tom for the worst news in relation to Amos. The Red Cross had reported that many Japanese prisoners of war were being murdered across the Far East or were being inhumanly mistreated and that many of the guys who had been stationed in the Far East were either dead or not expected to survive. Bill told Tom that Phil had also heard this news and that Phil was finding this news hard to bear.

Bill related how Phil seemed to be affected more than the last time Tom had last seen Phil. Bill told Tom that he was at a loss as to what to do for Phil, but he made regular visits and wrote to him daily when away from London. Sadly, Phil was not replying to his letters. As Tom read, he too thought how strange to was, because he too had not received any letters from Phil.

Montgomery began the British arm of the Allied invasion of the Italian peninsula by crossing the Strait of Messina landing at Calabria—the 'toe' of Italy. As Montgomery's Army began its invasion of the Italian mainland the Italian government had agreed to surrender. However, the Allied advancement through Italy proved to be a terribly slow and costly affair.

Of the many offensives which took place, Tom and his group were amongst those who tended to be pushed forward first. Tom recalled his first kill to Bill. Although understanding the need to stop the enemy and to preserve his own life, taking the life of another was never an easy thing. The first would remain with Tom for ever, as the unfortunate guy had taken a round directly to the head. Tom saw as the bullet impacted, throwing the recipient backwards with a jolt, then collapsing in a heap.

The only redeeming feature was that Tom knew the guy had died instantly and possibly didn't even know what had hit him. Others after were not so lucky, some would die slowly, while even more would be maimed for life. Tom escaped several near misses, mainly from mortar fire and from flying shrapnel rather than bullets. A number of the guys from his platoon had been severely injured, some with bullet wounds and one or two stabbed by bayonets when fighting at close range. According to Tom, at least fifteen men had died or had suffered fatal injuries, dying soon after in the field.

Rome did not fall until June the following year, by which time a stalemate ensued. Tom and his company spent much time involved with more and more skirmishes, moving forward slowly then retreating before moving forward again. Tom's involvement became more intense, and he became more skilled in identifying trouble spots. Tom was also not afraid of taking the initiative, which was noted by his commanding officer. Tom was promoted in the field. He too, like Bill became a colour sergeant.

The British 8th Army made relatively easy progress for a while up the eastern coast, capturing the Ports of Brindisi and Bari, as well as airfields around Foggia. Although involved with fighting, Tom loved Italy. Tom loved Brindisi, especially its natural harbour. The harbour penetrates deep into the Adriatic which always was of a deep blue hue.

The weather in Brindisi was always fair. Summer heat could reach high as 86 °F during July and August and the winters there mild. The light winds cooled and moderating the summer heat and during the winter, did intend to increase the wind chill.

On 11 September 1943 and following the Armistice of Cassibile, Bari was taken without much resistance, even though some Italians still remained loyal to the Germans. Tom, along with his squad were able to take a decent rest once Bari was secured, camping just outside of the town. The men took stock of what they had been through and experienced, were able to sort out their gear and spent much more time relaxing, playing cards and only occasionally conducting manoeuvres.

Horace Hersey, a close friend of Tom's, ended up doubling up with Tom in their make-shift camp. Horace, a 6' 2", stunningly good-looking man, who hailed from Stafford was a quiet individual but had become close to Tom. Horace had shown real determination and grit when it came to engaging with the enemy and liked Tom for the same reasons.

Horace was never far from Tom's side, which Tom appreciated unreservedly. Horace was also like Tom in that he liked to maintain his gear and living space immaculately clean, well as clean as could be in the circumstances. Horace also liked privacy and time to reflect. He was a deep-thinking man but held his emotions close to his chest. Tom admired Horace and thought how lucky he was to have such a great friend.

At night, Horace and Tom would talk quietly after lights out and to ensure no one was disturbed by their talking. They would move their beds close to one another so that their conversations were audible only to each other. Having Horace close, Tom sometimes thought of Bill. Being close to Horace and thinking about Bill had an instantaneous rapid effect on Tom, who found that he would become easily sexually aroused.

Tom would never say that being close to Horace aroused him, but still, he would fantasise about Bill and also what it would be like to make love with Horace. Horace was aware that Tom liked to be close to him and suspected that Tom sometimes got horny. Horace could tell by the change in Tom's voice when it happened. When this did happen, Tom always seemed to get a dry throat and his breathing changed. Horace, a vehemently committed heterosexual was not put off by Tom's change in behaviour but wondered why this was happening.

Horace also on occasion had become more than just aroused himself but kept quiet, not telling Tom. One night, as Horace and Tom were talking, Horace asked Tom about his girlfriend. Horace was aware of the many love-letters Tom was receiving and began probing to find out about this never-spoken-about other half. Horace was curious. Horace had had girlfriends in the past, but now, was single.

Tom tried to change the subject, not wanting to disclose who his true love and partner was and did not want to lie to Horace either. However, Horace was persistent. Tom held fast keeping his secret but thought that at some point he would open up to Horace and would have to tell Horace the truth about himself, but for now, he was keeping his lips sealed.

During the latter part of November, plans had been made for Tom's troop to move forward. However, before they actually moved off from their camp, and on the night of December 2, the Germans bombed the port in Bari, sinking seventeen ships and killing more than 1,000 American and British servicemen and hundreds of civilians. Caught by surprise, an American Liberty ship, which was carrying a secret cargo of 2,000 mustard bombs exploded.

The Luftwaffe's lucky strike released a poisonous cloud of sulphur mustard vapour over the harbour and liquid mustard gas into the water. In the crush of casualties that first night, hundreds of survivors from the bombing had jumped or were blown overboard. Those that survived the bombing of their ship tried in vain to swim to safety. After reaching shore and clambering out of the water, many were mistakenly believed to be suffering from shock from being immersed into the oil filled sea.

Unbeknown to those survivors and their rescuers, these men had been affected by the concoction of poisonous gas and chemicals released from the American Liberty Ship. Many minor casualties were given morphine, wrapped in warm blankets, and left to sit in their oil-soaked uniforms for as long as 12 or even 24 hours, while the seriously wounded were attended to. It was tantamount to marinating those men in mustard gas, but all remained ignorant of their peril.

Tom, along with Horace and their troop were called upon to lend a hand moving casualties and isolate the bodies of those who had been killed. By dawn the next morning, many of the survivors who had swam to safety had developed red inflamed skin and blisters the size of balloons. Within 24 hours, the field hospitals and the hospitals with Bari were full of men in excruciating pain, eyes swollen shut and becoming more unwell by the minute.

Doctors did suspect some chemical irritant was at play, but these men did not present typical symptoms nor were they responding to standard treatments. Unease deepened when notification came from headquarters that the hundreds who were burnt and displaying unusual symptoms should be classified as 'Dermatitis N.Y.D.' (not yet diagnosed). To Tom and many others, this notification raised serious concerns, not least that Headquarters was keeping something under wrap.

Then without warning, patients in relatively good condition began dying. These sudden, mysterious deaths left the doctors baffled and at a loss as to how to proceed. Rumours began spreading that the Germans were using an unknown poison gas. With the daily death toll rising, British officials in Bari placed a 'red light' call alerting Allied Force Headquarters of the medical crisis. After a couple of days, divers were sent to pull up fragments of fractured gas shells, the casings were identified as being from 100-pound American mustard bombs.

Not only was the gas from the Allies' own supply, but the victims labelled with 'Dermatitis N.Y.D.' had suffered prolonged exposure because of being immersed in a toxic solution of mustard and oil floating on the surface of the harbour. Churchill refused to acknowledge the presence of mustard gas in Bari and with the war in Europe entering a critical phase, the Allies agreed to impose a policy of strict censorship on the chemical disaster: All mention of mustard gas was to be struck from official records and troops who had been affected and those who worked to support casualties were never informed.

For several days, Tom and his crew worked tirelessly helping out the medical teams. The psychological and emotional effect on those supporting the injured was telling. Tom and Horace in particular found the whole incident trying, as they not only helped with the sick, injured and dying, but also had to motivate the men under their command who were visibly scared. Finally, when relieved of their duty, the men of Tom and Horace's troop returned to camp.

They were then told to prepare to move forward. The night before they began their next push forward, Tom and Horace began their nightly debate, moving their beds closer than they had ever done before, more out of providing reassurance than for any other reason. Both men were so psychologically drained by what they had experienced they began to open up to each other about their fears and anxieties.

"God, that was frightening," Horace began. "I've never witnessed anything like that before."

"Me neither," Tom replied.

"Seeing all of those guys in such a state and seeing them in pain and dying has really hit home." Horace went on.

"Are you scared that it might affect us?" Tom asked, meaning that they too might succumb to the physical injuries they had seen.

"Yes," Horace said with a tremble in his voice.

"Me too," Tom replied. There was silence, and then Tom said, "It's got me thinking. I don't know about you, but this dam war is getting to me. Something like we have witnessed could also happen to us at any time."

Horace hung on to every word Tom had said and replied, "You're right their mate."

After a brief pause, Tom looked at Horace and asked, "Can I confide in you?"

Horace looked at Tom and replied, "Of course you can mate. I think that we have been through enough together these last months to be able to trust each other."

"Yes, I know," Tom said thoughtfully, "but this is personal, and I don't want it to affect our friendship."

Horace looked at Tom rather confused. "I don't know what you mean! You know that our friendship could never change, not after all that we have been through and what we might still have to face in the future," Horace said.

"Well," Tom began. "This is something that I have never told anyone, and I want to get things straight just in case something happens to me."

"Fuck sake mate," Horace said sounding really concerned. "What the hell is it?"

Tom took a deep breath, as if it were his last. "Well," he began, "you know all of the letters I get?" Tom paused, "They are not from a girlfriend." Tom paused again, fearful of the response he might get from Horace. Tom forced the next statement out of his mouth as his stomach churned, "They're from another man." There, he had said it.

Horace looked kindly at Tom and said, "Funny, I thought that's what it might be, even though you don't look or act queer. You never talk about your relationship like the other guys, and I suspected that there was something different going on."

Tom stated, "We've been together for a while now. It's a mate from home. It just happened and I love him so much. He's in the army too, stationed in Aldershot at the moment. He served with the 'Desert Rats' in Egypt. I guess he should have been with us here under Monty, but he has been lucky enough to have time at home." Horace listened as Tom told him about Bill. "I wanted to ask you a favour" Tom went on. "If anything should happen to me, will you make contact with Bill and will you make sure that all of my letters are sent back to him? I don't want this to get out," Tom said in trepidation.

"Leave it with me," Horace said, "you can trust me and your secret is safe with me." A feeling of relief overwhelmed Tom. He would never be able to thank Horace enough for accepting him the way he had.
"I can't explain what a relief that is to me. It's even more of a relief that you know now and that you're ok with it, and that you are not judging me," Tom said. "I've never told anyone before and holding it in has become a pressure that I don't want." A longer silence followed, and then Horace said, "Will you do the same for me, let my family know if anything happens to me? I would rather it came from you. At least, you really know me, having lived with me for so long."

"Of course, mate, you can depend on me," Tom replied smiling. Horace then did something quite unexpected; he rolled forward towards Tom, placed his arm over Tom and hugged him, kissing Tom gently on his cheek. Tom was a little taken aback at first but recognised that the hug and kiss was Horace's way of sealing their deal. That night, Tom and Horace slept holding each other close. Tom sensed that Horace was becoming sexually aroused and at that point, he too felt movement in his own pants. Horace's hand slipped down touching Tom's now hardening member.

Tom was in two minds about stopping Horace but thought it was something Horace really needed right now. Tom reciprocated, moving his hand to touch

Horace's now throbbing tool. Tom had seen Horace naked, but he had never seen him aroused. Tom was shocked at how much Horace's penis had expanded, standing now at about nine inches and the girth of his penis too large to fit into Tom's grasp.

The boys began masturbating each other, reaching their splendid climax at about the same time. "Thanks Tom, I needed that," Horace said quietly, as they lay together breathing heavily.

"Yeah, I needed that too," Tom said. For the rest of the night, the boys lay together, still wet, sticky, and hot but both feeling satisfied and relieved, and for once relaxed.

# Chapter Fourteen
# Phil's Ordeal

Working for the War office, Phil had come across and was privy to lots of disturbing and troubling information. Rumours about atrocities that were being conducted by the Nazis, in secret; particularly stuff relating to possible genocide of Jews, Homosexuals, Gypsies and people with disabilities were being branded about but little action was being taken to fully gain the extent to which this was happening.

Phil's had also come across other news, yet unconfirmed, that the Japanese were also carrying out atrocities on the civilian populations of the countries they had invaded and on prisoners they had captured. Concerns were also being raised at the higher levels of command about such acts being carried out by the Nazis and Japanese, but those in power had other considerations on their mind, not least, protecting Great Britain and putting an end to this war and to determine what influence each of the allied countries would have on the 'new world' once the war was complete.

Government officials knew that a new world order was on the cards and that by protecting the sovereign state, its empire and commonwealth, they could secure control for the future, without losing their position within the world. The loss of individuals at the hands of the Nazis and Japanese was part of the price that would have to be paid.

Phil understood where the government were coming from, but his main concerns altered because of the relationship he had with Amos. Phil's job saw him monitoring all information about the rise of the Japanese and the aggressive nature of their attacks. Like many others, and before the Japanese made their move, Phil thought that Britain was better prepared and ready for anything that the Japanese could throw at Britain and because of this, when Amos was first posted to the Far East, Phil really did not have major concerns.

However, following the Japanese attack on Pearl Harbour and the activities that was developing in China, he was now beginning to have uneasy feelings about how Britain might respond should the Japanese attack Malaya and Singapore. Yes, he knew that Britain held superior manpower within the region, but worried that its naval presence was insufficient. When Phil got the news that Singapore had been taken, Phil's heart fell. The sudden blackout of letters coming from Amos also added to Phil's feelings of anxiety. Somehow, Phil knew that something dreadful had happened or would happen to Amos.

Whether he had been killed, injured, or had been captured or had managed to escape and had hidden himself only exacerbated Phil's feeling of unease. After all, Phil and Amos were a couple. The love Phil had for Amos was greater than any love he had experienced before. Even the love he had for his parents dwindled in comparison. The sinking feeling Phil was experiencing just got worse as time went on. Phil was happy that Tom was around at that time and was also happy when Bill was able to be take time to be with him.

However, even with their support, Phil headed into a downward spiral. At night, Phil had been over thinking what might have happened to Amos and could not shift this deep sense of foreboding. Phil's sorrow was so great that each and every night he would cry uncontrollably. He found it difficult to sleep and when he was able to sleep, would experience the most horrific dreams. This nightly routine was taking its toll on Phil's physical ability to function. At first, it began with a lack of motivation to get dressed, tidy-up, and make his bed, shave and wash.

This was followed by leaving uneaten food on plates around the house and being disinterested in going out, especially to work. Although Bill had initially chivvied Phil to do some activities, when Bill left, Phil fell back into his dark place. Even when Bill called to see Phil, he had negligible impact on Phil's motivation and mood. Bill spent most of his time being concerned about Phil but tended to concentrate on just cleaning up all the mess left around. Bill attempted to unearth what was going on in Phil's head but with trivial effect.

Bill understood the sense of loss Phil was experiencing, after all, he had lost comrades who had been close and could imagine the depth of feeling Phil was going through not knowing what had happened to Amos. Bill's empathy was real, as he pondered about what it would be like should he ever lose Tom.

Phil's depressive state became more overwhelming when he received information whist at work about some of the things that had been reported by the

Red Cross. The thought that Amos may have been mercilessly murdered by the Japanese or that he was being tortured at their hands was horrifying. Amos, although a strong, tough individual, was also so loving and affectionate, caring, and supportive. Without Amos, Phil could not imagine life without him. When alone, Phil began to imagine all sorts of things that might have or was happening to Amos; the pain becoming unbearable.

Towards the end of 1943, Phil had reconciled within his mind that Amos was gone forever. Phil had tried endless ways to get more information, particularly from Amos's family who became quite angry with Phil for even attempting to get in contact with them. Phil realised that his grief was his alone, which caused him to follow his own path of reconciliation. The only way to describe how Phil was feeling this loss is that he had lost interest in all previously known rewarding or enjoyable activities such as friends, family, hobbies, work, food, sex, and laughter, but this description paled in comparison to Phil's real-life experience.

It was actually pretty difficult for Phil to explain his feelings of nothingness to people. Phil was feeling empty, dead inside, emotionless, as though he had nothing to contribute to the world, or as though he could not relate to the feelings and emotions of others; Phil was finding it more and more problematic to interact at any level. One night while in bed, Phil decided that the only conceivable way to escape from this feeling of nothingness would be to end his life. Once the thought of suicide came into Phil's thinking, it would not go away. After just a brief few weeks, suicidal thoughts encompassed his every thought. Phil contemplated many different ways to die and to end his misery.

Before deciding just how he would end his life, Phil began preparations by ensuring that all of his business was in order. Writing letters of farewell and altering his will. Phil spent some time with his solicitor, not letting on to him that he intended to end his own life, but used the war as an excuse, just in case anything should happen to him. One good thing was that Phil's solicitor knew about Phil's sexual orientation and Phil's relationship with Amos. This enabled the solicitor to word all documents carefully enough to make sure Phil's wishes were conducted to the letter.

On Christmas eve, Phil sat thinking about his life, the rebuke by his parents for being homosexual and the way he had been cut off from them. Phil also thought about the many casual love affairs that he had had over the years and the loneliness he had felt. These times had not been easy for Phil. The casual sex had been gratifying at the time, but Phil had always wanted a full, long-term, loving, monogamous relationship. A relationship that was focused on one person and with whom Phil could share and spend his life with. It had not been until his meeting with Amos that this fulfilment had been achieved.

With Amos, Phil felt fulfilled, secure, loved and part of something much bigger than himself. Amos had become the centre of Phil's universe. Someone who was everything to him. Now it seemed after all the loss he had experienced; this loss was by far the most painful and all encompassing. Phil could no longer live without the love of his life. That one special person who had fully connected with him. This dammed war had taken his love away for good.

Phil knew this emptiness would never go away, he knew that he would never recover and did not want a future. Phil picked up the letters he had written, put on his coat and walked to the end of the street to the post box where he posted the letters he had written. One letter to his own parents and one to Amos's parents giving full details of his love of Amos and his feeling of life without having him about. Phil apologised for any hurt that he had caused to both his parents and to Amos's family but at least the truth had been said.

Phil ended his letters with his finale goodbyes. Phil had also written to Bill and Tom. Phil thanked them both for their friendship, expressing his love for them and hoping that they would have a wonderful life together once the war had ended. Phil conveyed how grateful he was to both Tom and Bill saying that their friendship had contributed to the happiest time of his and Amos's life.

He ended his letters to Tom and Bill by telling them that he had decided for them to gain an inheritance from him after his death and hoped that they would share memories of him and Amos when they were there together. Finally, Phil said that he hoped Bill and Tom would remain in love and that they both would return safely from the war.

Phil returned home after posting the letters and decided to dress the house as if Amos was there. He spent hours preparing for this last Christmas by meticulously setting out each bejewelled bauble he could find, placing decorations around the hall, living and dining rooms. He set the table with his finest dinner service, one place setting for him and another for Amos.

Phil then went into the kitchen, cooked the final Christmas lunch, then once dinner had been prepared, Phil placed Amos's meal on his place setting and ate his meal as if Amos was there with him, even talking to the empty space where Amos would normally have sat. Phil even poured wine into the empty glass set for Amos and cleaned away each course as if the plates were empty. Finally, after finishing with a glass of port, Phil cleaned-up, putting everything away in its place.

He then went into his living room, where he drank one last brandy. Over the weeks preceding today's event and leading up to Christmas, Phil had accumulated a stock pile of medicines and pills which he had kept hidden in his bedroom and which he knew, if taken in such quantity and together, would end his life. Phil left the living room, walked back into the kitchen and took a large glass of water to take to his bedroom.

Once upstairs, Phil placed the glass of water on the table next to his bed. Sitting for a while on his bed, Phil began to empty the many bottles of tablets onto the clean bedspread. Phil began taking the many tablets, firstly one at a time, then several at a time, swilling them down with the water from the kitchen. Whilst taking the tablets, Phil's mind remained blank. All he could focus on was the bliss in knowing that the end would come, and that darkness would encompass him.

After taking all of the tablets, Phil emptied the last contents of his glass and lay back on his pillow, lifting his legs to rest fully on his bed. Phil began to think of Amos and of all the happy times that they had spent together. He thought about Bill and Tom too and how they had brought new life into his and Amos's life. True friendship like theirs was hard to find. Phil began to feel nauseous and had a cramping feeling in his stomach.

Knowing that this was the effects of the medication he had taken, he fought hard to stop himself from being sick and held his stomach tightly until he began to drift into a deep restful sleep. All thoughts of Amos disappeared as his sleep took Phil into a coma. His breathing shallowed as his body succumbed to the concoction of killer medicines.

Phil's breathing began to become shallow, struggling to maintain rhythm, his hands and feet started to get colder, and his skin began to look mottled and blotchy, slowly working its way up his arms and legs, his heart struggled to pump blood around his body and as his blood pressure dropped, his skin cooled, growing colder. His lips and nail beds began turned a bluish, purplish tint as saliva and mucus built up in his airway.

Phil's death rattle began and lasted for just a few minutes as he became too weak to clear the secretions that now lay at the back of his throat and into his lungs. Phil's arms and legs twitched in the closing seconds of his life. Then stillness. What had been Phil was now gone. His personality, his vibrant life source, his being had drifted off into another place. All that was left of Phil was his corps, the physical being that was flesh and bone, now busily commencing the initial stages of decomposition.

On receiving Phil's letter, Bill immediately contacted the Police station located near to Phil's house. Bill managed to get leave, travelling to London to meet the police. However, the Police had already entered Phil's house before Bill's arrival and had found Phil dead on the bed. When Bill arrived, Phil's body had been moved to the morgue awaiting identification and post-mortem. Phil's parents had also been contacted but they had refused to visit their deceased son.

Phil's parents saw Phil's life and death as being shameful and selfish and although they would grieve in their own way, they were determined to have nothing more to do with the whole episode. It was left to Bill to identify Phil and to make the final arrangements for his burial. Bill had anticipated the reaction of Phil's parents after finding an envelope and letter addressed to Bill in Phil's house. The letter explained how Phil's parents might react and of their possible rejection of reality. The letter also contained money and instructions for the disposal of Phil's body.

Bill followed Phil's instructions to the 'T', contacting the undertaker and asking for a quiet affair. Also within the envelope were instructions for Bill to contact Phil's lawyer. Phil's lawyer had also been left further instructions to follow after Phil had finally been laid to rest. Bill stayed at Phil's house while arrangements were made having to return to barracks just three days later. Bill then had to plan to return to London for Phil's committal and burial.

The burial, when it arrived, was an incredibly sad affair. Only Bill and the vicar were present. Even the funeral directors looked on in shock as these two people paid their last respects. At the grave side, Bill threw a handful of soil onto Phil's dark wood coffin, shedding a tear for his dear friend. Bill turned and thanked the vicar and after shaking his hand, he walked silently away from the grave.

Both Tom and Bill were totally saddened by the action Phil had taken and surprised that Phil had indicated that he had bequeathed a gift for them. However, just what this gift was, would have to wait until the reading of the will was completed. When Tom heard about Phil's passing, he turned to Horace for comfort and reassurance. Phil's death, as sad as it was, was just another death to deal with for both Bill and Tom.

The greatest impact on Tom and Bill was the fact that they could not share their grief with one another, could not comfort each other or offer each other support. For Tom especially, this feeling of inadequacy and failure would linger for some considerable time, always having the fear that should something happen to Bill, he might not be around to be there at the final closure, nor would he ever be able to show his true love and affection towards the man that he loved most in the world.

# Chapter Fifteen
# Preparing for Normandy

During the weeks and months before the Normandy landings or D-Day, the Royal Air Force prepared occupied territory in Europe for the invasion of ground forces by going behind enemy lines to attack strategic targets such as railway lines, troop trains and other transport carrying equipment. The RAF's main targets were the main rail systems in France and Belgium, used by the Germans for transporting troops and equipment. The Germans later wrote of the 'crippling' of the transport systems and the destruction of railways and road communications.

The R.A.F. successfully stopped the German reserve troops from getting to Normandy prior to and during the landings and prevented the Germans from building up troops for some time afterwards. By the time D-Day arrived, Normandy had been virtually isolated by the combined Allied fighter and bomber offensive. Allied fighter squadrons also flew systematic and debilitating attacks on German fighter airfields, aiming at German planes on the ground in France, as well as waging battle in the air.

The RAF fighters had destroyed around two thousand enemy aircraft over the English Channel and surrounding countryside. Southern England was becoming littered with downed German aircraft. The bulk of the Luftwaffe still remained and was busy on the eastern front fighting the Soviet air force, which meant that by D-Day the Allies had supremacy in the skies around England and the French coast.

By 1944, Britain was beginning to run short of soldiers. Campaigns in the Mediterranean, North Africa, the Far East and the war at sea had all but drained Britain of her manpower reserves. The army that was to be sent to Normandy lacked for nothing in terms of armament, but inadequate reserves of fighting troops were to be their greatest fear. Though well supplied with weapons, vehicles and equipment, the army could not afford to take on huge losses. Everything had to be done to minimise casualties and preserve the army's fighting strength.

One of the saving graces for the British Army was the vast reserves of US manpower coming on stream. It was vital for Britain's interests and national standing that her field army was strong enough not only to engage and defeat the Germans but also to provide a sustainable army of occupation once the Allies had taken root in France. As much of the current British army was untested in action, having spent long years training in the UK, orders were given to those veterans in senior positions of the intended invasion.

It took people like Bill to sort and deliver a force that had the morale and fighting spirit similar to their counterpart German soldiers who had been fighting on the Russian Front. Bill was ordered to set about driving his recruits in preparedness for what might be coming ahead. Bill knew that any attack on the Germans would involve the Sherman tanks of the Staffordshire Yeomanry and that these tanks would carry the infantry forward. Unlike other armoured divisions, which would be used as a driving force in full scale battle, the independent armoured brigades such as the Stafford's, would primarily be used to function as close support for the infantry.

Bill recognised the importance of this and that the infantry was likely to ride into the battle zone on the backs of these tanks, 'de-bussing' when within range of the enemy. And so, Bill trained his troops to use the armoured divisions as both transport and as protection. This new way of warfare not only boosted the morale of his troops but also gained admiration from Bill's commanding officers. Training his men hard resulted in Bill gaining total respect from his troops and given that he had already witnessed combat, made him a trusted N.C.O.

Training for the anticipated invasion of occupied territory became a deadly affair, amid live-ammo mishaps and landing craft sinking's, troops were being lost at a frightening rate. Compared with their opponents, the Allied servicemen who were preparing to invade northern France experienced an incredible degree of rugged and realistic training that put them at the peak of physical fitness, acclimatising them to battle and equipping them mentally and physically to win. Bill concentrated more on those men who showed fear and bewilderment.

Bill knew that these boys needed psychological strength as much as physical prowess. Bill was well known by his troops to be supportive as well as tactically sound. Bill knew his men were to be involved in the largest seaborne invasion in history, marking the beginning of the campaign to liberate north-west Europe from German occupation. One particular guy, Tony Walsh appeared to be afraid of his own skin and Bill paid Tony special attention to him. Not only did Bill help Tony to build him into a formidable soldier, he also helped him to overcome many of his fears and anxieties.

Bill took time to talk to Tony, not directly about his worries, but got to understand where Tony was coming from. It appeared that Tony had always been a sickly child but had also never found favour with his father, who was a brute of a man, often drunk and who would use his fists on his children to 'toughen' them up. Bill's quiet approach towards Tony resulted in Tony's ability to recognise his strengths and abilities and after some weeks, Tony looked on Bill as the father he had always wished for, kind yet firm, without being over controlling.

As D-day approached, some 7,000 vessels were gathered to be used in the landing: 1,213 warships and 4,127 landing craft of various types and sizes along with 23,000 airborne troops. The airborne troops were too be dropped in enemy occupied France as 132,000 men landed on the Normandy beaches. A staggering 12,000 Allied aircraft was also to be used, of which two-thirds of the aircraft; more than three-quarters of the landing craft and 892 of the warships involved were British.

With increasingly large Allied forces now in the Mediterranean and following the assault on Sicily and with the vital capture of airfields in southern Italy, Italy began to wobble. Allied strategic air forces worked in tandem with bomber forces operating from Britain, tightening the noose around the Third Reich. Gaining air superiority over all of Western Europe was a non-negotiable prerequisite for any invasion into France and it was not until the spring of 1944 that these conditions had been met. It was also not until early June 1944 that the Allies had sufficient weight of men and materials as well as the control of the skies which allowed the Allies to invade.

Bill had achieved his goal in preparing his men to fight, helping his troops through the many rehearsals for invasion. His ability to relate to his troops was outstanding. Bill knew most of his troops by name and had singled out those who were homosexual. He knew of some that were having sexual relationships and he also knew those who had not come to terms yet with their own sexuality. Bill was impressed by the way these guys acted and responded. These guys were as tough as any heterosexual under his command dispelling any notion that to be homosexual was to be weak. Bill worked with his youngest troops, giving them special attention, which was noted by higher command.

Higher command recognised that by giving extra support to troops, particularly the weaker guys, helped in preparedness, improving their abilities faster than by using old fashioned bullying tactics. Amongst these few men, Bill also realised that another young chap, John Perkins, was especially vulnerable. John displayed homosexual tendencies and had taken a lot of stick from his fellow troops because of his effeminate ways. Bill realised that it was not the fear of fighting that caused John to show anxiety but that it was mainly due to the fact that he had been bullied.

Bill took action against any bullies under his command, stressing that when they were to engage with the enemy, all would have to provide support for each other, whether they liked an individual of not. Bill was always telling his troops that, "Even the weakest will do their part and their part might well be the most crucial, saving the lives of others in the troop." Bill's emphasis on providing individual training for John, (unlike other sergeants) and taking a softly-softly approach was showing real positive results.

This enabled young men like John and Tony not only to catch up with the rest of the guys but also provided Bill with personal satisfaction. It also caused Bill to have some personal difficulties, in that the relationship between these men and Bill was becoming emotive rather than pragmatic. Bill saw that John had responded well to his one-to-one approach but sensed that John was forming an attachment to Bill that was not healthy, so too was Tony. John, was a 'pretty' looking boy, was endearing, attractive and charming. It seemed to Bill that John also saw Bill as a father figure, although the age difference was not that great.

John on the other hand was beginning to see Bill as his protector, carer and confident. On several occasions when working alone with Bill, John had become too close, almost flirting with Bill. Bill realised that there was physical attraction on both of their parts and Bill had also recognised that on occasion, John had become sexually aroused; Bill too had a similar response but fought back to control himself. Bill realised that it would not take much for them both to become entwined in sexual activity and so Bill made sure that the opportunity did not arise. Bill also felt guilty because of the promises he had made to Tom. Having to juggle command with support was difficult for Bill, but he learned many new lessons from having this responsibility, including fidelity.

When orders did eventually come through, Bill had to inform his men that they were to be the second line of the invasion force. Bill explained carefully to his men their target, men from all other allied countries also set about preparing themselves mentally for what lay ahead. The Allies amassed their vast forces, but despite the thousands of warships and landing craft, only a fraction of Allied strength could initially be transported across the Channel. Allied intelligence was superb and so long as the exact location and timing of the invasion remained secret to the Germans, they felt that as attackers they could achieve total tactical surprise when the landings began in Normandy.

As things panned out, this actually proved the case, but thereafter, the race was then on as to which side could build up a decisive weight of force in Normandy first. When Bill was informed that his troops was not needed for the initial wave, he breathed a sigh of relief. But as his men were expected to be ready to follow immediately once the beaches were secure, Bill knew that his men would be first to see the atrocities first hand. Bill also knew that this second wave needed to secure the headland after witnessing the blood shed of the beaches and prepare his men to push forward as soon as enough men and equipment were landed.

Although Bill was relieved that his men were not to be at the forefront of the invasion, he did realise that their job was potentially going to be more difficult, especially if the Germans were able to reinforce quickly. Bill recognised the psychological effects of having his men pass dead bodies and potentially severely maimed comrades. Bill was sure that he had been able to motivate his men enough to fight, even after seeing such carnage.

When D-Day finally arrived, tensions were high as his group were loaded on to a troop carrier. The weather that day was not good and when the troops were informed that the landing had been delayed, there was a wave of tense relief which enveloped the ship. None of the men were allowed to disembark from the ship but had to settle down in any space that they could find. Once Bill had settled his troops, he found himself a vacant space next to one of the large guns on the upper deck. To his amazement, John Perkins suddenly appeared, grabbing a space next to Bill.

Bill next to him, John felt secure and relatively happy. Bill was not completely at ease but also found that being near John did gave him comfort. That night was to be one of the longest nights either Bill or John had experienced. It was also a night when confessions would be made, initially from John, who disclosed his sexuality to Bill and who also professed his desire for Bill. Lying close together on the cold steel deck, John asked Bill if he could get close to him. At first, Bill rejected John's request, but as the night drew in and as the chill in the air engulfed them, Bill relented. "Are you cold?" asked Bill. "Yes, a little," John replied. "Please can I get close to you? I think that by being close, we'll both warm up. I think that I'm more nervous than cold," John confessed. "Ok" Bill said, thinking at the same time, this is the wrong thing to be doing. John moved towards Bill and got as close as was physically possible. The close proximity of the two men seemed to calm their inner anxieties. Both were facing each other. Bill could feel John's warm sweet breath enveloping his face.

"You have been so kind to me," John sated. "I'll never be able to repay you for all that you have done for me or for showing me such kindness," John said in a quiet caring voice.

"I've only been doing my job," Bill replied.

"Yes, but you have gone beyond your duty, and I know that you have not had it easy from the other N.C.O.s for putting so much time and effort into helping me," John went on, hoping that Bill would feel comfort from his words. "I feel it's time that I tell you something that I have never told anyone before, and I need to tell you now, just in case something should happen to me. I need to get it off my chest," John said.

Bill almost anticipated what John was to say next. "You don't have to tell me," Bill responded. "I think I already know what you are about to say and its ok by me."

"You know that I'm attracted to men?" John asked, knowing that Bill must be aware of John's inclinations.

"Yes," Bill replied, "I think that it's quite obvious and the stick you have been taking during training has been confirmation for me."

"Doesn't it bother you?" John asked.

"Not really," Bill said, "each to his own." John looked at Bill as if he was about to ask Bill his sexual orientation but hesitated.

"You do know that I have a crush on you?" John blurted out.

"That might be so," replied Bill, "but I don't think this is the time or place to discuss such matters. I've got other things on my mind at the moment."

John realised that going any further with this conversation would not prove productive but recognised in Bill that there was something in Bill's character that was being hidden by him. John sensed that like him, Bill had probably become sexually aroused. After all, the proximity of their bodies next to one another must surely have warranted some sort of response and Bill had not moved after John's advancement. Bill closed his eyes and thought about Tom. This intimacy and conversation with John had been to close a call for Bill.

Whether it was because it had been so long since he last had sex or whether it was the build-up of adrenaline in anticipation of the landings, Bill could not make out. All that Bill knew was that he had struggled to keep his hands off John and he had found it difficult to control the swelling in his trousers. Bill had never wanted Tom more than he did now. What he would not give to be lying next to Tom holding him close: never wanting to let Tom go. Bill reaffirmed to himself that once the war was over, he would remain with Tom forever.

Bill silently prayed for Tom to be safe and prayed that Tom also wanted the same as him, a lifetime of happiness together. Bill fell into an uneasy sleep, being woken suddenly to find that the troop ship had set sail for Normandy. Bill knew that the crossing would not take long and that soon he would be facing danger and would have the added responsibility to ensure that his men stayed as safe as possible. An empty feeling engulfed the pit of Bill's stomach as the realisation that for some, this would possibly be the last day of their young lives.

John opened his eyes. He had not moved from Bill. Bill had fallen asleep and he too had managed to get some rest. Now John looked at Bill fearful of what the day would bring. "What's happening?" John enquired.

"We've set sail. It won't be long now before we see the French coast. Are you scared?" Bill asked.

"I really don't know," John replied. "I'm not sure whether I'm scared or cold. I just know that I'm shaking and that frightens me more that meeting up face to face with the Germans." Bill grabbed John and hugged him, kissing him gently on the forehead trying desperately to reassure John, but knew in his heart that nothing could be taken for granted.

Out in the English Channel, the ship stopped and waited. Bill could see barges towing large blocks of concrete. These blocks were to be locked together to form a 'Mulberry Harbour' to enable equipment to be landed. Other equipment such as tanks and Lorries were also being transported. Following these, landing craft started to pass by. These craft were full of Marines who were to spear head the attack. Bill was filled with admiration and concern for these guys.

If anyone was to take the brunt of the Nazi forces, these were the guys who were first in line. Once the landing craft had passed, the ship quickly got up steam and began moving forward. Bill passed the word for everyone to be prepared. Bill's troops scampered on the decks quickly gathering their equipment together ensuring that everything they needed was tightly pack and that their guns were at the ready. There was little noise coming from his men, only the scampering of feet and the sound of bags being hurriedly packed.

Everyone was lost in their own thoughts of the impending outcome and of their loved ones. As the ship neared the coast, Bill began to order his men to muster near to their allocated landing craft. Bill stood patting each man on the back as they boarded. "Keep your heads down men. Wait for your orders. Don't move until you are told and if by any chance we hit problems, make your way to the beach as fast as you can and stick together. I don't want to see any of you chasing after the French girls before I arrive," Bill said, trying to make light of the event.

Once everyone was boarded, the front of the landing craft lifted. Bodies were crammed into this formidable steal box and the mutterings within it became louder as the engines began to rev up. The landing craft manoeuvred and entered the waters of the English Channel, heading for the shore and the coast of France. The bombardment from war ships had started, the loud booms from naval ships burst in a crescendo followed by further loud booms as the explosives hit their onshore targets.

As the landing craft progressed closer, several other landing craft vessels were hit by underwater mines. Young soldiers were in the water screaming and crying out for help. Some of the lucky ones were killed immediately as the mines struck. Others were maimed and would die of drowning, while others fought to get to shore. Some of the latter would make it, but the majority lost their fight for life in the freezing waters of the channel. Any thought of rescuing these poor souls was the last thing to be done.

Bill prayed that his landing craft would be spared and that at least he and his men would have a proper fighting chance of survival. Suddenly, as Bill's craft moved towards the shore, one of the sailors on Bill's craft leapt from the front of the craft as it slowed, taking with him a rope. This rope was then attached to a much thicker rope and as the sailor clambered onto the beach, he pulled for all his might as he waded through the icy water towards the beach.

The thicker rope being hauled by the sailor was to be used by Bill's men to help them forward. The landing craft swiftly turned in the water and the ramp began to open. Bill urged his men forward, shouting, "Come on men, run like crazy and keep your fucking heads down." The sea was about six feet deep at this point and the men had to hold up their rifles with one hand to keep then dry whilst with the other hand grabbing the rope that had been secured by the sailor.

Each man had been issued with rubber rings to keep them afloat and they bobbed in the water being pushed forward by the man behind. As the men approached Sword Beach with all of their gear on their backs and their rubber rings, they eventually managed to touch the seabed, and was then able to move easier for the last few feet before reaching shore. Some of the guys did not make the short distance. Some were blown out of the water, and some were drowning through shear panic. Bodies were floating everywhere but many of the men took little notice fearing that if they did not move quickly, they too would be floating with their comrades.

Led by the Marines, Bill and his troops were led off to rear up the forward group. Shells were exploding everywhere, but the men continued to advance. Once the men were able to regroup, they were held there for a brief time by Bill who encourage them to keep low. They had to wait for the marines to finish their job before they could advance further. The men remained fixed in once place as shells exploded around them and as bullets passed heading towards those men still at sea and who were struggling to get to shore.

The job of the marines was to push the German's back, which they did with profound effect. Bill's group, as part of the second wave then had to take over from the marines when ordered and hold the line, before the third wave overtook the second to do the same thing. As the men moved forward, they managed to reach the coastal path. Once there, they recognised that there seemed to be lots of French people about. Many of them dead, injured and many just wandering about shell shocked and confused.

Why these people were here was a surprise to both Bill and his men, as they had thought, they would have run towards the interior, rather than being on the edge of the battle. For two days, Bill and his men, along with many other brave allied souls held the lines while the mulberry platoons were erected, then tanks and other equipment was mobilised. When the tanks arrived, Bill made sure his men were ready to follow behind them. In all, during those first two days, Bill had either lost twenty percent of his men to enemy fire or they had been seriously injured unable to fight further.

Bill's men had waited on the beach until the road was clear, had made their way to the muster point at the top of the headway before counting heads and identifying those who had not made it. His men looked ashen, cold, and fearful. Now, his main concern was to build up his men's morale in an attempt to prepare them for the next stage. Each man looked at Bill and even though Bill was trembling inside, he managed to put on a brave face praising his men for their effort and bravery. His men looked on in admiration to a man who was their stalwart.

# Chapter Sixteen
# Battles, Lust and Nights in Cairo

Tom's reaction to Horace's embrace and kiss was one of relief. Tom desperately needed affection, particularly from another man. It had been so difficult for Tom not having Bill around. Each night Tom's thoughts had been about Bill and how they had loved each other. Tom wanted that strong firm embrace again and needed to experience that sense of security which he had never gotten from anyone else. For Tom, no love could be the same as the love he had received from Bill. Horace's embrace had reminded Tom of just how special his relationship was with Bill.

Tom recognised that Horace also craved love and even though Horace was definitely heterosexual, he sensed that even Horace wanted more. Whether Horace was considering his own mortality and the fact that that he might never be able to have another intimate time with a woman, Tom could not tell, but clearly Horace was not withdrawing from his embrace with Tom. Horace edged his hips forward as his grip on Tom intensified. Horace's groin pushed forward, and his swelling manhood pressed on Tom's thickening erection.

Horace was breathing faster now. His cheek slid along Tom's moving his mouth ever closer to Tom's. At any second, Tom knew that he and Horace would be locked into a full-on kiss. Although Tom wanted this to happen, he kept thinking about Bill. Guilt swept through Tom making him now feel uneasy. Tom pulled his face from Horace and at the same time pulled his hips back so that their members could not touch. Tom looked directly at Horace and in a sensitive voice said, "Please don't do anything that you will regret later. I know that we both need this but I'm not sure that you will be able to cope with the aftermath. You're not even attracted to men."

Horace began to sob, his body shaking, trembling as he held on to Tom. "I just need to be close to someone," Horace replied as he gasped for air. "We have gone through so much shit together and after seeing what happened to all those guys has made me realised that tomorrow, it might just be me. I don't want to die without knowing that I have loved and have been loved."

Tom knew exactly how Horace was feeling because he too was feeling the same way. "You are loved Horace, and I'm happy to hug you and keep hugging you. You're not going to die! You're far too lucky to let that happen," Tom said in an attempt to lift Horace's mood. "If we did more than we have just done, I'm sure that after, you would not be able to look me in the face without feeling guilty. I'd also feel guilty because I have committed myself to someone and promised that I would remain faithful to the end of days."

Horace listened and nodded in reply, still holding on to Tom. "You are right Tom, but can we just hold each other? I need this," Horace replied in realisation. Nothing more was needed to be said; Tom squeezed Horace in a tight bear hug. Their sexual arousal began to subside and each felt more comfortable with each other. "You are like a brother to me Tom. I will never forget what we have been through and will love you forever," Horace pledged.

Tom nodded in agreement, saying, "Me too brother." Tom realising that by saying this, he at some point would have to confess everything to Horace; his relationship with Bill and how they had decided to commit to each other for life.

The whole of southern Italy was now in Allied hands. By early October 1943, the Allied armies stood facing the Volturno Line. The Volturno line ran from Termoli in the east, along the Biferno River through the Apennine Mountains to the Volturno River in the west and north of Bari. The German forces had set up a series of defensive lines across Italy, following the Allied invasion of Italy. The German intention was to delay any Allied advance. These defensive lines which ran across Italy were from which the Germans could fight delaying actions, giving ground slowly, thus stalling to complete their preparation of the Winter Line, their strongest defensive line situated south of Rome.

The Winter Line was a series of three lines designed to defend a western section of Italy. The focus of these defences centred on the town of Monte Cassino. The important Highway 6 was central to this defence as it ran uninterrupted to Rome. The primary line of the three was the Gustav Line, which ran across Italy from just north of where the Garigliano River flows into the Tyrrhenian Sea in the west, through the Apennine Mountains to the mouth of the Sangro River on the Adriatic Coast to in the east. The other two subsidiary lines, the Bernhardt Line and the Hitler Line ran much shorter distances from the

Tyrrhenian sea to just Northeast of Monte Cassino where they would merge into the Gustav Line. Relative to the Gustav Line, the Hitler Line stood to the North-West and the Bernhardt Line to the South-East of the primary defences.

Tom and Horace, along with their respective troops made ready to move forward. The troops were soon back fighting their way up to the Volturno River. On a number of occasions, there were hold ups because bridges had been blown and crossing the river became difficult. Tom and Horace were ordered to dig in near the river. One afternoon, N.C.O.s were given orders that their troops would be making a night crossing supported by artillery. Tom and Horace were informed that their sections would be amongst the first to cross.

That night, the men prepared to move forward, slowly by quietly. As the small craft loaded with men moved mid-stream, the quietness was interrupted as the Germans opened up, shells began flying overhead; the Germans opened up their machine guns and six-barrel mortars. Bullets began whizzing overhead as the boys in the boats desperately tried to speed their crossing, hurrying to safety on the far bank. Tom and Horace managed to land their troops without mishap. However, some of the other guys were not so lucky, as their boats were blown out of the water.

Tom and Horace managed to find a ditch, shouting to their men to get down and return fire. After much heavy fighting, Tom and Horace ordered their troops to push forward, making an assault on the German lines. The Germans fell back but not before they had taken out several of Tom's men and more of Horace's. The following morning, Tom along with three of his men were ordered to try to make contact with the battalion to their right. The men moved off and about half a mile on, they spotted a small, isolated farmhouse. As the four approached the house, it was visible that someone was moving about.

From the house, a mortar was fired towards the four. Tom immediately told his men to withdraw, not before he was able to throw a couple of grenades. The men fell back, firing as they retreated and reported back to the platoon. Tom was angry with himself for not reaching their destination and having to turn back to their platoon. That afternoon Tom and Horace we ordered to take their men to try to find out exactly where the enemy were located, but to their disappointment they were not able to locate them.

On their way back, they came across the house that Tom and the other three guys had attacked that morning. Tom sent Frank Sharp to investigate. Frank was a stocky guy but light and nimble on his feet. Frank was also extremely willing to take risks, he was one of Tom's trusted troops, fearless and determined. Tom had another guy; Steve Walker follow Frank. Steve was armed with a Bren gun with Tom and the others following behind. Just a little way inside the side gate of the Farmhouse Tom noticed something on the ground. Tom immediately shouted, "Look out, don't anyone touch it."

As soon as those words left Tom's mouth, there was an almighty explosion. Frank was blown into the air and Steve was knocked backwards about six feet. Tom could see Frank writhing in pain, holding his hand in the air with blood running down his wrist. At the same time, Steve began screaming. Tom ran towards Steve to find that Steve's right leg was missing, and his back covered in blood. Tom attempted to stop the flow of blood from Steve's amputated stump with a makeshift tourniquet applied to Steve's leg but Tom could not stem the bleeding from Steve's back.

Tom tried all that he could to save Steve but within a few minutes he died in Tom's arms. Covered in blood and with tears running down his face, Tom then set about tending to Frank. Frank was patched up then Tom immediately dispatched Frank to the medic station where his wounds were dressed, and small pieces of shrapnel removed from other appendages.

Frank spent two months in hospital being treated and getting some well-earned convalescence. Steve's body was taken back to his platoon, where preparations for his internment were made. This incident affected Tom badly from then on. Many nights Tom would wake up screaming, shouting for help.

Just after Christmas, Frank was declared fit and returned to duty. When Frank arrived back, the battalion were preparing to go back up the line. Tom greeted Frank with a smile. "Glad you're back mate, we've missed you." Frank laughed, "You can't get rid of me that quick. I've had to come back so that I could bring you some new babies to look after," Frank responded. Indeed, Frank had come back with a number of new recruits who stood looking in some amazement of the activities going on around them.

Tom looked at the new recruits realising that there was not much time to get to know the boys he would be leading into battle. Tom had learned that he, his troop and Horace's troop would be involved in attacking Monte Cassino. That night both Tom and Horace did not sleep well, they were afraid of what was to come. For a second time, Horace moved close to Tom, unseen by the other men as they huddled in their tent.

Horace asked Tom, "Do you mind if I cuddle you again?" he said sheepishly. "I have this dreadful feeling in the pit of my stomach that something bad is going to happen to me," Horace stated with a tremor.

"Ok," Tom replied. As Horace got closer to Tom, Tom could feel Horace's body tremble as if he were on a cakewalk at the fun fair. As they lay close together, Tom said, "Horace, I have something to tell you and you might not like it." Tom paused; Horace was all ears. "Horace, I'm queer," Tom blurted out without a second thought. Horace did not move, and it appeared that his trebling subsided. "I have a boyfriend called Bill. He is the love of my life. I do not understand why we are so much in love, but we are. It just happened. I need you to know because I want you to tell him about me when you get home, especially if I don't make it out of here."

Horace immediately responded by saying, "You are going to get out of this mess, and I will make sure you are safe."

Tom continued, "All you need to know; you will find in my letters from Bill. I just hope that you don't hate me?" There, Tom had said it. He had told Horace the thing he had wanted to say for so long and now it was done. Horace at first did not reply but also did not let go of Tom, remaining in his close embrace.

"I'm glad that you have told me," Horace said after a while. "I wouldn't have guessed, not in a million years. Even after what we have done together. Ordinarily I would have probably smacked you in the face and called you all sorts of vile things. I would have probably reported you and would have told everyone to make your life hell, but how could I do that to you? You are my dearest friend, my brother; whatever you are, you are still my rock and I have to say that I have loved being with you and I have also loved having our intimate times together." Tom's relief was tantamount to having Monte Cassino lifted off his shoulders.

He knew that Horace had meant every word and that his secret was safe. "Can I ask you something?" Horace asked.

"Of course, you can, anything," Tom replied.

There was a short silence then Horace asked, "Do you fancy me?" Tom laughed.

"Well, I think that you are a stunning looking bloke and I think the world of you, but you are my mate. I have enjoyed having fun with you, but I don't want you as my lover. I've already got one," was Tom's reply.

"But have you ever fancied having full sex with me?" Horace went on.

Tom thought for a moment then said, "Well we did come close to it, when we were in Bari. Do you remember?"

"Yes," Horace said. "I can't get that night out of my head. It was me who was instigating it if I remember. God I was so horny that night and I know that you were feeling horny too. I'm glad that you stopped me and that you didn't go any further that night. I don't know if I could have lived with that on my conscience; especially because I didn't know about you then, well about you being queer and all that." Tom squeezed Horace as a way of thanking him. Horace reciprocated and said, "You're one hell of a guy Tom."

"You too mate," Tom replied. Both men hugged drifting off into a restful sleep.

The following night the men moved up to their start line. Soon after the artillery opened up and Tom and Horace's men were ordered to move forward and started climbing. The terrain was rocky, making it difficult to climb. When the enemy shells and mortars started and landed, many men were injured or killed. Mainly because of shrapnel and splinters of rock which rained down on them like a hailstorm. Eventually, Tom's troops managed to reach the summit followed by Horace and his troops.

As they looked down, they could see the Gariagliano plain. No more resistance was met until they reached the river which had to be crossed. The men managed to get across with few casualties and started to dig in, in a field just over the riverbank and over a road which ran parallel to the rivers course, the men began to dig. While digging in, one of the guys hit something hard, initially thinking that it was a stone but then realised that it was a mine.

The guy shouted, "Mines stop digging," everybody froze. One of the officers then ordered everyone to fall back retracing their footsteps in an attempt to avoid any other mines that might have been planted. Happily, all of the men managed to get back on the road without any mishaps and the guy who had hit the mine had not caused it to explode.

The men pushed on, treading carefully, then were ordered to come out of the line. They made camp not too far from the front, what was termed the second line. This gave the men chance to bathe in a stream which ran close by, to relax, eat a proper meal and to write a few letters home.

Tom and Horace decided to take a swim in the river. They walked some way from the camp where they found a secluded spot, stripped off naked and took a dip. Tom was reminded of the times he and Bill had swum in Jacob's pool.

Looking at Horace, Tom was reminded of how Bill looked; how his strong muscular frame had glistened in the cool air, his manhood hanging thickly set and free. Tom, looking at Horace could do nothing but stare and admire him too. Then Horace realised how intently Tom was looking at him, not deterred, Horace arranged his stance so that he faced Tom full on, parting his legs a little; he then put his hands on his hips allowing a full view of his manhood to be visible to Tom.

In a way, Horace enjoyed Tom's voyeurism. As Tom moved to the edge of the river Horace watched as Tom got out of the water, he too looked at Tom, admiring his body and the strength of the man. Horace's face began to redden as he caught himself looking at Tom's manhood. Horace had never thought of looking at another man's private parts in a sexual sense before, but Horace was particularly appreciative of Tom's length and girth. Horace thought in his mind's eye of Tom's size when erect, and how it had felt when they had masturbated each other. After all, he had felt just how big it had become when they had cuddled together in Bari.

Horace suddenly realised that he was becoming semi-erect so turned and began to get dressed slowly. Horace's semi-erection had not been unnoticed by Tom, who was also showing signs of an erection. As Horace sat getting dressed, Tom walked over to collect his clothes. Horace reached out, grabbed Tom's now extending manhood and began stroking it. Tom was in two minds whether to pull back to stop Horace but then enjoyment took over from his logical thinking. Horace then did the unimaginable. He pulled Tom closer and took Tom's now fully swollen tool into his mouth, taking the whole shaft deep into his throat, Tom moaned with pleasure.

Still with Tom's manhood in his mouth, Horace pulled Tom down onto the floor, Tom on his knees and Horace lying on his side. Tom manoeuvred himself around placing his knees either side of Horace's head. Tom head and torso leant forward as he lay himself on top of Horace. Tom grabbed Horace's now throbbing member and reciprocated, taking Horace into his own mouth. They sucked, kissed and licked around each other's genitalia until they both climaxed; the release of pressure erupting like volcanoes.

Tom fell full onto Horace resting his head on Horace's thighs. Horace lay flat on his back, head tilted to one side to slow down his breathing. After a short while, the lads got up, went back into the river, washed again and dressed. Neither of the boys said anything to each other but it was obvious that both were satisfied. Happily, both men ambled back to camp, happy to be together and happy to be alive. Once both were back at camp, the boy's grabbed some food from the mess tent, taking it back to their own tent to eat.

They ate with gusto, fastened up their tent securely, chatted and played cards for a while before settling down for the night. That evening was different from any other evening they had spent together in that both men seemed far more relaxed, joyous in each other's company. It was clear to both men that during their card game, they had even looked at each other differently than they had ever looked at each other before; both had caught each other looking deeply at each other's facial features, each having thoughts about what it would be like to engage in more sexual play.

As they prepared for bed, both men stripped off to their underwear, something that they had done every night before. Usually, they slept with t-shirts and their underwear but tonight, both decided to sleep totally naked. Neither of the men said anything to each other, they just undressed without even thinking about the possible consequences. Horace lay down first, stretching his arm so that as Tom lay down, Horace's arm could support Tom's neck.

There was a nervous tension in the air that was not disturbing but which produced warmth and comfort.

"Can I ask you something?" Horace enquired.

"What?" Tom replied in anticipation. "When you're with Bill, what do you actually do in bed?" Horace felt uncomfortable asking Tom but was desperate to find out the intimate detail of his relationship with Bill.

"I guess it's the same as when you make love to a woman," Tom said, "the only difference is that neither of us has the same appendages as women, so we just use what we have got. I suppose I like it because it feels stronger having another man holding on to you," Tom said, thinking about Bill's strength as well as his gentleness.

"Who takes the woman's role?" Horace asked, feeling a little more uncomfortable but realising that just by asking, he was getting physically aroused.

"Ha! That is an interesting question," Tom began. "Neither of us are women, so neither of us take a woman's role." Horace seemed confused by this but allowed Tom to continue. "If you are asking who penetrates who, then that depends on how we are feeling. We both touch and fondle each other, and we both enjoy oral sex; but it was Bill who penetrated me first, if that's what you're asking." Horace was shocked by Tom's honestly and openness. It seemed that Tom was not afraid to tell Horace what he wanted to know.

"Does it hurt; being penetrated?" Horace asked.

"I guess it was a little painful at first but when the moment takes you, it's a fine line between pleasure and pain," Tom responded. "Have you ever had anal sex with your girlfriend?" Tom asked.

"Not with my last girlfriend, but the girlfriend I went out with before her let me do it once," Horace recalled.

By now, Horace and Tom's erections were so hard that they were beginning to hurt. Horace's free arm pulled Tom closer. They were now facing each other, Tom almost on top of Horace. They could now feel each other's manhood pressing against each other. Horace was so excited that small globules of seminal fluid began seeping out.

"Horace!" Tom cried. "I can't go all the way with you. I'm committed to Bill. I think the world of you and in any other circumstances I'm sure that I wouldn't have any hesitation. And another thing, I don't want to feel guilty for getting you to do things that you wouldn't normally do."

"You're right," said Horace, "but I would enjoy just getting some relief." The moment took hold as they embraced. They kissed, rubbing their bodies together and feeling each other's erections with their hands. Without knowing, they locked together, naked and hot, kissing, hugging, sweating and both climaxing without any intention, then falling exhausted in each other's arms.

Tom rolled off Horace, grabbed his underwear and wiped them both clean of their off-loaded tension.

"Thanks," Horace said. "I hope that you are, ok?"

Tom thought for a while before responding. "Yes, I'm fine thanks. I hope you are ok too. But I don't think we should be doing this anymore. I really like you, Horace, but you are my friend, my best friend in war. I still have Bill."

Horace nodded in agreement. However, this did not stop them from cuddling up next to one another, happy and content with what had happened.

All too soon, the men were back on the line taking part in more battles. The men took up positions in the ruins of the town trying to fight their way through and up the mountain that lay at the other side. As on other occasions, they got pushed back again due to the intensity of shell and mortar fire. To add to their discomfort, it seemed to rain the whole time. Attack after attack was put in.

It was clear that that the Germans were occupying the Monastery and a decision was made that the Monastery must be destroyed. The American's first bomb drop missed the target and the town was bombed instead. Finally, the second wave managed to destroy the Monastery. Seeing this beautiful building being turned into rubble was heart breaking. Hundreds of years of monastic life was gone in minutes.

The next day, another attack got Tom and Horace's troops halfway up the mountain, their men had to take shelter as the intensity of gun shots increased and mortars rained down. The men stayed sheltered until nightfall, then, under the cover of darkness, they made their way back down the hill taking with them their wounded. The following night, the men were instructed to move off the hill completely and under heavy shell fire from the artillery they once again fought their way back up to a position overlooking the Monastery. The Germans continued their attack, but the Allies managed to hold them off.

After two more days of heavy fighting, another battalion took over. The whole division to which Tom and Horace was a part was to be taken back to Naples. Tom immediately thought that his guys were going to be given a rest period but instead his men were taken directly to the harbour. After a brief rest, they were boarding landing craft. Tom's men were being taken north to make a landing at Anzioin in an attempt to cut off the supply route to Monte Cassino.

Two days later Tom's troops set off in convoy from their last position, they were landing on the Anzio beaches. Luckily, they were not met with opposition and pushed on. After several miles they were halted and told to dig in once again to form a defence position. Their instruction was to stop and wait for the supply group to catch up, leaving the Germans time to organise and launch a heavy attack. The American forces who were also there took most of the assault. After two weeks of heavy fighting, the Allies were nearly pushed back to the beaches but managed to break out and pushed on to the out skirts of Rome. The British were then halted, not being allowed to push into Rome before the Americans. To the British, this move enabled the Americans to get full credit of liberating Rome.

Tom and his troops managed to get a few days rest in Rome before they we told that they were being redeployed to Egypt. For Tom, the two days in Rome were unforgettable. The vast majority of Italians in Rome were relieved that Mussolini was no longer in charge and even greater relieved that the Germans had now gone. This allowed the Italians to show their gratitude to the Allies, who were keen to take any allied troop into their homes. Tom was happy to wonder the streets of Rome taking in the sights and history of this great city. The tranquillity Tom took from his wanderings allowed him to mentally recuperate after all that he had gone through. Tom felt rested and at peace for a short while.

Tom's division were transported to Taranto before being boarded on troop ships and then setting sail for Port Said. Arriving in Egypt the men were then to be taken by train to Cairo then by lorry to a camp in Beni Usif. Beni Usif was located about four miles from Cairo and within walking distance of the Pyramids in Giza. During Tom's time at Beni Usif, Roosevelt, Churchill and Stalin held a conference in a hotel near to their camp and Tom's group was detached to provide security. Reinforcements also started to arrive and within a couple of weeks, they were back to normal strength.

During the time Tom spent in Beni Usif, Tom took several days leave in Cairo. Apart from looking around places of interest and exploring different areas, Tom also became aware of just how many British soldiers were being accompanied by younger Egyptian men. Tom wondered just how many of those men were having sexual relationships with their 'boys', as they were referred to.

Many of the men were able to rent rooms rather than staying in hotels. This suited the men as it was cheaper and provided more privacy. Tom managed to rent a two bedded apartment that had a substantially large living room and kitchen facilities, albeit basic. The apartment lacked windows muffling the noise from the street as a result; the only real noise coming from the mosques when prayers were called. Tom was amused when the songs of prayer were shouted out from the minarets. The sound not being unpleasant but did happen five times per day as the muezzin called the faithful.

The apartment Tom found was owned by a guy called Abasi. Abasi had been sitting outside the apartments he owned and had seen Tom walking alone. Abasi was quick to take the opportunity to gain Tom's attention, encouraging Tom to rent rooms from him. Abasi was a pleasant man and had a son Ammon. Abasi ordered his son to take care of Tom. Ammon, who was about 18 years old, was a handsome young man, smooth-skinned, had a full head of jet black tight curled hair and beautiful straight white teeth, which seemed to sparkle when he smiled. Ammon's eyes appeared to glisten as he smiled.

Ammon could not do enough for Tom, showing him the apartment with pride. Once the agreement had been made with Abasi, Ammon became Tom's batman, errand runner, cleaner and all-round maid.

Ammon shopped, cleaned, and cooked for Tom, made his bed and ran any errands Tom wanted. Tom realised very quickly that Ammon would be hard to avoid. In fact, to Tom's surprise, Ammon moved into Tom's apartment with him. Ammon hardly left Tom's side. At night, Ammon went into the second bedroom to sleep but during the night, he would make his way to Tom's room, sliding in bed next to Tom without invitation. The first two nights Tom did not detect Ammon getting into his bed and as Ammon awoke earlier than Tom to attend prayers and make breakfast, Tom had no idea that Ammon had even been there.

It was not until the third day that Tom recognised Ammon's bed had not been slept in and that the bed had remained exactly as it had been the night before. Tom was curious and asked Ammon where he had slept. Ammon without any hesitation and smiling, replied, "With you, Sayyid. You are very nice to sleep with you, Sayyid." Ammon went on in broken English.

Tom looked astonished. He was more astounded because had been sleeping naked due to the temperature of the night air and had only been covered by a thin cotton sheet. It was even more shocking to hear Ammon say, "Sayyid has nice body, nice ass and big qadib."

Confused, Tom asked Ammon, "What is qadib?"

Ammon smiled saying, "Qadib, qadib," while pointing down towards his own penis.

Tom's jaw dropped finding it difficult to say anything, then he asked, "Do you also sleep without clothes?"

"Oh yes Sayyid, very nice feeling. Ammon likes being without clothes when sleeping with Sayyid," Ammon replied. "Sayyid's qadib is very big when sleeping. It is very nice. Sayyid also has lovely ass."

Tom was dumbfounded. Here he had been thinking that he was safe and alone, when all along, this young Egyptian boy had taken advantage of him exploring his body whilst he slept. Tom then began to smile, thinking, *The audacity. Cheeky fucker!* Tom began smiling, which quickly turned to laughter and Ammon laughed along with Tom. Clearly, Ammon was unaware of what Tom was laughing about but felt it right to laugh along with Tom to keep him happy.

That night, after Tom went to bed, he fought hard to stay awake. Lying motionless Tom heard Ammon creep into his room; then Tom heard the sound of Ammon's sandals being flicked off his feet; then the sound of sliding as Ammon removed his thawb (the long robe frequently worn by Arab men). Tom knew that underneath the thawb, Ammon was naked, as most Egyptian men were. Ammon then slid into bed behind Tom, who still lay still, pretending to be asleep. Ammon curled up close behind Tom getting his knees to interlock with the back of Tom's.

Ammon placed his arm around Tom pulling himself close to Tom so that the whole of Ammon's front was touching Tom's back. Ammon manoeuvred his semi-erect penis so that it fitted neatly between Tom's inner legs and close to Tom's arse. Snuggling down, Ammon's hand moved down Tom's chest and stomach until he reached Tom's hard erection. Ammon grabbed Tom's manhood clenching his fingers around Tom's shaft so that the whole of Tom's member was enfolded into Ammon's palm. Ammon moved his hand gently, rubbing Tom slowly. Ammon's now fully erect penis touched the underneath of Tom's scrotum moving Tom's balls forward.

Once comfortable, Ammon stopped, kissed Tom on the back of his neck and slept. Tom's breathing had become short and fast but still he did not move. Tom found it difficult to sleep feeling horny but did nothing to advance his desire. Ammon was soon soundly asleep, and Tom knew that Ammon was content just being next to Tom. It would have been easy for Tom to engage in sexual activities with Ammon, but it did not feel right to take advantage of Ammon, particularly as it had been at Ammon's father's behest that Ammon was staying with him.

Tom thought to himself that this had not been Ammon's first experience of being in bed with a man and began to reflect on Ammon's behaviour during the days previous. Clearly, Ammon had indulged in full sex with a man before and Tom knew in his own mind that Ammon would have been happy to be the recipient of anal activity. Two more nights were spent with Ammon. However, it was Tom, who assumed the position behind Ammon in bed, replicating how Ammon had settled that third night. Ammon appear content as was Tom. No sexual activities took place, but each knew that there was a special bond between them. Leaving the apartment following Tom's leave was more difficult than Tom had imagined but he did promise that should he get more leave; he would be more than happy to stay with Ammon.

The road back to camp followed along the Nile, where alligators and other exotic wildlife could be seen along its banks. Tom had loved being in Cairo and wanted to return. Not because of Ammon, but because he had found solace in Cairo from the troubles of war. Tom managed to write a few letters to Bill and to his parents. Tom told Bill about his sexual contact with Horace, begging Bill to forgive him. Tom also told Bill about his stay in Cairo and about Ammon. He also spoke of Egypt and how he would have liked Bill to have been with him.

Bill's response was one of forgiveness, knowing that things like Tom had experienced could possibly happen and was please that Tom had been truthful and honest with him. Bill also told Tom about his close encounters too. It seemed that jealousy between the two would not break the bond that they had.

All too soon, Tom was to be moved again, going back to Port Said. It was while Tom was in Port Said that he received a letter from Bill telling him that the invasion of Normandy was about to commence, and that Bill would be amongst the many who would be fighting the Germans for the liberation of France. Tom knew the dangers Bill would be facing but had peace of mind that Bill had already had experience of heavy fighting and knew that Bill would be as careful as he could. However, Tom was still concerned. This push on France had to work and in Tom's heart, he knew what this meant, if successful, the invasion of France would be the start of Germany's decline and demise, and the end of the war.

# Chapter Seventeen
# France

Bill and his men were now part of the 50th Division, whose objectives were to cut through the Caen-Bayeux highway, then to take the small port of Arromanches, before linking up with the Americans from Omaha Beach to the west at Port-en-Bessin. The plan was to link up with the Canadians who had landed on Juno Beach to the east. The 50th Division were also ordered to take the Longues battery from the rear. La Rivière had already been taken by the British, as had Le Hamel by mid-afternoon.

The speed at which the British had moved pleased Bill. He was proud of what they had achieved so far. Adrenalin had kept Bill focused. He had taken orders, related them to his men and had maintained momentum. Bill's troops had followed him to the letter trusting him implicitly. Bill knew that in order to keep his men safe, he had to show true grit. Any sign of weakness would be picked up by his men and Bill knew that it was possible that the chaos might trickle through the ranks. Bill, although scared, remained focused. Bill was informed by his Commanding Officer that 47 Commando had already passed south of Arromanches and Longues and were pushing west. They were now within a kilometre of Port-en-Bessin.

The good news was that the guns at Longues were now not in action thanks to the efforts of the cruiser HMS Ajax, which had fought and won an outstanding duel with the German artillery. This news allowed for some relief, as Bill knew that had the guns not been obliterated, he was sure that many of his troop might not have survived. By the end of the day, the 50th Division had managed to land 25,000 men, had penetrated 6 miles inland and had managed to hook up with the Canadians from Juno Beach. They reached the heights above Port-en-Bessin but had not been able to cut the Caen-Bayeux highway as planned, nor had they been able to link up with the Americans from Omaha Beach. This impressive start was exhausting, and Bill was glad to be able to report than since landing, his troop losses had been low.

Still, Bill felt inner pain for the men he had lost. John had remained at his side and had fought well. John looked completely done in and Bill suggested that he should rest. Bill could see the fear in John's eyes and as he looked at the rest of his men, they all appeared to have the same expression but still willing to follow Bill's orders. The following day, the 50th Division now occupied Bayeux advancing 3 miles south. Bill, along with his men joined a column from the division and began to move south over the Caen-Bayeux railway into the Bocage, advancing towards the bridges between Tilly and Saint-Pierre.

When they arrived at the bridges, they were joined by the 8th Durham Light Infantry. The advancement made by the 50th Division had been so successful that this has resulted in placing the division in a salient facing the Panzar Lehr Division and the SS Hitlerjugend Division. A salient, which the men knew as a 'bulge', is a battlefield feature that projects into enemy territory. The Division was surrounded by the enemy on multiple sides with troops located within, occupying the salient.

This move by the division had now placed them in a vulnerable position. The column still moved forward and was able to capture Saint-Pierre. Bill's men engaged in much close-quarter fighting to achieve their goal. Several of Bill's men had been injured; some being inflicted with shrapnel wounds from mortar fire, some receiving bullet wounds, and some bayoneted because of the closeness of the fighting.

Bill had to kill three Germans in close order fighting, each being run through with Bill's bayonet. At the time, Bill had no thought for his opponents, realising that if he had not killed these men, he would have been the one to be killed. There was little time to rest or take stock as the men moved forward and moved as one.

After two days, the Germans counter attacked. Bill realised that they were surrounded. This counterattack blunted their advance to Villers-Bocage and the 69th Brigade attack on Cristot. The division fought forward to hold a line between La Belle Epine and a point to the north-east of Saint Pierre. Fighting became more ferocious, the men had to fight like crazy, going into farm buildings with fixed bayonets, fighting face to face with the enemy. Casualties were so heavy that two composite companies of the Durham's had to be formed from the whole battalion.

By sheer determination and grit, Verrières was captured but Bill had lost several of his men. Only when Bill had time to rest did he think about his opponents and the lives that had been lost on both sides. In darkness, Bill would breakdown. Bill had the strength of character to overcome his grief and feelings of horror before the light of morning resulted in him taking charge of himself and of his men.

On 16 June, the 69th had advanced against stiff resistance to Longrave, about halfway to their goal; a road to the south and on 18th June the division finally took Tilly. By 19th June, the division, and the equally exhausted Panzer Lehr settled into a lull allowing for some respite. Near to the Tilly Bridge lay a small hamlet; this had been taken through hand-to-hand combat. Bill gathered up his troops together and hurried them back to the hamlet. There, they found an old cottage standing alone with a small brook running through a field to the left.

Bill told his troops to make camp in the empty cottage, allocating some of the men to clean up inside. There were several dead German soldiers still in the cottage and the men removed their corpses outside, laying them to the rear of a small barn. Outside, the apparent occupants, an older man and a woman lay dead in the field near to the stream. Bill had a couple of his men dig graves in the field where the old couple lay. The other men who had removed the dead Germans dug a pit at the rear of the barn for their remains. Bill saw that care was taken by his men in digging and lying to rest the assumed occupants.

Bill took charge to ensure that the owners of the farm were carefully covered; their bodies wrapped in blankets which had been found in the cottage and after the burial, the graves turfed once they had finished. They also made crosses to mark where the graves stood; Bill and his men standing in silence for a short time honouring their dead. The German soldier's bodies were not given the same respect. Once the hole was dug, the three bodies were un-ceremonially thrown into the pit and covered with the dirt that had been excavated. The only marker for them was one of the Germans metal helmets which was kicked onto the side of the mound. No prayers for them, and no honouring of their lives.

Inside the cottage, the rest of the men had moved broken furniture, piling up the broken wood next to the fire. A fire had been lit and several pots of water had been placed on and around the fire ready for hot drinks to be made and for food to be prepared. The men found potatoes, onions, carrots, and turnips in the barn across the yard. John had taken it upon himself to begin making a vegetable stew.

As John prepared the meal, several shots were heard from outside. At first, there was general panic as the men dived for their guns in readiness.

Then Bill's voice was heard. "Don't panic, lads," he reassured them. "It's only Mick, he's just potted us a couple of rabbits."

"Fucking idiot," said a voice from inside the cottage. "Scared the shit out of me."

John looked from where the voice had come from and said, "Well, at least you're going to have fresh meat with your dinner." Mick walked into the cottage smiling and holding up two plump Coneys. Mick looked as if he had won a gold medal from the Olympics as he presented his catch to John. Another guy took out his bayonet, grabbed the still warm rabbits from John, went outside and began skilfully skinning and dressing the evenings fare. Skinned, gutted, and portioned, along with the edible offal was presented to John, who proceeded to add the meat to his now simmering stew.

John had found salt and ground black pepper in a small cupboard located in the cottage and had seasoned the stew to perfection. When some of the men who had been working outside returned to the cottage, they also brought with them a handful of fresh thyme which they found growing in a small vegetable patch. This was also added to the now cooked potage.

While dinner was still cooking, all the men found spaces to bed down. Bill decided that he would use the barn, allowing his men to have time without him and for him to collect his thoughts. Bill had already set up a bed for himself using straw to soften the area. He had also built a small fire using stones as a hearth. In the barn, Bill found an old tin bath and decided that he would try to relax in this bath before getting some rest. He collected water from the brook, boiled water in two exceptionally large iron pots and prepared for his quiet time. *This was to be the best bath of his entire life,* he thought. Alone, undisturbed and with just the fire light casting shadows around the barn.

After preparing his bath, Bill undressed and got into the bath. Bill lay in the warm water thinking of Tom. His mind drifting back to when they had first met; of their runs together, their time swimming in Jacob's pool and of the Christmas they had spent together and of their time with Phil and Amos. So much had happened since that first meeting. Bill thought how much Tom meant to him, realising that the love he had for Tom was increasing day by day. Even with all of the chaos that had been around since the start of this darned war had started, the only constant thing in his life was Tom.

As Bill and his troop relaxed around the cottage, the 2nd Essex, along with the 6th Devonshire Light Infantry, supported with tanks from the 24th Lancers and the, the 2nd Essex regiment, preceded on in a rolling barrage. On 19 June, two attempts were made to take Hottot, 1-mile south Tilly by the 231st Brigade and then by the 2nd Devon's. Both attempts failed, being forced out of the ruined village by German armour. The division was now arranged with 231st Brigade north of Hottot, 151st Brigade around Tilly and the 69th Brigade south of La Belle Epine. This stalemate still required patrolling and it was left to Bill and his men to identify danger areas and report back. There was sniper fire and mortar fire exchanged from both sides.

One of the main sources of discomfort was the large number of dead cattle lying around which resulted in an overwhelming stench. Any attempt to remove the offending beasts attracted more German fire. In many ways, Bill and his troops had learned the hard way about how to avoid enemy detection. They, like their counterparts becoming more attuned to the possibilities of becoming exposed. The next major attack took place on 11th July. The Devon's and Hampshire's both reached Hottot with help of the Cheshire's but were counter-attacked by Panzer's and Panther's. They were also accidentally rocketed by Typhoons from the British side, being forced to retire as night fell. The Hampshire's alone had 120 casualties, including forty-three dead. However, on 18th July, the Panzer Lehr abandoned Hottot after suffering huge losses. By August, the 50th Division advanced towards Villers-Bocage with the 43rd Division and the 59th Division. Later that month, the division was taken out of the line for the first time since D-Day and given three days' rest.

The 50th Division performed well during the Normandy campaign, not suffering the initial problems of the two other divisions. Many veterans were now running out of energy and in some ways courage. Bill's men along with others from his division had fought in six major attacks without being fully hit by the Germans, but many knew that the odds of surviving another six would be particularly slim; however, they pushed forward towards Paris and to its liberation. The division passed through the Falaise Pocket and Argenten mopping up bypassed Germans. Small actions were fought at Picquigny and Oudenarde.

By the end of August, the allies crossed the Seine and entered Brussels taking part in the ceremonial liberation parades. The three-day rest period coupled with more time given as a result of Brussels being taken allowed Bill and his men to fully take stock. Not only did they rest and recuperate but this time also allowed the men to reaffirm their friendships with one another. Bill used this time to try to build up morale focusing on the positive moves they had made against the Germans rather than pondering of the losses that they had incurred, or on the horrific scenes they had witnessed.

Some of the men found it particularly difficult to face the fact that they had killed other humans but also realised that without taking this action, they and their friends could have been the one's that would have been either buried or left lying to rot on grounds that was not their homeland. Bill took time to write to Tom, who he was missing dreadfully. In Bill's letters, he only provided Tom with the advancements they had made and to point out that his only goal was to ensure that he and Tom would be together soon. Bill realised that Tom must also be going through similar difficulties but in another theatre in another part of Europe. Bill wanted so much for Tom to keep safe and for him to keep his spirits high. Bill was keen to tell Tom just how much his letters had kept him going and how, by reading Tom's letters over and over, he felt that Tom was close to him.

It was during this time that John, who had always made sure that he slept close to Bill, made his advances. Bill allowed John the opportunity to fondle him and Bill reciprocated. They engaged in rigorous foreplay but halted at Bill's bequest to fall short of full penetrative sex, although John was ready for Bill and Bill ready to provide what John wanted. After, they both agreed that this was the last time would push for sexual favours. Bill realising that sex with John was not like it was with Tom and John realising that any further advancements would not result in what John really wanted, a full relationship with Bill.

The Division was soon to move off again forcing a crossing across the Albert Canal, then being given the task to force their attack towards Geel. As the brigade advanced towards Geel they faced resistance. The men were forced to expel the Germans by house-to-house fighting. As the action progressed, and because of continued counter attacks, the unit was forced to hold back for a while. By the 12th of September, an order was being prepared for the 50th to withdraw from the Geel bridgehead. However, the German's fled, leaving the Division to enter Geel unopposed. The American infantry, British tanks, and artillery, working in unison were now able to drive the enemy back. The Germans suffered heavy losses, and this allowed the brigade to re-join action pushing on towards Nijmegen. There, the Division took over from the Yanks.

As they crossed one bridge, they were met with a dreadful sight. Many dead American paratroopers were laid out. The men were ordered to dig in on both sides of the river and held their position for a number of days. Frogmen were called in to enter the river to blow the bridge but were spotted by the Germans. As Bill and his men sat in their trench, they witnessed those brave divers being potted off one by one by sniper fire. The situation worsened because of supply vehicles being held back, resulting in Bill and his men having to rely on eating captured German rations. These rations were not the best by any stretch of the imagination, as much of the food they had captured was rancid.

The 50th Division was now tasked to keep the road open between Uden and Veghel. Here, along with Americans, they fought for the next two days. Bill found himself working closely with an American G.I. from New York, Dwight Houser. Dwight, who was also a sergeant, admired Bill; having found that Bill had also been involved in action in North Africa. One evening, as they rested, some of Bill's letters from Tom fell out of his bag as he searched for rations.

Dwight saw the letters fall and clambered to retrieve them for Bill. Sharp-eyed, Dwight recognised that these were love letters and had been signed by 'T.' Later Dwight asked Bill if 'T' was his wife or girlfriend. Bill, without thinking said, "No, 'T' is my boyfriend." In that split second, Bill realised what he had said and tried desperately in a light-hearted manner, to hide his mistake. "Only kidding," Bill said, laughing nervously.

"Each to their own," replied Dwight. It was at this point that Bill felt both angry and sorrowful at the same time. Why is it that he could not just be honest about his love for Tom? Other men openly and regularly professed their love for their girlfriends and wives back home, but he always had to keep his love concealed. The injustice of it all fell heavily on Bill's heart. His love for Tom was as great as the other men's love, if not deeper. From that point on, Bill decided that if anyone else should ask about 'T', he was going to be totally honest.

The next day, seventy tanks and the equivalent of an infantry division attacked the brigade. The 124th Field Regiment and 'B' Company of 2nd Cheshire's who had led the attack were now relieved by the rest of the 50th which continued the attack around Haalderen. The division was given the task to guard the bridgehead and for two months static warfare became the norm. Troops were now being rotated regularly, resulting in frequent bouts of leave being given. Since D-Day the 50th Division had suffered losses of 488 officers and 6,932 men.

In November, Montgomery made a speech to the division informing them that the 50th Division would be returning to England as a training division. Veterans who had served three and a half years or more overseas would be repatriated to Britain under the Python scheme or given generous leave. Three other categories of men were also drawn up. Those most recent infantry reinforcements were to be posted to other rifle battalions, whilst men requiring retraining could perform garrison duties. And so it was, and to Bill's relief, he, and the remains of the division returned to Britain in time for Christmas.

# Chapter Eighteen
# Leave and Reunion

Tom had received letters regularly from Bill, who had informed him of the pending Normandy landings. Tom worried about Bill, knowing that the invasion would not be a walk in the park and that there was potential for heavy losses. Tom, who was not religious, found himself praying constantly for Bill's safety. He himself had gone through so much and he also knew Bill had experienced similar things too.

Now, Bill would be facing even worse troubles ahead. It was difficult for Tom because not only was he worried for Bill; he too would be facing new difficulties in a strange and different world. The one redeeming feature that Tom had, was the fact that Bill had already told him about North Africa and at least Tom had some insight into what life would be like there. Tom's experiences in Egypt had not been as bad as he had first thought and in meeting Ammon, Tom had at least gained some comfort.

To Tom's delight, in the autumn of 1944, he was informed that he too would be going back to England. He was to be given extended leave. In many ways, Tom was glad to be going home, but before returning to England he wanted desperately to meet up, just one more time, with Ammon and his father before his departure.

Tom decided to travel to Cairo and take his chances in finding Abasi sitting outside his apartments and to see if he could rent the same rooms again. This time, he asked Horace to join him. Horace did not have to be asked twice. How great it would be to spend time with his friend and be away from army restraints. Horace jumped at the chance of getting away from camp and to explore Cairo with Tom. The train journey from Port Said to Cairo was quite pleasant. Both men were excited to be taking a well-earned rest.

Egyptian trains were well maintained and well looked after and Horace was particularly surprised by this, relaxing and taking in the views as they travelled. How different Egypt was to Italy and England. When Tom and Horace eventually arrived in Cairo, they soon made their way to the area to where the apartments were and where Abasi had first met Tom. Many of the locals tried to stop Tom and Horace along the way, in an attempt to sell them something or to get then to rent rooms, however, Tom was able to move them off and lead Horace through the crowded streets towards their destination. As they turned the corner onto the street where the apartment was located, Tom could see Abasi sitting outside, as he had been the first time Tom had been there.

On seeing Tom, Abasi jumped to his feel and ran towards him and Horace. "My friend, my friend, you have come back," Abasi shouted with enthusiasm.

"Yes, my friend," replied Tom. "Do you have any rooms?" Tom asked hopefully.

"Always for you, my friend; I have rooms but if I did not have them, I will find rooms for you, my friend. I have same apartment as you had before. You liked this apartment?" Abasi asked in broken English.

"Yes, I liked it very much. That is great news," Tom said. "This is my friend Horace," Tom stated, introducing Horace to Abasi. Abasi smiled at Horace, then grabbed Tom giving him a welcoming hug. Abasi then turned to Horace, kissing him on both cheeks before kissing him full on the mouth.

Horace was a little taken aback with Abasi's over familiarity. "Horus!" Abasi shouted, "Horus, the Egyptian god. Your eye is the sun and the morning star and your other eye is the moon and evening star. You are power, my friend. Welcome Horus."

Horace looked at Tom in wonderment and laughed. Tom too began laughing, telling Horace that he would explain later. "You come; I will take you upstairs to your apartment. Everything is ready." Abasi remarked as he began pushing the two men through the outer door and onto the staircase. "I will send Ammon; he will be pleased that you are here. Ammon will take care of you. Ammon enjoys taking care of his friend Tom from England."

"Thank you," Tom said smiling. Horace nodded, recognising that Ammon was the name of the boy who had looked after Tom during his first visit. Tom had told Horace about Ammon but had spared him the details of sharing his bed with him.

The men entered the apartment dropping their bags in the lounge and both dropped into the armchairs as if they had just completed a fifty-mile hike. Abasi ran out of the room muttering something in Arabic returning within minutes with water, coffee and sugar. Abasi went to the small gas burner that was in the kitchen area and placed a small metallic vessel on the gas. He poured water into the vessel before disappearing again. It took about five minutes for the water to boil. Before Tom had chance to make the coffee, Abasi had returned with Ammon.

Ammon ran towards Tom, kissing him and hugging him. "My friend Tom, my friend Tom, my life has been emptied without you. You have returned to me my friend and you have brought with you another like my friend Tom," Ammon shouted. Both Tom and Horace were shocked at Ammon's statement and the way he had greeted his old friend. After all, they were British and rather conservative, and here they were, being showered with hugs and kisses from a young Egyptian boy who was ecstatic, showing his love for the men freely.

Tom returned Ammon's hugs then introduced Ammon to Horace. "My lovely handsome friend Horus; I am gifted to be with you. You are very handsome. I am pleased that you have come with my Tom. We will make happy times together" Ammon grabbed Horace, hugging and kissing him in the same fashion that he had greeted Tom.

"Fucking hell!" Horace said quietly, looking at Tom for reassurance.

Tom burst out laughing, "It's not what you think mate, Abasi and Ammon are always like this. In fact, all of their friends greet you in this way."

"I bloody hope not," Horace said smiling nervously at Abasi and Ammon.

The lads had their coffee and chatted with Abasi and Ammon before Abasi looked at Ammon. Abasi then said something sternly to Ammon in Arabic before Ammon replied in his native language. Ammon then bowed his head to Abasi as if his father were deity. Abasi stood up saying that he was leaving, and that Ammon would take diligent care of both of them.

Ammon took the boys' bags into their respective bedrooms then returned to make them more coffee, by which time Horace stated that he was tired and went to bed. Tom and Ammon stayed chatting for a little while longer before Tom also retired. Ammon washed the glasses used for the coffee, tided up the living room then joined Tom in his bed. Tom was by this time fast asleep. Ammon climbed naked behind Tom, snuggling up as he had done before, locked into

Tom placing his arm over Tom as if he were there to keep Tom safe from predators.

Lucky enough, Tom woke before Horace and suggested to Ammon that he should go into the living room to sleep on the couch. Ammon smiled, grabbed a blanket from inside the wardrobe, making his way to the living room. Tom remained in bed until he heard Horace get up and heard him chatting to Ammon. Tom heard Ammon ask Horace if he had been safe in bed and that the bed was to Horace's liking.

"Yes, thank you," Horace had replied, sounding confused.

"Don't worry my friend; Ammon will make sure that you are safe and that your bed is fitting." After dressing, Ammon left the apartment returning with bread, cheese, and olives. Ammon set the food on an old newspaper which he lay on the flood inviting the men to join him to eat. The guys smiled as they looked at Ammon. Ammon clearly thought that he had provided them well with breakfast and that his service was by far the best the boys had ever had.

After washing and cleaning up, Ammon took the boys sightseeing. He took them to a Bazaar situated close to their apartment, where the guys were hassled. Ammon started shouting at the sellers in quite an aggressive manner making Tom and Horace think that they might end up fighting, but the arguing ended as abruptly as it had started and the three moved on. As they progressed through the Bazaar, the hassling and arguing continued. It seemed to Horace and Tom that this way of communicating within the Bazaar was just a matter of course, which the men found amusing. After buying food for lunch from a street seller, the boys made their way back to their apartment for a siesta. The heat during in the middle of the day felt far more oppressive in Cairo than it had done at camp and was draining.

Back in the apartment, Horace quickly stripped off removing his sweat-drenched shirt and shorts, took a quick shower and headed for bed. Tom did the same then headed to his own bed. Tom lay in bed expecting Ammon to join him, but Ammon did not appear. After about an hour, Tom got up to use the toilet. Passing Horace's room, he noticed that the bedroom door was ajar. Looking through the crack in the doorway, and to his surprise, there was Horace and Ammon, locked together, Horace on top of Ammon banging away like there was no tomorrow.

Shocked at first, Tom stepped away from the door, used the bathroom and went back to bed. Tom's mind was spinning. "Well, who would have thought that would happen?" Tom said to himself laughing. After their siesta, Horace and Ammon returned into the living room. Tom walked in smiling; Horace was quiet but somehow looked content; Ammon had a look of self-gratification on his face as he wondered around doing chores and singing some Arabic song of happiness. Horace never told Tom of his escaped with Ammon and Tom chose never to raise the subject with him.

For the next few days, the boys enjoyed their stay in Cairo before returning to camp. However, when it came to sleeping arrangements, Ammon would wait until both men were in bed, would spend time making love with Horace, who was apparently enjoying the experience, then when Horace fell asleep, Ammon would join Tom in his bed. Tom did not mind this at all, in fact, Tom was surprised with himself for not having any jealousy. *Why should I?* he thought to himself. *Ammon is just a lovely friend.*

Tom was happy for both Ammon and Horace. At least, they had enjoyed their time together. When Tom awoke on the last morning of their stay, Ammon was already awake, lying next to Tom, looking at his face. Ammon appeared to be crying. "Whatever is the matter?" Tom asked.

"Sayyid, you are leaving today, and I may never see you again." Ammon sniffed. "You will go away and forget Ammon."

"I will never forget you, my friend. You have always been so kind to me," Tom stated.

"Sayyid is not angry with Ammon for having love with Horus?"

Tom smiled at Ammon, touching his face, "No, I am not angry with you at all. In fact, I am pleased that you and Horus have enjoyed time together," Tom said comforting Ammon. "You are my friend, and I am happy that you and Horus enjoyed being together," Tom stated.

Ammon looked at Tom and said, "You are my love, Sayyid; Horus is nice man to have the sex. He is strong and enjoys with Ammon very much, but I do not love this Horace as I love my friend Tom."

Tom reassured Ammon, "I love you too, my friend, and I am happy that you and I are just friends. That is the way it should be. Our friendship will always remain strong" Tom hugged Ammon, kissing him gently. "Come on now, time to make a move."

Tom and Ammon washed then dressed before waking Horace. They ate breakfast together, packed their bags and began to bid a last farewell to Ammon. Ammon's father arrived just as they were leaving, happy in the fact that his

British guests had honoured him by staying in his apartment. Tom paid Abasi the money he owed and both Horace and Tom gifted Ammon some money as a thank you.

The journey back to camp went quietly. Horace was lost in thought and Tom chose not to engage in petty conversation. Tom could see that Horace was trying to process what had happed in Cairo. Tom thought Horace must be experiencing mixed feelings of confusion, guilt, enjoyment, and happiness all at the same time; similar conflicting feelings that he had gone through when he had first stayed with Bill and after their first night of passion.

Back at camp, life returned to the mundane until it was finally time to pack up and return to Blighty. Excitement had been building up for days and now the time had come to put behind all the troubles of war, at least for the time being. The troop ship carrying the men home was a welcoming sight as they boarded and the journey through the Mediterranean uneventful. As they passed through the Bay of Biscay, the seas became rough. Thoughts of home became more intense as the weather turned from warm and sunny to dark and inclement. *Typical British weather,* Tom thought.

On landing in Southampton, the men were greeted by the W.R.V.S who presented the men with hot tea and biscuits. From the dock side, the men mustered in a large warehouse where they were issued with money and a travel warrant, then transported to the railway station. Many of the men bid farewell to the men they had been fighting with when they reached the station while others waited to say their goodbyes when on the train. Tom and Horace chose the latter.

On arriving in the Midlands, Tom hugged Horace as the train pulled into Birmingham station. Tom's emotions were high, wanting to get his connection to home. Horace was filled with happiness too, along with feelings tinged of sadness. "Thank you," said Horace; and without saying another word, Tom understood that this 'thank you' was in recognition of Tom's loyalty and the fact that Tom had remained silent about their time in Cairo. Horace had been aware that Tom had seen him and Ammon together or had at least heard noises as he and Ammon engaged in their full-on intimacy. Horace was just grateful that Tom had not questioned him. Tom alighted from the train watching and waving as the train moved off towards its next destination. At about the same time, Tom was boarding his link to home, Bill was also boarding his ship to return home.

On Tom's arrival at his home station, he was greeted by his and Bill's parents. Tears flowed, kisses were plentiful and hugs abundant. On the bus home,

Tom chatted away with his and Bill's parents. Tom's parents were insistent in telling Tom all that had been happening at home. They went on about the food shortages and the bombing and about how everyone was working endless hours to produce all sorts of stuff in support of the war.

Tom's mother went on and on about how women had taken up the role of men and how many of the women were now becoming more independent. She gave great detail of the bombing of the munitions factory and of their lucky escape and of those who had lost their lives. Tom chose not to say anything about his experiences of Italy and of North Africa apart from the geographical sights that he had seen, the climate and of the many friends he had made along the way. Tom was also happy when the conversation focused on Bill and his impending return. With luck, Bill would be home in another two to three days.

Before going home, all four called at Bill's parents' home. They too were overjoyed at the news that Bill would also be coming home. The relief for all four parents was tangible. Both boys were returning; both boys were alive; both boys physically unscathed. However, Bill and Tom's fathers were mindful of the mental scars that both of their boys would be enduring, both being aware not to push for details of what Tom had been through.

Two days later, Bill and Tom's parents along with Tom all waited at the railway station for Bill to arrive. They were all elated as Bill stepped off the train. As Bill was being showered with hugs and kisses from the four older members, all Bill could do was look intently at Tom. Tom in return looked directly at Bill. Both wanted so much to kiss and embrace Tom but knew that this would not be good to do out in the open.

When Bill eventually got away from his and Tom's parents, he walked directly to Tom, shook his hand, gave him a manly hug and whispered, "I love you, Tom. I have missed you so much."

Tom reciprocated, "I love you too."

Once off the bus, the boys walked together, a little behind their parents. They tried to catch up with news about what they had gone through but found it difficult to talk with so many people about. All that they wanted was to have time alone, but this was not going to happen, at least not for the time being. Tom's mother turned beaming; she looked at the boys and said, "Party tonight. We're all off down the Swan. It is a welcome home party for both of you."

Home at last, Tom joined Bill, helping him unpack. Alone together for a brief time, Bill and Tom were able to greet each other in the way that they wanted.

They hugged and kissed passionately, promising themselves to each other again and reaffirming their love for one another. It also felt good to be back in civilian clothes and to enjoy familiar surroundings. Bill's mother had cooked a special meal for the boys. Joe and George had killed one of the pigs a few days earlier which they had helped produce. Joan had roasted a leg joint and had prepared vegetables of roast potatoes, parsnips and carrots and cabbage from the garden, along with all the trimmings, including crackling and stuffing.

Tom's parents had also been invited to join them and the boys; both families celebrated together. It was an intimate meal for all six. Tom's mother had made a rhubarb crumble, which they had with custard. It was a feast for sore eyes. After dinner, Bill and Tom's mothers set about clearing up before they all headed to the Swan.

The welcoming party filled the pub. People were outside waiting for the boys to arrive. Bunting was strewn around the outside of the building and cheers erupted as the boys walked up the street. The party did not allow the boys to have much time together as everyone wanted to offer their congratulations individually. Halfway through the evening, Bill managed to grab Tom for a second and said, "You up for a run tomorrow?"

"Absolutely," Tom replied with a smile and a wink. The party went on for several more hours. It seemed that by the end of the night, everyone was either drunk or well on the way to becoming drunk. It certainly had been a night to remember.

The next morning, and still feeling hung over, the boys prepared for their first run together since the start of the war. For both, it felt that time had stood still. Before leaving the house, the postman delivered a letter for Bill. The letter, which looked official, but was not army related, was quickly opened. Bill read the contents. The letter was from a London solicitor who had requested Bill to attend his chambers three days hence. The letter stated that he had important news that would greatly benefit Bill and that until their meeting could not provide further details.

Tom also received the same letter. When the boys met, they were both intrigued and wondered what it was all about. Tom said, "We had better make arrangements to go down to London. We might as well stay for a couple of days rather than travelling down and returning the same day."

Bill agreed and before their run, they both informed their parents that they had to go to London for a few days on business but would be returning. Bill and

Tom's parents were intrigued as to why the boys had to leave so soon, wondering what the letters had said and who had sent the letters. Both Bill and Tom declined from giving details but stressed to their parents that it was not bad news and nothing to do with the army.

The boys set off on their run. The morning was bright, a little chilly but nothing that they could not manage. They ran along the canal remembering how it had looked the last time they had followed that route. They reached Jacob's bridge stopped and looked about them. There was not a soul insight, and the calm gentle breeze made the whole world seem to stand still just for them.

"I'm so happy to be back with you, Bill," Tom said.

Bill looked at Tom and without hesitation, grabbed Tom, kissing him full on the lips. "I'm never going to leave you again," Bill replied as they broke their embrace. Both laughed like school kids as they ran on towards Jacob's farm, through Yew Wood and on to their favourite swimming place. No swimming was done that day. The boys lay on the ground making love and enjoying each other's intimate touch. Although it was quite cold, their bodies radiated enough heat to make them both comfortable.

Two days later, the boys set off for London. Sadly, they thought that they could no longer stay at Phil's house so managed to book a room in a small hotel near to where they had previously stayed. They had brought with them their letters of invitation and took a cab to the solicitor's office. At the office, they were greeted at the reception by a stern looking woman who was busying herself typing letters. "Yes gentlemen, how can I help?"

The boys handed the women their respective letters which the woman read. "That's lovely," the woman said after checking the contents of the letters. "Mr Grimes is expecting you. If you would like to take a seat, I will see if he is free now."

The boys sat looking at the austere wood panelling which embellished the walls of the solicitor's office. After a little while, the woman returned inviting Bill and Tom to follow her. They were taken into a large office. Two seats had been placed facing a large oak desk which had a leather covered chair set behind it. The boys were invited to take the two seats and the woman left the room. After a few minutes, the woman returned placing a brown document folder on the desk. As she did so, a small, rather fat man, wearing thick rimmed glasses walked into the room. "Good morning, gentlemen. Thank you for coming," Mr Grimes stated, struggled to breathe as he walked to the empty chair on the other side of the desk.

Mr Grimes opened the document folder and said, "I understand that you were friends with the late Philip Thompson-Brown? Incredibly sad affair!" Mr Grimes went on to say; Bill and Tom looked at each other in amazement. Mr Grimes looked at the boys waiting for confirmation.

"Yes," Bill said nervously. "He was a good friend."

"Well, my dear fellows, it seems that he also thought of you both as good friends too. I have been instructed to inform you both, that prior to Mr Thompson-Brown taking his own life; he made adjustments to his last will and testimony. It has been a long, messy and very difficult process, if you ask me, but with you both being here today, it will enable me to conclude the final measures," Mr Grimes stated officially.

Bill looked at Tom and Tom returned his look. Mr Grimes continued, "Mr Thompson-Brown stated in his last will and testimony that you, Mr Harris, and you, Mr Taylor, have jointly been bequeathed joint ownership of his London property, including all of its contents and chattels, which I understand you are familiar with." Mr Grimes peered over the rim of his glasses awaiting confirmation.

Bill and Tom looked shocked, but both nodded to confirm that they were familiar with the property. Mr Grimes then continued, "Mr Thompson-Brown has also bequeathed each of you the sum of £10,000 pounds." The shock on Bill and Tom's faces could not be missed as they continued to listen. "There are a couple of provisos, that on accepting the house and financial recompense, that you do not try to make any contact with Mr Thompson-Brown's parents and that you can confirm that you will both reside in the said property and not sell the property unless absolutely necessary or until either one of you is deceased."

Mr Grimes again looked over the rim of his spectacles, coughing to gain a response from the lads. Once again, the boys nodded to confirm that they had heard and understood correctly. Mr Grimes looked down at his paperwork and proceeded, "Mr Thompson-Brown's parents have already arranged for the property to be secured but have no further wish to return to the said property," he said. "And, I am now in possession of the deeds and keys to the said property."

Bill and Tom remained silent, neither knowing what to say. Mr Grimes went on, "I have drawn up all the relevant documents and paperwork and once you have read them, agree their content and have signed, I can hand you the keys to the said property and give you each a cheque for the money that has been left to you. I presume that you will be happy receiving cheques rather than a bank note?"

"Err…yes," said Bill nodding, followed by Tom also agreeing in a similar way.

"Good," said Mr Grimes, who then presented each with the documents he had prepared. Both boys read the documents carefully. Once they had completed reading the documents, Mr Grimes asked, "Are you satisfied with the content of the documents and satisfied with the conditions outlaid?"

Bill answered first, saying just 'Yes', followed by Tom who also only said, "Yes." They were then presented each with a pen and each asked to sign each document in the appropriate places. Mr Grimes then countersigned each paper, then opened his desk draw taking from it another large brown envelope. First, Mr Grimes took out a set of keys from the envelope, handing them to Bill; he then took out two cheques, each for £10,000; handing them respectively to Bill and then Tom.

Finally, he removed a sealed white envelope, handwritten and addressed to Bill and Tom. The handwriting was distinctively Phil's. Mr Grimes then handed over the deeds to the house and then said, "Thank you gentlemen" as he began to stand. "This concludes our business here today and may I wish you a very pleasant day?" Mr Grimes held out his hand and shook Bill and Tom's hands respectively, edging the boys to the exit door. "I am sure that you will both be very happy with the outcome of this meeting," Mr Grimes retorted as he walked past them, going into another office.

The boys left the office and outside, both looked at each other in amazement and totally dumbfounded. It was Bill who spoke first. "Fucking hell, Tom, we've got a house and twenty grand between us!"

"I don't believe it," Tom said trembling. "What are we going to do?"

"The first thing is to go to the house, see if there is anything left inside and to take stock. I never expected Phil to leave us anything…" Tom stated, "let alone leaving us his house and giving us so much money."

"I'm shocked that Phil's parents haven't kicked up a fuss and have chosen not to contend the will," Bill replied. After the initial shock, the boys decided to leave their visit to the house until the next day, getting there early the next morning.

That evening, they stayed in their hotel room reading over and over the copies of the documents which they had both signed and the deeds to the house. They also looked at each of the cheques that had been presented to them. Both cheques had been signed by Mr Grimes as each cheque had come out of his business account. The boys decided not to open the letter from Phil, preferring to open it when they were in Phil's house.

The following morning, as they walked towards the house, both reflected on the happier times they had spent with Phil and Amos. Bill opened the door, then turned to Tom sweeping him off his feet and carried him inside. "I'm carrying you over the threshold," Bill said laughing.

"You daft bat," Tom proclaimed laughing. As they entered the darkness of the house, they switched on the lights. The house smelt musty and damp. They moved around the house opening curtains and windows to let in light and fresh air. All the furniture had been covered with dust sheets, which they removed, folding them and placing them in a pile in the corner of the room. They surveyed the house and its contents. Nothing seemed to have been touched since Bill was there last. "It's going to take some cleaning," Tom said feeling sad but also elated.

"We can make a start in a minute," was Bill's reply. "Let's open Phil's letter." They sat together on the sofa as Bill opened the letter, reading it slowly aloud:

*My Dearest Bill and Tom,*

*I am sure that by now, you are still recovering from the shock of finding that you are now the proud owners of a house in London and that you have a considerable sum in your bank account. It is my wish that you both have the opportunity to have a place of your own and I am hoping that you will both consider living here permanently. I have spent many happy hours in this house, and it has always fitted my purpose. The happiest times spent here was with Amos and when you both stayed with us.*

*I loved Amos dearly and unconditionally and knowing that we would never be able to be together again was far too much pain for me to bear, hence I have decided to join him. Please do not feel angry with me or condemn me for the actions I have taken, really it is for the best. As you know, I had little support from my parents who disowned me because of me being homosexual.*

*My parents never accepted this part of my life, particularly my father. They were never going to accept my love for Amos, and they would never accept gaining from my death either; hence I decided to leave the house to you both. You have always been so wonderful to me, and Amos and I hope that you will remember us both kindly. The love you have for each other is similar to the love Amos and I had, which should be never taken lightly. You have been my dearest friends and your love will remain with me for all eternity. Be assured, that now, I am happy, knowing that I will be with Amos. Please stay safe and love one another always.*

*Your friend,*
*Phil.*


Bill stopped reading and hung his head in silence. Tom sat motionless, tears running down his cheeks wetting the front of his shirt. Both knew the difficulties that Phil had experienced and understood fully why he had taken the actions he had done. Now, they felt it was their duty to honour Phil and Amos by accepting this gift and to have them both in their memory for all time. Bill broke the silence by saying, "Well, Phil would hate to see the place looking so shabby, I think we should start by cleaning up."

Apart for going out to buy provisions and to go the bank to open new accounts, both men spent the next two days cleaning and making the house ready to live in again. As they cleaned, they talked about how they could break the news to their parents. Bill came up with the idea that once they were both discharged from the army; they would remain in London to start a new life together; telling their parents that to come home would be far too difficult for them both after what they had experienced. Further, they would also tell their parents that they intended to start a business in London as being at home would restrict their ability to move on.

When Bill and Tom returned home after spending three days in London, both boys explained that they had been left money from a friend they had met and who had sadly died. They told their parents that their friend had no family or friends other than them, which was not totally true, but which did not need further explanation. Neither of the boys told their parents about Phil loving Amos, nor did they inform their parents how Phil had died, nor about his parents who had disowned him. They only said that Phil had died during the blitz.

It was difficult for both sets of parents to accept that their boys would not be coming home after the war had ended but were each reconciled that this was a good productive move for both of them. "After all, London was not so far away and they would at least be able to visit regularly," Joe stated when the news broke.

After hearing the boys' plans, George and Mary and Joe and Jean set about trying to make the boys comfortable before they had to return to Aldershot and their going back to the theatre of war. The days spent at home during this time seemed to be the happiest time for both families. Bill and Tom each gave their parents £1,000 each, enough to purchase their own homes and to have enough left over to keep them secure, if only for a fleeting time. Both boys did have a few opportunities where they could share a bed together, as on a couple of occasions, their parents were not around. Wednesday evenings was the best, as their mothers attended the Women's Institute, and their fathers were out on fire watch duties.

When it was time to leave, all were sad, but all were happy in the knowledge that at least something good had come out of the war, at least for their families.

# Chapter Nineteen
# Victory in Europe and New Beginnings

Following their extended leave, both Tom and Bill returned to Aldershot; Tom leaving several days before Bill. Life back in Aldershot saw Bill and Tom leading platoons, training new recruits to enter the war, and looking forward to seeing the war conclude. Happily, progress was being made with the fighting in Europe and the end of the war was in sight. After four long years, Bill and Tom were now stationed together. They kept their relationship secret, only daring to enjoy personal time together when allowed off base or when given leave, when they returned to their house in London.

On 7 May 1945, the formal act of military surrender was signed by Germany, ending the war in Europe. The next day celebrations broke out all over the world to mark Victory in Europe. In Britain, Churchill marked the occasion by declaring the 8th of May a public holiday. At the barracks, all training was suspended for the day; all troops were given the day to rest and celebrate; apart from a skeleton crew who were needed to maintained security. The sense of relief emanating from everyone was like a tsunami.

The men were elated, running about cheering, singing, and dancing with each other. The beer in the NAAFI ran out and more had to be bought in from outside. Trucks were sent from the barracks to a nearby brewery to ensure stocks could be maintained. Beacons were built and lit and fireworks illuminated the night sky. Bill and Tom joined in with the celebrations but made sure that they also took some time to themselves, sitting on a grassed verge happy with each other's company.

"It won't be long before we're both discharged from the army," Bill said.

"It will be strange," Tom answered. "But I can't wait. We'll be able to start our lives together and not be worried about what people will say."

Unfortunately for Tom and Bill, their discharge from the army was not to come as quickly as they had hoped. It is true to say that for some, the release process began about six weeks after the ending of the war, but for those individuals who had progressed to higher ranks, decommissioning was slow. By December, approximately 750,000 men had been discharged, the number doubling two months later after the Japanese surrendered. Decommissioned soldiers received their demobilisation grant and a set of civilian clothing, which included a suit, shirts, underclothes, raincoat, hat, and shoes. Tom and Bill were beginning to get frustrated at the slow pace that demobilisation was taking. They desperately wanted out and to start their new life.

Apart from the institutional problems of release, news was mounting that many of the service men and women returning to civilian life were facing all sorts of problems. Six years of bombing and shortages of basic essential living products, including food, clothing, and housing put a strain on family relationships. For many, the adjustment of being back with parents and spouses after many years apart caused divorce rate to soar. Tom and Bill were happy in the knowledge that at least for them, they would not be amongst the majority experiencing such problems. However, both Bill and Tom knew that they could not return to their old life back in the Midlands nor could they live with their parents again.

In January 1946, Bill was told that he would be demobilised; Tom had to wait until April before he was told that he could leave. Here in Aldershot, they had been able to be together again after such a long time apart, now they were being separated again, if only for four months. Bill decided to go home to visit his parents. Bill and Tom had discussed using the money Phil had left them to buy a small pub in London where they could build a business. Happy that they were both going to be together as business partners. Their parents were not so happy though, as the thought of life without the boys at home sunk in.

Tom's parents took his pending move worse than Bill's parents who had to come to terms with the fact that their child was no longer a boy, but a man who had not just grown up, but had experienced the horrors of war and had come through as an independent person in his own right. Although both sets of parents had been looking forward to returning to some sort of normality this was not to be the case. Rationing continued well into the 1950s and shortages of food stuff in particular caused a strain. Life without the boys being around would also mean hardships on an emotional level but they were happy in that they had secured long term friendships.

However, Tom's father realised that his suspicions about Bill and Tom's relationship was more than others imagined. He had seen the look in each of the boys' eyes, recognising their love for one another but dared to say nothing. Tom's father was content but also recognised that neither Bill's parents or he and his wife would ever become grandparents.

Bill returned to London after his leave and to the house that Phil had left them. He set about re-decorating and moving stuff around so that it would be more to Tom's taste than Phil had. Tom had often stated that he would change the colour scheme of the house and move items from one room to another, throwing away those things he hated. However, Bill could not throw anything of Phil's away, choosing to box them up and storing them in the attic. In doing this, Bill came across letters written to Phil from Amos.

At first, Bill did not want to read the intimate love lines, but one day, after he had eaten dinner, Bill sat and read each letter thoroughly. The depth of love that flowed in each line reminded Bill of the letters he had received from Tom. It was heart-breaking to read such letters, especially because of his and Tom's relationship with Phil and Amos. Suddenly, a sense of grief engulfed Bill. He was shocked and saddened that Amos had died in some strange country, tortured or even starved; poor Amos, who must have been alone, afraid and in pain.

Bill also became angry with Phil who he thought had chickened out, but soon realised how he might have reacted had it been him in Phil's position. Bill decided to hide these letters from Tom and packed them away with the other stuff that was not wanted. Bill placed the sacred letters in a box, sealed its contents and put them in the attic. Now he must concentrate on preparing for Tom to be back with him and for their future ahead.

As April approached, Bill began to get more excited at the thought of Tom being with him. Bill had explored the possibility for getting a pub but many were already occupied and there were lots more either demolished or had been badly damaged from the bombing. Bill was always in wonderment as he walked through the rubbled streets of London; children always seemed to be playing, finding all sorts of treasures to occupy their minds. Danger was still always present from falling masonry or from the occasional unexploded bomb. Bill knew that it would take years to make the streets safe again and for new buildings to be erected, making Bill realise that it might take a while before Tom and Bill's dream of owning a pub would come to fruition.

Following the late winter of 1945–46, cold winds, floods and rain arrived, continuing until March. It was not until April until the sun came out at last. It seemed to Bill that this was an omen of things to come, and that the warm weather had held out for Tom's return. On the day Tom was eventually discharged from the army, Bill headed for Waterloo station. Bill was early, anxious to see Tom again. Eventually when Tom arrived, they hugged and kissed openly on the station platform, happy to be together again. Before going home, the boys went to the Elephant and Castle pub for a few drinks. Tom was given a warm welcome, receiving a rapturous applause from the bar staff and customers.

It was clear to Tom that this was the first time, he and Bill had felt true acceptance as a couple. Once home, Tom saw the effort Bill had made to make their home comfortable and was pleased with the outcome. However, time to gloat on the new decor would have to wait. There were more important things to do. Bill took Tom by the hand, leading Tom upstairs to bed, where they remained until the next day. After christening their marital bed, they slept, cuddled and wallowed in each other's presence.

From now on, they could stay and sleep together every night for the rest of their lives, not ever having to wait for opportunities, or to be worried that they might get caught out. Here was their sanctuary, their love nest, their safe haven; protected from the outside and relieved that there were no more wars on the horizon. A new world order was beginning and within this new world order might come a realisation that love could prevail and that with luck and time, their love for one another might one day also be recognised.

Milton Keynes UK
Ingram Content Group UK Ltd.
UKHW020233281123
433366UK00007B/179